No Mean Affair

ROBERT RONSSON

FOXWELL
PRESS

Copyright © Robert Ronsson 2012

First published by
Foxwell Press
1301 Stratford Road
Hall Green
Birmingham
B28 9HH

ISBN 978-0-9570934-3-0

A CIP catalogue record for this book is available from the British Library.

Typeset in Cambria by print.uk.net.
Cover design by Stuart Bache
Book design by Adam Davis

No Mean Affair is fact-based fiction. Descriptions of people, places and historical events are based on the sources listed in the bibliography. One person's name has been changed to avoid confusion. The story is imagined.

In loving remembrance of Dad.
And to Daisy Ireland Byrne, welcome.

PREFACE

Dad was dying. His face was caved in and jaundiced. His cheeks, after I shaved him, had a waxy sheen. His breathing rattled, but still he fought to break the surface of consciousness and talk. Mum patted his hand.

'You know, Norah, the more I think about it, the more I believe that MP in Glasgow was my father,' he said.

Dad died on July 22, 2003.

In his papers, we found a photograph of Britain's first Labour Government of 1924. One man's resemblance to my father sent a chill of recognition down my spine. This man stood on a platform at the back, one of only three in the topmost row, his head forming an apex to the grouping. The other men focused on the camera but his eyes, my father's eyes, seemed to look out beyond the garden at 10 Downing Street as if his was the only mind set on the future. Ramsay MacDonald, who sat below and in front of him, may have been Prime Minister but it was the man at the back, John Wheatley, who looked most at home.

Until then, I had always understood that my paternal grandfather was a drunkard and gambler, disowned by the family decades before. My grandmother had abandoned him and her three older children when she fled to London with my father. Could I actually be the descendant of this John Wheatley, who was such a prominent political figure? Was this picture a clue as to why my kindly, eccentric 'Nana' had wronged my father's siblings so badly?

Motivated by these questions, I combined historical fact and family lore to create this work of fiction.

ROBERT RONSSON

One

Saturday February 19, 1912

The dark mood settled its claws into William's shoulders as he bent over the milk churns at the end of his working day. In the cold of the Glasgow winter, he had lost all feeling in his hands and his flesh-empty fingers looked as if they had been stained with ink. He had already sluiced down the platform of the handcart and was now shining up the insides of the containers ready for the morning.

At this time of year, William had only one round a day but Charley, his sister's husband and his boss, always laid off half the workforce in October so the rounds took twice as long. William kept his job but resented the extra work.

On the walk home, the pain from his hands put a grim look on his thin features. He pushed through a group of street-corner wasters to turn into Duke Street and felt the men's resentment cling to his back like a swirl of fog. He was an incomer who had robbed one of them of work. He could swank along with his pockets clinking with silver, while they, having started the day with a futile vigil at a factory gate, had to pin their hopes for a night's drinking on the generosity of others, or the speed of a horse on a distant English racecourse.

They marked him as different because of his complexion. His skin was dark and his hair black. Street legend had it that people with his looks were descendants of shipwrecked mariners from the Armada, so it naturally followed for him to be known as 'The Spaniard'.

William and his wife Mary had lived in Dundee but when that town failed to recover from the depression of 1908 and he lost his job, they moved to Glasgow. This was two years ago. With wee Billy already on the way, Charley's offer of work in the milk depot was the only way to stay off parish handouts. Now, as if slaving for his brother-in-law was not enough, he and Mary were living in the single-end next to Charley and Lou's two-roomed 'house'.

Today was the anniversary of wee Billy's death. Since it happened, William had lived his life in the same glades of gloom as the men around him. Yes, it raised his spirits when one of his prettier customers shyly opened her shift to offer an alternative method of payment. He was always happy to take his chance when a man had pocketed the pennies his wife had set aside for the milk bill but the effect on his morale was fleeting.

He turned into the shadow of the close, paused to allow his eyes to grow used to the darkness, and followed the steps upwards, feeling the creeping cold of the dungeon-like sandstone walls. He paused at the door. The brass hand-plate shone; it was a bad sign. Taking a deep breath, he went in.

By rights, he should have been greeted with the smell of cooking. The table should have been set. Today though, Mary sat with her back to him. The only smell in his nostrils was the clog of wax polish. He looked round. The sternest sergeant major could find no fault in the few square yards of this pin-bright room. Even the tablecloth folds hung as if a gauge had been used to test their symmetry.

She must have known he was there but still she kept her back to him. He crept the few paces to the chair furthest from the door and sat down.

She looked up. Her eyes, which before the boy's death had been piercing and bright, were dulled, the skin around them red and blotchy. 'It's you, William,' she said. It looked as if the minimal effort of greeting him had sapped her energy.

He sighed and unwound his muffler. 'Aye, it's me.' He glanced at the range. The ashes in the grate looked like snow compared to the gloss of the polished surround. 'You let the fire go out, hen.' He tried to keep his voice light, free of reproach. 'I'll start it up and put the kettle on.'

She put out a hand, blue-veined, too old to belong to a woman of only twenty-two. 'No, let me. I'll think about your tea.' She stood and turned to the press alongside the range. 'Look!' She sounded as if she had discovered a seam of gold in a coal mine. 'I can do something with these.' It was plate of potatoes in mince gravy. 'I can fry these up in no time.'

'There's not enough for both of us.' He knew how she would respond.

'Och. I had a piece earlier. I won't be eating the night.'

She had always been a small woman but now, after a year of what seemed to him like fasting, she was so frail. He'd been shocked when, pretending to be asleep, he had spied on her bathing. Her body hung from her shoulders like an empty sack.

'You should try to build yourself up.'

'Why?'

'Maybe we could try for another bairn.'

She nodded but her eyes focused beyond the grate, which she was stuffing with kindling. She put a match to the bundle and sat back on her heels.

William came to the chair alongside the fire and leaned forward, laying a hand on her shoulder. 'Try to pick yourself up, Mary.'

She turned to face him. There were tears on her cheeks. 'Why? So we can stay and kill another child with the foul air hereabouts?'

'You know what they said. It was wee Billy's Dundee lungs couldnae cope. A bairn born here will stand a better chance. There's enough children make it through here, for God's sake.'

'Aye and whit have they to look forward to? If he's lucky, a boy will have a life of toil to make a rich man richer. A girl will be expected to keep a home and a family – never be anything more than a shadow of the men aroon' her.'

'Politics!'

'Aye, politics. And why not? It's only working-class bairns die. Our Billy died because of politics.'

He kept his voice gentle. 'See sense, hen. It's the way it is.'

Her head slumped forward. 'You're right. I ken. But it doesn't mean we cannae want it different.'

'Different?' He shook his head. 'Not for the likes of us. It's that Guild, isn't it? Filling your head–'

'It was you who said I should find something to take my mind off things,' Mary broke in. 'The work we do feeding the poorest bairns and giving them treats goes so far. But when the men from the Labour Party come to talk it's about more. We can change the system.'

He knelt alongside her, his arm now encircling her shoulder. 'Time was you would have been happy with what we had, Mary.'

She looked at him and her lips separated in a smile but the hollowness in her eyes betrayed it. 'Aye, I'll get over it. It wasnae so bad here with wee Billy in my arms and you cuddling me like this.' She snuggled in to him. 'Sometimes I think about Dundee and the times you came down to the laundry to meet me after you'd done your shift in the mill. The girls waiting with me would dig me in the ribs and make saucy comments as you came along. If one of them'd asked me, I would have said all I wanted in the world was to be that man's wife.'

'I'm still that man, Mary.' He allowed his voice to show his exasperation. 'It's you who has changed.'

She pulled away from him. 'What do you expect? I was alone. I had nothing to do except go over my loss – time after time. When I go to Guild meetings we hear about big ideas – about the way the world is put together–'

'Listen to yourself, woman!' His voice was raised now. Charley and Lou would be able to hear everything through the wall. 'You think a bunch of harridans from the steamies are going to march on London? When I said to join the Guild it was to help organise Christmas parties and trips to the country.'

'Aye, women's work.' Mary's voice was scathing. 'Well, if the men are too scairt to take the fight to the boss class, we will have to do it.'

He stood up. 'You know full well you're talking nonsense. There's no way out of this. If you stopped your politics you'd be better company for the other women around here. You would make some friends.'

Mary seemed to unfurl her body and throw back her shoulders so she was effectively spitting the words at him. 'And what if the friends I made were "friends" of yours, William? What then? What sort of friendship would that be?'

He'd known she was probably aware of what happened on his collection round but she had never voiced it so openly. He brushed past her. 'Ah've had enough of yer blether, woman. Ah'm away to Craib's Bar and I make no promises about my mood when I come back.' He grabbed his cap and muffler and made sure to slam the door behind him.

Two

The alarm clock's corpse-stirring clatter brought William to a sitting position even before he was fully awake. He scrabbled for the hook to stop the din.

He rubbed his eyes, unseeing in the dark, and pushed open the cavity bed door to step down onto the icy linoleum. After rousing the embers in the range, he put the kettle on its stand and hurried off to the lavvie. At this time in the morning, even with four families using the same facilities, he was confident he would be the only one there.

When he returned, Mary was up and the tea was mashing. She was stirring the porridge she had cut from a batch made for the week. The wooden spoon's mesmeric scraping filled his head. He had downed a few last night and his thinking was fuzzy, but he was sure it was nothing like the swollen heads many of the other drinkers would be waking up to.

He remembered his plan for how their conversation should go this morning and he began cautiously, 'There was a poster up in the bar about the kiddies' summer trip to Easterhouse.'

She came to the table with the pan steaming in front of her. She shook her head. 'Aye, an' I hope there's a big whisky bottle full of copper to pay for it.'

'Aye, there is a bottle but it isnae full.'

She smiled. She was doling out the porridge into two bowls. 'Well it's early days.'

He sprinkled sugar onto his porridge, carved off an edge and chewed on it as he spoke. 'Take some sugar, by th'way. It'll build you up.'

She put the lid back on the sugar bowl, twisting it so the

teaspoon handle was just so. 'You know I prefer mine as it comes from the pan.'

William put down his spoon. 'When the outing comes around you'll have done your part. It'll be time to start thinking about us starting a family again.'

She studied her porridge. 'The Guild was your idea.'

'But it's filling your head full of nonsense.'

'Only to you. I want more out of life than scraping by, breathing the foulness that killed our Billy. There can be a way. The Labour Party–'

'I don't want to hear to hear any more aboot the bloody politicians! I'm talking about us.'

'Don't you see, William? I have to get away from here. I don't want to lose the next bairn the way we lost Billy.'

He sighed. The conversation was not going the way he had planned. 'Can't you see, Mary? It's the politics making you unhappy – worse not better. Whit I'm saying is, well – it has to stop. You're not going to the Guild if they carry on with the politics. You can help with the kiddies' outings but no more.'

Mary pushed back her chair and stood with her back to the range. She crossed her arms. 'I'm your wife, William, not your lackey. I will do as I please.' Her voice softened and she uncrossed her arms and placed her hands on the table. 'But to show what a dutiful wifey I can be, I will stop going to the Guild and get a job. There, that's fair.'

William's shoulders slumped and he put his palms flat down on the table. 'How many times, Mary? No wife of mine is working in a laundry or going into service while I can bring in a proper wage.'

'But I have to do something. I'll go out of my mind otherwise.'

'Plenty of wives aroon' here would die to be in your position, woman. I bring in a wage. I give you the housekeeping regular as clockwork. Most of the men, who are lucky enough to work, have gambled and drunk their money away before they get home on a Friday night. Perhaps you'd rather be married to a waster so you *have* to work.'

Mary seemed to fold into herself as she sat lower in her

chair and pushed the half-eaten breakfast to one side. 'Of course not, William. I know you're a good man and I'm lucky, but there must be something better for me than this.' She looked round their one room with the doors to the bed still open wide. 'You can't be happy with what we have here. If I work, the money I bring in will help us get away.'

'There is a job for you and it's bringing up our children – and it's only going to happen if you pull yourself together and start to think about *my* feelings and *my* needs.' He pushed his chair back as he stood, pleased that it grated jarringly on the linoleum. 'Now, I'm off to work and I expect things to start being different around here when I get back.'

His boots sparked on the steps and he hurried out of the close. All around him was inky blackness except for the glow to the north from Beardmore's foundry. The cold bit into him and he pulled his jacket tighter. It was a bad start to the day and he wondered what sort of welcome there would be for him when he returned. But he had been right. The Co-op Guild had put ideas into Mary's head and it would have to stop. And she wasn't going to work either. What man in his position would allow his wife to take a job? No, the only solution was another bairn. That would put her right.

Three

Sunday June 16, 1912
William staggered out of the rear door of the Auld House. He looked up, accustoming his eyes to the mid-summer brightness after the smoky backroom. The short alley took him down to Westmuir Street and he stopped at the corner to lift his chin from his chest and set his shoulders straight. He still had enough wits about him to know that if he looked tipsy any lurking temperance snooper would have the excuse to report Davie Anderson for serving on a Sunday.

He watched steam and smoke from Beardmore's scudding low across the sky. At a higher altitude, the mackerel scales of cloud glinted green and blue. It raised his spirits despite the fact that he was already contemplating the ferocity of the headache that would greet his early rising. It had been a good day. Many of the men of Parkhead and Shettleston had spent it in unaccustomed alcoholic companionship because, like him, they had been freed from family shackles. Mary and her Guild companions had been away with the Co-operative outing to Easterhouse.

Now, shortly after ten o'clock, he imagined how the carts, dragooned into service from East End tradespeople, would be ferrying the picnic party back from Gartcraig Wharf. Bundled together in heaps of belly-full and dozing humanity, the bairns would be swaying in time to the stamping feet of the horses. William pondered the wisdom of stretching the children's dream horizons to include canal-boat leisure rides, clean-water lochs and a village where the sky was wide and the air so fresh it made them sneeze. How many of them would see the like again?

He felt a belch rising and tried to hold it at the back of his throat, his chest puffed up like a bantam. It escaped in a sonorous and satisfying rasp across his tonsils. Tonight, he decided, he would tell Mary that enough was enough.

The single-end was dark so he lit the gas mantle, roused the embers in the grate and put the kettle on its stand. The store held a good supply of coal and he sorted a few smooth-faced lumps and watched them spurt into flame. He prided himself on being able to afford quality – none of the dust and grit that many in the tenements had to make do with. Sometimes, when he broke into a coal and its insides leaked out like treacle toffee and spluttered with a rich orange flame – well, it was one of his pleasures in life. Like a half of heavy with a whisky chaser – his hof n'a hof – it was something he could afford. He sat back and waited for her tread on the stair.

The scratching of a key in the door woke him. He started up and, realising his surroundings, settled back as Mary swept round the door.

'All right, hen?' he said. 'I've put the kettle on.'

Sure enough the water was burbling and Mary busied herself making the tea while her coat was still on. She passed him the mug with a spot of milk in and the sugar to sweeten it himself. 'Would you like a piece to go wi' it?'

'Aye. An' some dripping.'

She took off her coat and bonnet and hung them behind the door. He watched while her fast hands sawed a slice from the loaf and flicked a spread of dripping over it.

'Salt!' he demanded.

She nodded, sprinkled it with two good pinches and folded the bread over. She took a small plate from the press and handed over his supper.

'You not having anything?' he said.

She blew air from her sun-bloomed cheeks. 'No, we took too much for the picnic. Even with the bairns filling themselves to bursting there was enough for everyone and more.' She poured his tea. 'Aren't you going to ask me how it went?'

He cleared his throat of some troublesome phlegm and spat into the fire. The oyster-like mass bubbled and hissed. 'Okay, hen. How was the outing?'

She smiled. 'The weather was kind. The air was fresh as a laundered sheet. We didn't lose any bairns and nobody drownded in the canal so we must call it a success.'

He nodded. 'It's a good time to leave then.' He flashed her a fierce-browed look so she would take his meaning.

Mary sighed and fussed at the edge of the tablecloth. 'Please don't start, William. It's been a long day.'

'It's been a day of your own making, Mary. First it was the Christmas party and no sooner was that finished than you started with the outing. Well you've done it and now it's time to put your home and your man first.'

Tears welled up in her eyes. 'Please, William, not now. We'll talk tomorrow.'

But he had steeled himself, rehearsed his lines as the drinks went down. 'We'll talk now, woman, and you'll do what I say. You're leaving the Guild. It's taken over your life.'

'You don't know the half of it, William.' She wiped the back of her hand across her eyes. 'You think I'm there because of those raggedy kids with their backsides hanging out of their breeks? I'm there because it's a place where working women can hold up their heads. We can organise.'

He brought his fist down on the table, making his supper plate rattle. 'Organise! You're speaking like some councillor from the Hall of Corruption in Glasgow. You think they organise for you? They organise for theirselves – to make money on the deals that go through that place. Yon politicians? Don't fool yourself they care about you and your likes.'

'Have you met any of them? Of course you haven't. Labour men have taken the pledge. You won't find them drinking themselves stupid.'

He sighed. 'There you go, woman – trying to stop my simple pleasures. Ah'm telling you those do-gooders are in it for theirselves.'

Her tears were flowing now. 'You *won't* talk about my comrades like that. *They* are men with principles. Men who want to see us do better for ourselves.' She looked around, her face twisted with contempt. 'Are you satisfied with this, William?

Is this all we have to look forward to? A life of drudgery in a single-end? Surely, even you can see this is no way to bring up a family?'

He felt a jolt in his chest and his mouth didn't seem capable of working fast enough to blurt out all he wanted to say. 'Family! Chance would be a fine thing. Many a man round here would take what he needs but not me – I've been too soft with you, woman. It's been your way for too long.' He stood up and saw Mary pull back in her chair. 'Aye, you can cringe.' He leant forward and jabbed a finger towards her face. 'You can blether all you like aboot your "comrades" and what they're going to do for you. But it's over. You think yon politicians care about one tenement biddy more or less? From now on you look after me and this house. You're going to have bairns and bring them up. One way or another I'm going to keep you in your place.'

She sat stiffly with her jaw set and said nothing.

'Now, we're going to bed and you'd better make it a warm one or you'll feel the back of my hand.'

She stood up, her hands bunched into tight fists, her shoulders trembling. Her eyes flashed their dark fire. 'I ken what I signed up for, William.' She hissed the words through clenched teeth. 'I'll warm your bed and I'll bear as many bairns as providence brings but you shall not stop me trying to make my way out of this God-forsaken city. I'll go to the Guild and I'll fight for our bairns to have something better than this.'

The blood roared in his ears and he made a fist, pulling back his arm. This would be no namby-pamby slap. She deserved a lesson.

She flinched and turned her head to accept the blow. In an instant his rage cleared and his shoulders sagged. 'Aw, Mary,' he said, lowering his arms and wrapping them round her. He hugged her with all the force he had been ready to put into the punch, wanting, without knowing why, to crush the bones of her.

Danny

One

Sunday June 30, 1912

Mary Ireland edged into Danny McAleer's vision carrying a soapbox. She was hugging close to next door's garden wall and stopped as if she recognised that she now encroached onto the bigger house's stretch of pavement. Danny watched the tendons in her delicate wrist strain as she swung the crate down on the Yorkstone slabs. She stepped onto it, ignoring the hands of the men who had followed her as they proffered them in support. She raised her black-bonneted head and harangued the backs of the mob. 'Come on, then – I'll take on the lot of you. Come and smash another face. Take on the smallest woman in Parkhead.' One by one, as her screech swept over them like a wave, they turned back to face her. She stood like a statue, arms rigid, fists clenched at her hip.

'Who's that, JW?' Danny said.

The man standing alongside him held back the lace curtain. 'I don't know but she has a sense of timing. They're not likely to go home peacefully now.'

The woman could not know it but the men who watched her, Danny and his boss John Wheatley, had already sent the rabble on their way. Now it was if she had put a flame to the fuse of the mob's resentment.

For Danny, the events of that Sunday had started after lunch. He had been in his attic room in the Wheatley house tapping his good foot to the beat of the military band music that drifted into an open window from Tollcross Park. He was in the doorway, the only space where he could stand upright, contemplating the ladder-like stairs down to the house proper. His clomping on the bare boards irritated Mrs Wheatley. Every other villa in the street had a maid in the attic room and his occupation of the space as JW's resident muscle was an affront to the lady of the house. But he could not mind it, he had heard activity in the hallway and his job was to be there.

Danny lifted his left leg carefully but still winced when it hit the tread. The dull thud, punctuating every other step, was the rhythm of his life. He crossed the landing to the top of the house stairs. There the scent of lavender wax-polish was overlaid with the meat-heavy, gravy smell of Sunday lunch. From the faint clanging of pans, Danny could tell that his mother, the Wheatley's Sunday cook, was finishing up in the kitchen.

With the banisters for support and the carpet muffling his step, Danny relaxed. As he descended, his shoulder brushed the rose motifs cut into the wood-panelling. His boss stood at the foot of the stairs, adjusting his bowler hat in a rosewood-framed mirror.

Wheatley turned and looked up. 'There you are, Danny'. He patted his stomach with both hands as if checking the pockets of his waistcoat. Danny had once observed to a drinking pal, 'JW wears his prosperity as a layer of fat. His belly is always the first part of him to enter a room.'

Mrs Wheatley stood to one side with her hand on the doorknob. She wore a brimmed hat and a formal three-quarter-length coat. She was smiling but her body jittered with impatience.

'Catherine and I are going for a walk,' Wheatley said.

'The branch delegation will be here any minute,' Danny said.

Wheatley flipped his watch out of his waistcoat pocket. 'Which is why we shouldn't be. If we're here when they come, it'll look as if we are expecting them.'

'But you are.'

Wheatley tapped the flat palm of his left hand with the index finger of his right. 'Listen, Danny. Our party comrades spontaneous demonstration of support is meant to be a surprise.' He tapped the finger again. 'They're due here at five forty-five. Catherine and I shall return shortly after.' Another tap placed the next element of the argument on his palm. 'I shall look suitably moved by their gesture and make a modest speech about how delighted we are to see them. This will send them on their way with their hearts lifted.' He passed his right hand across the open palm sweeping away the case he had built. 'That's how it works.'

'You're an operator, so you are,' Danny said. He held the door as Mr and Mrs Wheatley stepped out arm in arm. Wheatley's blue eyes squinted behind his gold-rimmed spectacles. The pall of grime that habitually hung over East Glasgow had thinned and drifted north.

'Don't you worry. The weans will be all right with me,' Danny called, waving as his employer turned towards the sound of the band. Danny checked the other direction towards Shettleston Road. The redstone crags of the tenements loomed at the junction only fifty yards away. He knew well how the ragged valley of dark buildings shambled two and a half miles to the west, progressively crowding in on top of each other until they reached the congestion of the city centre. It was a similar distance in the other direction, through the mining town of Baillieston, before the country opened up and the air freshened.

Danny was at the kitchen table sharing a pot of tea with his mother when he heard the percussion of marching boots through the open windows. He knew instantly that events would not go the way Wheatley had predicted. His boss's Labour Party comrades were mostly soft-booted tradesmen and teachers. They did well to muster twenty. The scuffing and striking of working-boots on the cobbles of Anstruther Street signalled the advance of anything up to a hundred working men. Danny's finely-tuned ear told him a rammy was in the offing.

'You slip out the back way, Ma,' Danny said. He bustled her through the tradesmen's door and across the paved courtyard to the back entry. He pulled the heavy door open and leaned out. 'It's clear, Ma. Hurry home now. See you next Sunday.' He bolted the entry and hop-skipped back into the house, locking and bolting the back-kitchen door. He clomped through to the hallway and leaned against the banister post.

'Lizzie! Patrick!' His fast breathing made him bark the words out more sternly than he normally would have done.

'We're here, Uncle Danny.' It was eleven-year-old Lizzie. 'What's wrong?'

'You stay in your rooms, now.'

She appeared at the top of the stairs in her Sunday dress covered by a smock. A blue ribbon held back her hair, the colour of a collie's coat.

'I said to stay in your room.'

'What is it?' Her blue eyes were wide.

'It looks as if there will be trouble in the street; some local hooligans come to have words with your father.'

Patrick appeared at his sister's side. He was taller despite being two years younger. His dark eyebrows looked fierce. 'You'll need me to help face them off, Uncle Danny. I'll come with you.' He started down the stairs.

'No.' Danny signalled like a constable, making the boy hover in mid-step. 'These are hard men, probably from Parkhead way. You two stay up there at the back of the house or I'll tell your father. Come on now, I've no time for an argument.'

Danny turned to the front door and took a deep breath. If these men were from Parkhead, or worse Garngad, they would be looking to spill blood after their trek. His fighting instinct calculated he would be facing overwhelming odds but he had learned as a boy not to show fear. His inner self may have been taunting him with how many ways he could be hurt by a rampaging mob but there was no outward sign of it. He checked the calliper joint at his knee and the leathers on his forearms. He filled his chest with air so his jacket lapels fell back to his shoulders. He was ready.

They were at the gate when he opened the front door. Only fifteen feet of lawn and a low stone wall with wrought iron tracery stood between him and a steaming mass of hard-faced men shuffling in on each other and filling the road. The man at the front was roughly the same age as Danny, early twenties. The grime was deep in the pores of his stubbled cheeks. His jacket and trousers, from different suits, were shiny with dirt polished into the fabric. If his clothes were ever washed they would fall apart. The ends of a red, cotton scarf, tight at his neck, flicked up as he spoke. 'Where's your man? Where's Wheatley?' He stumbled forward as the mob surged. He turned. 'Hold back there!'

Danny weighed his options. He could tell them there were children in the house. They would let the weans out before they swept past him, as if he was no more than a lamp-post, and trashed the place. Or he, the Boot of Garngad, could stand up to them. It would buy time. If the delaying tactic failed, he could always tell them about Patrick and Lizzie before they could do any damage. He planted his feet apart.

'He's oot – he's no' here.' Danny said it loud enough for the mob to hear and turned back to the thug in front. He dropped his voice. 'What do you want?' He had his good leg ready to take his weight and hitched his trouser so the man could see the boot on his left foot.

The ruffian caught the movement and glanced down. When he looked up, his eyes had lost their edge. He took off his cap and stuffed it in his pocket. A man unfamiliar with the ways of a Glasgow tough may have interpreted this as a gesture of deference. Danny knew better. The cap would soften the blow should the man attack using the preferred first move – a head butt inflicted with the speed of a striking cobra. Danny was distracted for a second by the way the waves of the man's red hair shone with grease.

'When's he back?' the man said.

'I don't know.' Danny was once more focused on the confrontation.

There was another surge and murmurings of dissent. The man held up a hand, broad and calloused from work. 'We'll wait.' He squatted on his haunches and the men followed suit.

Danny leaned over him. 'What's it about?'

The man spat at his feet. 'Father O'Brien is fed up of Wheatley's blether. We have come to make a fellow Catholic see sense.'

There was a commotion at the back of the mob. They stood and yielded the crown of the road. Danny thought the police in the park might have noticed the crowd and walked down to them, but no; it was Wheatley holding his wife's hand and acting as if they were still strolling beside Tollcross Mansion. He nodded to the men massed on either side, wished them a good afternoon and commented on how clement the weather was for a Sunday walk. He came alongside the man at the front who rose slowly until he was a good half-a-foot taller than Wheatley.

'Good afternoon,' Wheatley said and shook his hand. 'It's good of you to come to see me.'

The man stepped forward until his nose was no more than six inches from Wheatley's forehead. 'You'll no' be thinking it's such a fine day when we have finished, John Wheatley. Every man here is a God-fearing Catholic. We have no time for your communist ways. We have come to teach you a lesson you will no' forget.' There was a low growl of confirmation from the rabble.

Wheatley blinked up at the man from behind his glasses. Without breaking eye contact, he spoke in the broad East Glasgow of his upbringing, his high-pitched voice loud enough for the crowd. 'I see you've worked the coal. I was down there in the dark when I was eleven. I have been there in the narrow seams breaking coal until my knees locked. I have worked, eaten and shat,' he nodded an apology to Mrs Wheatley, 'all in the black hole. All to make a profit for a man in a mansion.'

Wheatley stepped onto the kerb. 'I know from first hand how the miners were robbed. Miners, labourers, all working men, suffer in the machinery of capitalism. Your cheap labour makes other men rich. Why, the pit owners care more for the horses than they care for you. You may be had for nothing and retained only for your keep. They pay you just enough to keep you working, just enough to feed your children who are next in line to serve them. And what's your reward? The workhouse or an early grave.'

Some of the men bowed their heads, others started shifting their feet. Wheatley took off his hat. His hair was flat on the crown of his head. Mrs Wheatley, who stood alongside the gate, watched her husband intently.

'I am not your enemy. God gave us all life and the green fields and sunny sky we enjoy today.' He looked up and raised his hands, palms upward. 'It's the factory and pit owners who have stolen His gifts from you. Not me. I am not your enemy.'

Wheatley leaned forward and spoke in the ringleader's ear.

After a long pause, the man nodded. Wheatley took his wife's hand and led her up the path to the door. With one defiant look at the mob still crowding round the gate, Danny followed them inside.

Wheatley wiped the sweat from his brow with a handkerchief, took off his glasses, polished them with a fresh corner of the same cloth and breathed out through puffed cheeks. 'Thank God I can remember that stuff in a crisis,' he said, his words clipped in the new way.

'It was a fine speech, JW,' Danny said.

Wheatley laughed. 'Almost word for word what I wrote in *Forward* two weeks ago.'

Lizzie and Patrick were at the foot of the stairs hopping from foot to foot.

'I told you to stay in your room,' Danny said, wagging a finger. He turned to their parents. 'I telt them to stay at the back of the house.'

Wheatley smiled and patted him on the back. 'You did right, Danny. You went out to face them. That took gumption.'

Mrs Wheatley's hand was clutched to her bosom as if she was testing her heartbeat. 'Those dreadful men, John. What possessed them to waste their Sunday afternoon coming out here?'

'The devil, Catherine – in the form of Father O'Brien maybe, but the devil no less. Come away in the drawing room.' The children followed them. Wheatley called out over his shoulder. 'If Mrs McAleer has gone home, perhaps you will be good enough to make us a cup of your best tea, Danny.'

When Danny entered the drawing room, carrying a tray of tea things, the family was seated round the cold fireplace. Wheatley's chair was empty. He was standing by the window looking through the lace curtains.

'Ah! The cup that cheers,' Wheatley said, rubbing his hands. 'Will you pour, Catherine?' Mrs Wheatley took the tray from Danny and set it down on a side table. Lizzie and Patrick perched on the edge of the settee. Their heads bobbed like parakeets as they tried to see what was happening outside.

Wheatley signalled Danny to join him. 'The delegation from the party is overdue. Let's hope they saw that rabble and went home.'

'Are they still there?' Danny said.

'It's turning a wee bit ugly.' He pulled the curtain aside an extra inch so Danny could see. The leader was holding up an effigy that had been cobbled together from a shirt and trousers stuffed with newspaper. He was trying to light it with a match. One of the men stepped forward with a small bottle and doused the material.

Danny checked Wheatley's face. The muscles in his cheek throbbed with tension. Danny's throat was tight, his voice pitched high. 'What should we do? Shall I go through the back alley, up to the park and bring back some polis?'

Wheatley laid a hand on his arm. 'No. I want you here in case it starts up again.'

Mrs Wheatley spoke quietly, trying to keep the tremor from her voice. 'Can't we do something, John? Are we to be turned out? What about our lovely house?' She clasped an arm around each child.

'Hush, Catherine. They won't harm anybody while Danny and I are here.' He turned back and whispered to Danny. 'I suppose it's meant to be me they are trying to set light to. I only hope that red-haired goon has the brains to heed my warning. If not, we're in trouble.'

The effigy flared into life and the leader held it aloft, dodging the flames. A shorter man took up the burning figure with a stick and it danced above the crowd as the fire took hold. Patches of cloth fell away and the leader jigged amongst the flames. The crowd behind him clapped in time to his feet and shouted encouragement.

'What did you say to him?' Danny asked.

Wheatley had one eye on his family. 'I told him he could have his fun in the road but if he or any of his crew so much as land a toe on my property, he will be my enemy. If he lives in East Glasgow, he'll know well enough what it means.'

Danny shook his head. 'He's a gangster from the tenements, JW. Maybe not Garngad, or the Gorbals, but Parkhead is still rough enough. You dinnae want to cross him.'

'I was hoping it would take the heat out of their blood when I told them I'm as Catholic as they are.'

'And a miner,' Danny said.

'Twenty years ago.' Wheatley pushed his spectacles back up his nose and blinked his hooded eyes.

The two men turned to the window again. The ashes drifted in the road like discarded cigarette papers. The mob began to slink away. They faced a hot trudge home without having had the excitement of trashing the rich man's villa. Then, in one movement, they lifted their heads to catch a screeching noise behind them.

This was the moment Danny and John spied Mary Ireland stepping on to her soapbox in front of next door's garden. She was short and tiny-thin. Her face was sharp and her eyes shone like chips of anthracite. If she had been wearing a pointy hat instead of a wee black straw bonnet, the mob would have thought to burn her at the stake. Even though to some it might look as if she was dressed in widow's weeds, Danny recognised the tenement woman's Sunday best and did not hesitate to guess her age at around twenty.

The woman's chin jutted forward with her bottom lip curled out, her thin right arm was raised, fist clenched in the direction of the departing men. Her voice was scratchy and high-pitched and Danny struggled to make out the words through the window. But he recognised the screech. It was a tenement holler. She was sending the men on their way with a sherricking – a public haranguing of a man by a tenement wife.

Wheatley eased open the bottom pane of the window and her holler came clear. 'On you go, you bully-boys. You've finished your little party. Now go and take on a gang of your own size – if you're men enough.'

The leader stepped back bunching his fists. Danny knew the thug wouldn't hesitate to give her a belt to shut her up.

A group of men was hugging the fence behind the woman. It was the deputation from the local party that Wheatley had expected earlier. He tapped Danny's shoulder. 'Look over there, third man along – Andrew Fleming.' Branch secretary Fleming had dried blood masking the lower part of his face.

The woman started up again. 'Go on home, you sorry excuses for the working class.'

Danny's heart was pounding. He marvelled at the fiery little woman's reckless courage. He turned away from the window.

'Where are you going?' Wheatley held Danny's arm.

'She is going to take a kicking unless I do something.'

'Wait, she may talk her way out of it yet.'

Danny shook his head. 'You don't understand these men.' Without Wheatley's restraining hand he would have been at her side already.

The shrill voice peaked. 'Are you too stupid to tell who's on your side?' She pointed at the house. 'The man here is one of us. He started down the pits. He lives in a big villa now, but he's no less one of us for that. He fights for you on the City Council. It's the other parties who are in cahoots with the factory owners and the landlords. The Labour people are for the working class.

That's who John Wheatley is for.'

The ginger-haired man stood in front of her, head cocked, feigning interest. His fists were clenched and his chest open as if, any moment, he could throw a punch.

The woman looked directly at him for the first time. Her voice was still pitched high but she spoke softer. 'You should be ashamed of yourself, Bobby Craig, come here to take on a politician.' She spat the last word contemptuously. 'This is going to be telt as a bedtime story to the tenement bairns.' She put on a mocking, sing-song voice, 'D'ye ken the time Bobby Craig and his gang beat up on the pollytishun and his family?'

Craig's severe look slipped and his mouth dropped open to reveal blackened stumps.

'Aye, you can laugh,' she said.

She smiled and Danny found himself smiling with her, willing her to take advantage of the moment and leave the field.

Wheatley spoke. 'Well, I never! He's backing down. Incredible.'

With a feigned laugh and a dismissive wave of his hand, Bobby Craig turned back towards the bottom of the street and started to herd his men away.

'Let's hope she knows when to stop,' Wheatley said.

The woman screeched, 'When socialists are running this country, we will have the power. We won't be afraid to turn the boss class out of their big houses.'

Wheatley sucked in his breath as Bobby Craig hesitated.

'We're for it now,' Danny said. 'They won't be sent away a third time. The silly biddy!'

Wheatley threw up the sash window and signalled for the Labour Party deputation to run into the house. The men, realising the danger she had put herself in, swept the woman from her soapbox and scurried up the garden path. Danny opened the door for them. He gave a quick nod to the tiny woman in black and stepped outside leaving the front door ajar.

Danny put all his tenement swagger into the six steps that took him to the open gate. He accentuated his limp. He knew the front man, Bobby Craig, had recognised his boot but now he needed the others to be sure.

He stopped and pushed his left leg, rigid in its calliper, forward. He hitched the trouser as he had done before.

Bobby Craig again cut a glimpse at the boot. His eyes moved quickly. He would be in no doubt about Danny's reputation. He would have heard how Danny preferred to charge his opponents, leading with his protected forearms covering his face and neck. Craig would know that when he was on the floor, the bone-crushing boot would take over. Danny's trademark was to stamp on an arm to disable it.

Danny waited to see whether Craig's temper was up enough. Maybe his followers would have the sight of some blood that evening. Danny may have looked calm but his stomach churned at the danger. The numbers massed against him meant that, if Craig was willing to take a broken arm, Danny would be overwhelmed by his gang. He had no doubt the men would trample him with their heavy boots as they surged into the house. He would be lucky to survive to see the next day and the hooligans would be free to turf the family out and sweep through, like a swarm of cockroaches, smashing whatever took their fancy.

Danny locked his eyes onto those of his adversary. He noticed the sweat break out on the freckled forehead. If Craig made a move now, no matter how slight, Danny would charge. All the thug had to do was raise a fist or tense the muscles in his neck to launch a headbutt.

Craig looked down. 'You're lucky I'm in a good mood after all that caterwauling, Danny McAleer,' he said.

Danny felt the tension drain out of his straining shoulders, his clenched fists, his good leg.

'We'll be on our way back to Parkhead Cross then. You and your red friends can sleep soundly in your beds tonight – but only at my say-so.' Craig hawked and spat a gobbet of phlegm on the path.

Danny nodded and stepped back to allow Craig to save face in front of his cronies. 'Take your fine words with you, Bobby Craig,' he said. 'Count yourself lucky my boot hasn't put you in the infirmary.'

Danny and Craig bobbed their brows to each other one last time like stags on the rutting ground, before turning away. Craig surveyed the rabble pressed close around him. 'Let's go, lads. We've seen as much action in Shettleston as we're going to. I know a wee woman in Parkhead who's fretting to sell us a few beers to take the taste of this damned place out of our throats.' He hawked and spat theatrically. The crowd gave a murmur of assent before ambling after him towards the junction with Shettleston Road. Danny watched the last of them pass the other villas and turn left towards the city.

For a few seconds Danny contemplated the empty road. He took a deep breath and considered what might have been. No question, he had averted a full-scale rammy. He looked down at his foot, the source of his hard man reputation, the reason he was known in the tenements as 'The Boot'.

His childhood polio had been a blessing in disguise. He had built his upper body and developed a fighting technique to compensate for the weakness the illness had left him with so he could survive on the streets as a young tough. Before that, when he was in quarantine, the nuns had taught him to read and write. Without his fighting prowess and his education he would not have his job with JW. Without the job he would have been a no-mark.

He turned and went back through the front door.

In the hallway, Andrew Fleming held a bloody rag to his face. The little firebrand speaker stood alongside him, now as timid as a Rabbie Burns mouse. Mrs Wheatley came from the kitchen with a clean cloth and handed it Fleming.

'You're a sad sight, Andrew. What happened?' John Wheatley said.

Fleming wiped the blood from around his mouth. 'They jumped us in Shettleston Road. Us twelve against – how many of them?'

'And who is this brave lass?' Wheatley turned to the dark-haired woman standing alongside his wife.

'This is Mary from the Co-operative Guild,' snuffled Fleming. 'Mrs Mary Ireland.'

Two

Sunday June 30, 1912 – evening
One by one, the comrades shook hands with Wheatley, tipped their hats at his wife and took their leave. Most of them lived in Shettleston or Tollcross so had only a short walk home. Danny was fretting about wee Mary Ireland. What if Craig and some of his mob recognised her when she went back to Parkhead?

'Where do you live, Mrs Ireland?' Wheatley asked.

'Please, call me Mary'

'Mary it is then. Now, where do you stay?'

'I stay in Parkhead, Mr Wheatley,' she answered, her voice now no more than a whisper. 'Off Westmuir Street before the Cross – near where Bobby Craig and most of his goons stay.'

Her eyes were downcast and the lids stretched to cover them. The skin was so delicate Danny could see a faint tracing of veins. She was still trembling after the confrontation and it brought to his mind the vitality of a greyhound held ready for the release of the hare.

'Well, as to you getting home, I think our man Danny can look after you. Eh, Danny?'

Danny's heart lurched in his chest at the thought of escorting the young woman. He kept his voice even. 'Aye, JW. I'll see the lass arrives home safe.'

They caught a tram in Shettleston headed towards Glasgow. Summer insects and cloth-winged moths swarmed to the electric lighting and, caught in the warm capsule of golden air, darted crazily between the lightshades. Mary kept her shawl wrapped about her and her eyes fixed on the floor. Danny, who had sat down gingerly so as not to crush her against the side, turned his head towards her from time to time. Her face was in profile, with no more than the peak of her nose visible beyond the curtain of hair that hung below her bonnet. Following her downward gaze, Danny studied her stockinged feet, which were tightly buttoned into cracked, black shoes with uneven heels.

Danny was desperate to know more about this strange wee woman. He could see out of the window that her stop would arrive all too soon and his mind raced as he tried to think how to start a conversation. Finally, he settled for the mundane. 'You did say you stayed by Westmuir Street?'

She turned to him, her eyes catching the light. 'Aye, but it's a shorter walk if we stay on 'til Duke Street and double back towards the Cross.'

Danny held up the tickets. 'But I only paid to Westmuir.'

'Aye, I ken. We'll have to take a chance.' She smiled at him shyly. Danny slid lower in the seat. Mary jostled him with her elbow. 'Don't worry. They'll not turn you off. Not with your reputation. I'm safe as long as I'm with The Boot of Garngad.'

'How did you ken?'

'Few men would have faced up to Bobby Craig and that gang on his own – the callipers an' aw.'

'I must have been away too long,' Danny said. 'Is Bobby Craig the new man?'

'Aye. He took over from Cameron McBride. Bobby's the new Razor King.'

Danny shook his head. 'That's all behind me now, thanks to Mr Wheatley. He took me out of it two or more years ago.'

'How so?'

'It's a long story. Let's just say he needed somebody to look after him doing his collections just when I was getting a reputation on the streets.'

'As a hard man?'

'Aye, I suppose.' Danny looked out of the window of the lurching tram. He didn't want her to think of him as on a par with Craig and his gang. 'Anyways, how is it a young woman like yourself is mixed up wi' politics?'

Mary looked up sharply, 'Yeh should be asking how can

anyone in the tenements of East Glasgow *not* be in politics. Just because I'm a woman –'

'Whoa! Where did that come frae? I meant with you not having the vote an' aw.'

'Sorry, Danny.' Her voice softened. 'See, my mam made sure I could read and write – I know whit's going on. The women hereabouts accept what little they have so readily – it doesn't have to be this way.'

'You sound like JW.'

'Aye. It's Patrick Dollan from Mr Wheatley's Independent Labour Party branch who comes and talks at Guild meetings. He wants us women to spread the word through the tenements. It was he suggested we turn out for Mr Wheatley today.'

Danny tried to animate his voice so she would see how much he already admired her. 'But it was only *you* had the gumption, Mary.'

'The women *will* change, Danny. We'll have our time.' She looked up as the tram jerked to a stop. 'C'mon! With all this blether we nearly missed our stop.'

Danny stepped back to let her out and she led him off the platform. She scurried into the first turning – Duke Street. Like its neighbours, the road was lined with reddish brown sandstone buildings blackened by soot. At ground level, the shop windows were interspersed with doorways leading to the closes. Even though it was a Sunday, Beardmore's ironworks and the Garngad chemical factories belched sulphurous smoke. The smuts floated down around them. Danny found himself quickening his pace to keep up with Mary's light step.

She slowed down. 'So what did you do for Mr Wheatley to get you out of this little piece of hell and into his plush villa?'

'Like I said, he needed some muscle when he started publishing *The East Glasgow Gazette*. Local businesses paid a subscription to advertise. My job is to make sure they keep paying.'

'And if they refuse?'

'Let's just say it can be awfy inconvenient if your shop window is put in shortly after you have cancelled your advertisement.' He fell in alongside her again, dragging his heavy leg as quickly as he could.

She jutted out her chin, 'I don't care how Mr Wheatley got where he is. All I know is that he's a man who can change things for the better.'

'Aye. Well he's up for Glasgow City Council next. He'll shake them up, all right.' He was tiring of her admiration for his boss. 'But tell me, Mary, how come *our* paths havnae crossed before?'

'William and me were out in the country; we moved to the city a year or so ago. He came to work with his sister's husband. My man delivers the milk to the closes aroon here.'

'The Spaniard? Your man's William the Spaniard?'

She sighed. 'Don't mind his dark looks. He's as Scottish as you or me.'

They arrived at the opening of a close with nothing to distinguish it. It was one of the middling tenements, not too low but certainly not a lace-curtain address. Danny pictured the dark landings and heavy doors. His nostrils prickled with the remembered sour stench of families crowded on top of each other.

'We're here,' she said. 'This is our close.'

'Aye, well...' Danny wiped his palm down his trouser leg before taking her hand. He wanted to find any reason to stay in her company. 'I'm sure JW appreciated what you did for him today.'

'I hope so. Because I'm thinking of tapping him to donate some money to the Guild for our outings and the Christmas party. Whit d'you think?'

'It can't do any harm. He owes you, right enough,' Danny said.

'For nearly getting his fine villa burnt to a pile of cinders, you mean?'

'Aye, that.' He chuckled and started back the way they had come.

A group of louts was standing in the light from the doorway of Craib's Bar on the corner. There were five of them, all with their hands in their pockets. Danny could tell by the shape of them that they had a leader and he was preparing to step in the way. Danny hop-skipped faster, hoping to pass them before they made up their minds whether he was worth rolling.

The leader blocked the path and puffed up his chest. It was Bobby Craig. His arms held back the lapels of his jacket to reveal a razor handle glinting in each pocket of his waistcoat. Danny slowed and instinctively exaggerated his limp. He felt the familiar tightening in his throat and buzz in his ears as his body closed down his finer senses and kicked his survival instinct into gear. His mind was in turmoil, though. How many more of these confrontations would he survive? Would this be the one to leave him spurting blood in the gutter? He consciously swept his mind clear. Self-doubt was a killer.

Craig was smiling. 'I knew you'd be telt to bring the Ireland woman home.' His thumbs caressed the hooked ends of the blades.

'Ah, let's not go through this again, Bobby,' Danny said. He sized up the four men behind. None of them appeared armed or ready to back up the main man.

'Bobby, is it? You're awfy friendly all of sudden, *Mister* McAleer.' He put one fist inside the other in front of his chest and snapped his knuckles theatrically. Then, reversing the grip, he did the same to the other hand.

Danny did not allow himself to be distracted. He scrutinised Craig's face. 'Let's just go our own ways, eh?' He made to step past him.

'Hold on, Danny.' Craig moved to block his path and spat on the ground at his feet. I'm no' standing down again –'

Danny made his voice sound tired. 'I know you have a reputation hereabouts, Bobby. I heard about McBride. So you're the Razor King – of the moment. It's a dying breed, by th'way.'

'Not yet. There are still a few lessons to be dished out.' He crossed his arms in front of him and in a split second the blades were there open in his hands.

The four goons stepped back across the door to the bar. It was just Danny and Craig.

Every razor man Danny had ever fought chose to have a wall behind him for cover while his slashing blades did their work. But Craig, crouching, wheeled to his left so the open street was to his back. He beckoned Danny with the right blade which flashed in the light from the bar window.

Danny's breath shortened. He calculated that Craig knew his style and was giving himself room to step back and to one side, so he could slash his razors from the flank as Danny charged.

Nevertheless, he ran at Craig roaring with his forearms up in front of his face. Danny's instinct told him when the razor man would slip to the side and, in that moment, Danny flung his protected arms up and wide in great arcs. Craig moved right and his left blade caught Danny's left forearm. The razor looped away.

But Craig's weight was on his right foot and gave him the leverage to swing his right blade up behind Danny's arm. Danny felt warm liquid trickle down his neck. He still had the swing in his right arm and it came through to the back of Craig's head. With the smaller man's weight already going that way, the blow was enough to make him lose balance. Danny followed through, crashing his forearms down on his opponent's back. Craig slumped onto his hands and knees.

Danny wasted neither time nor effort. A stamp from the boot on the back of Craig's leg was enough to make him roll in agony. Then a kick to the breadbox and he was flat enough for Danny to select an arm. Craig's right had done the damage and Danny went for retribution. One stamp from the boot brought a satisfying crack. Normally, it would have been enough but the razor man had to learn a hard lesson. Danny kicked the bent arm twice. He knew it was enough for the broken end of bone to be out through the skin. The injured man's screams brought faces to the bar window.

Danny stabbed one look at Craig's cronies to make sure they stayed put. Then he put his hand to his neck to staunch the blood and limped away.

By the time Danny arrived at the Royal Infirmary, his muffler was scarlet with blood that seeped into a growing stain across his chest. He was dizzy. The doctor pulled his hand away from his head. 'Razor?' he said.

'Aye,' Danny said. 'Three goons jumped me.'

'Did you pick up the missing bit?'

'Missing bit of what?'

'Of your ear – the missing bit of your ear?'

'What?' Danny frowned.

The doctor passed him a mirror. 'You'd better take a look.'

Danny's left ear lobe had gone. There was a cut to his cheek as well but it was the straight edge of open flesh and cartilage that drew his attention. Blood pulsed out across the open surface. His head swam and it was only the smell of hospital carbolic stopped him fainting.

There was a commotion outside the cubicle. Danny recognised Bobby Craig's voice, low and hurting. 'My arm. Get somebody to look at my arm.'

The nurse's reply was indistinct.

'For the love of God, woman. Look for yourself. You can see the bone. Get a doctor for pity's sake.'

The doctor's shoulders slumped. 'You would think it would be quieter on a Sunday night.' He pressed a dressing to the side of Danny's face. 'Hold this against your ear. It'll need stitching.' He pushed aside the curtain and was gone.

When the doctor returned he eyed Danny suspiciously. 'That was a bad one,' he said. 'The bone was sticking right through. Somebody set about him with an iron bar, so he said.' He glanced down at Danny's calliper and boot. 'I don't suppose it's anything you'd know about?'

Danny shook his head.

'No point calling out the polis, then?'

Danny gave him the wide eyes and shrugged. 'Nae point as far as I am concerned. Nae point at all'

There was only one light visible in the house by the time Danny returned. It shone in the first floor window and, with the curtains open, lit up the road enough for Danny to see the scorch marks where the Parkhead men had burned his boss's effigy earlier in the day. Danny could make out the silhouette of Wheatley's head and shoulders low in the window, looking as if a bust of him was perched on the sill.

Danny limped down the back alley and let himself in the tradesman's entrance, which had been left unbolted for his return. He crept through the kitchen, up the unlit stairs and doubled back on the landing towards the study. He knocked and entered.

Wheatley was at his desk, his back to the window. He looked up and stiffened. 'What happened?'

Danny told him. Wheatley tutted and shook his head.

'I'm slowing up, JW. I'm getting soft without regular action.'

'After today's events I was thinking something similar. I think you've earned a rest from the heavy work, don't you?'

Danny nodded.

'What say you keep the collections but if an advertiser needs some persuasion you hand the job to someone else? What about your new friend Bobby Craig?'

Danny sniggered. 'He's going to need a change of direction if his arm is as busted as I think it is. I'll have a word with him. Thanks, JW.'

'And the girl. Is she safe?' Wheatley asked.

'Aye, back with her man she is.'

'She's a fine specimen, that one; the sort we need in the party.'

Danny reached up to touch the rough stitches in his ear then moved his hand quickly to cover a stifled yawn. The last thing he wanted was his boss launching into a speech.

'There will be no big change as long as the party is run by tradesmen and teachers. We need more of the street in it. Even if it's the women.'

'Well, I'm for turning in.'

'On you go. Put a towel over your pillow. If there's blood on it in the morning, Mrs Wheatley will give me hell.'

Danny left the small room and, taking care with his stiff leg, climbed the narrow stairs to his room. It was only when he was in the bed, freed from his calliper and with the creak of the springs accompanying every shift in his position, he allowed himself to think again of Mary. She was a spirited lassie, the like of which he remembered from his days in the tenements. You were either a fighter or you allowed the people around you to scramble over you to the top of the heap. Not many women had the fight in them Mary had shown. He remembered how she had seemed so frail as he sat next to her on the tram. She was thin, but still had a womanly figure on her. As the sleep overtook him, the presence of a wedding ring on her finger was no more than a small cloud on an enticing horizon.

Thursday July 4, 1912
Wheatley and Danny walked to St Paul's to see Father O'Brien. Shettleston Road bustled with horse-drawn traffic of every description. There were teetering loads of household paraphernalia, rails of swinging animal carcasses and stacks of finished goods of tin or steel. Other carts trudged to the tenement houses with milk, meat or vegetables. Among those carrying raw materials to feed the factories, some bore straw-packed demijohns of chemicals bound for Garngad. Then there were the tottering, towering loads of hay to fuel the engines – the skin-and-bone horses that plodded warily to avoid the scurrying, stop-go progress of the rail-bound electric trams.

The sharp tang of electricity was a high note soaring over the baser aromas of animal dung and man-made detritus – soot, iron-dust, eye-stinging chemicals and constipated sewer systems.

When they arrived at the manse, Danny was sent to have tea with the housekeeper while the two men talked together in the minister's study. Afterwards, walking back, Danny asked Wheatley if the troubles with the Father were over.

'Och, Danny, who was it once said, "who will rid me of this troublesome priest"? Nae, don't take it as an instruction.' He laughed. 'Father O'Brien and I have agreed to differ. I'll go to confession tomorrow and be in my place alongside Catherine and the weans for mass on Sunday. I'll pen my weekly Catholic Socialist notes for *Forward*. No change for me.'

'And Father O'Brien?'

'That hypocrite will continue to forget he is a pawnbroker's son and will, no doubt, get up in the pulpit and denounce me for pulling myself up by my bootstraps.' Wheatley's voice rose as if his collar stud had been pulled tighter. 'Och, Danny, that man has the rare power to make me forget myself. He calls himself the friend of God's poor but if they show any appetite to better themselves, he sees it as a deadly sin.'

'I did read the last edition of *Forward*, JW.' Danny said. 'I ken what you wrote.'

Wheatley chuckled. 'You're right, I'm preaching again. Let's just say I told him to look after the working class in the next life and leave it to me lead them out of hell in this. He has the message. There will be no more visits from the heavies.'

Three

Thursday May 21, 1914

Danny stepped down from the tram leading with his straight left leg, making sure it was firm before shifting his weight onto it. It was a comparatively bright day but here at Westmuir Cross, with the factories belching their filth, the sunlight was no more than a sick candle's flutter seen through a dirty screen. He joined the hustle of working men at the end of their shift and the stench of their oil-tainted sweat filled the air.

He had left the Wheatley house without being able to tell JW where he was going. He didn't want to interrupt a meeting. Wheatley's Labour Party cronies Jimmy Maxton, Davey Kirkwood and Geordie Buchanan were all there. Danny knew what it would be about – these days they talked only of storm clouds building over Europe and how a capitalist war had nothing to do with the working men of Glasgow.

Over the last two years Wheatley had changed. As his influence on the City Council had grown, he had less time for business. As far as Danny could tell, Wheatley's enthusiasm for the pursuit of money for its own sake had waned. He had appointed his younger brother Patrick to run the legitimate publishing house of Hoxton & Walsh and his brother-in-law Paddy to oversee the less savoury interests in East Glasgow. Wheatley was still skimming his share from the top of both operations so he would never be short of a bob or two.

His boss was still a mass of contradictions. He was a wealthy business man who talked passionately about bringing down the boss class. He was driven but his pudginess made him look feeble. He seemed nervous behind his spectacles but Danny had seen him carry a crowd. The people knew the legend of how the boy Wheatley had walked to night school after each day down the pit. The working men revered him because he had remade himself and was no longer one of them.

Stepping carefully to avoid the carthorse droppings, Danny recalled how Mary, the woman constantly in his thoughts, had persuaded Wheatley to support the Guild's summer outings to Easterhouse and the Christmas parties in the Co-operative Hall. Wheatley had insisted Danny arrange two meetings each year so he could hand over the cash personally. Mary missed only one, in the spring of 1913, when she had recently given birth. She came to the next meeting with the girl Ella in her arms.

It still hurt Danny that, at their first meeting after the rammy, Mary hadn't commented on the new scar on his cheek or his disfigured ear. Instead, and it was the same each time, Danny had watched enviously as she shook hands with her benefactor, looking up at him with those wide, black eyes. Danny could see Mary was mesmerised and she would almost curtsey to Wheatley before heading back for her tram. For his part Wheatley would watch her leave with a flush on his cheeks as if the hand he had held had taken years off him.

This day, Danny was in a hurry because, unusually, Bobby Craig had sent a note to the Wheatley house summoning him to The Auld House bar. The note said there had been disruption in the Ireland house.

Craig's being on Wheatley's payroll had given him back the status he had lost when his mangled arm meant he had to put away his razors. He had become a 'man who knew a man' and made his money from introductions. His network of contacts gave him access to the gossip in the steamies and closes and from it Danny had built a picture of the woman who intrigued him.

When he reached The Auld House bar and turned in, Danny found it was full of working men stopping off on their way home. Many had been paid that day and the drunken clamour indicated that they had already drunk their way through more of the pay packet than their families could afford. The reek of a putrid mixture of stale beer, tobacco smoke and sweat would have made a non-tenement man gag but Danny welcomed it as the perfume of his home.

He spied Bobby Craig and elbowed his way alongside him. 'What're you having?'

'Hof n'a hof.'

'Heavy?'

'Aye'

Danny lowered his head and shouldered his way to the bar. He didn't care if he spilled a man's drink. He still had sufficient reputation here for any offence to be forgiven.

'What's happened?' Danny said, setting down the four glasses.

Craig reached forward with his left hand. 'Slanje!'

'Slanje!' They each took a sip of beer and then repeated the toast offering up the whisky glasses.

'Tell me. What has happened?' Danny said.

Craig wiped the sleeve of his good arm across his mouth and leant in so he could talk directly into Danny's ear. His lips brushed the straight edge where his razor had done its work.

'The Spaniard's telling that woman, you and your boss are so interested in, to toe the line.'

'What d'you mean?'

'You ken I telt you about how she's the talk of the steamies? How she's fallen under the spell of this city councillor who speaks up for the tenement folk even though he's loaded? How she tries to throw them off by talking about his fat stomach and his piggy eyes but they're too sharp to be conned?'

Danny knocked back the rest of his whisky. 'Aye, and the rest.'

Craig grinned. 'Aye, the stuff like–' he mimicked a woman's high-pitch, '*Och he has such a fire in his eyes, girls, and such strength in his character. He'll be the man to lead the working people of East Glasgow when we rise against the boss class* - aw that rubbish.'

He jostled Craig's bad arm. 'Cut out the theatrics, Bobby, and get to the point.'

'Mind the arm there, big man. The point is that the Spaniard has heard about it all – probably from one of his more friendly customers – and he's no' a happy man.'

'How d'you know?'

'I was on the landing. I'd been visiting Charley about a job and heard their bust-up.'

'Whose?' Danny pulled his head out of the way as Bobby tossed back the last of his whisky.

'The Spaniard and the good lady you're so interested in.'

'What kind of bust-up?'

'Raised voices. Maybe raised fists as well.'

Danny felt the old tension fire into his neck and shoulders. 'Go on.' He circled his head like a boxer preparing for a bout.

'I heard him asking about the money from Wheatley.'

'The Co-op Guild money.'

'If you say so. Anyways, the Spaniard said she shouldn't be taking money from him. People would ask what she gave in return.'

Danny could feel the colour rising in his face. 'He can talk – he'll stick it in any hole. What did she say?'

Bobby looked at him sharply, his eyebrows raised. 'I havnae got a transcript.'

Danny put up his hands. 'I know. I know.'

'She shouted back at him about listening to gossip from the gutter and how Wheatley is twice her age. He came back with how she wouldn't take his money if she knew where it came from.'

'What did he mean by that?'

'As if you don't know, Danny. He told her how he lays his bets on with Joe Massey in Craib's Bar.'

'So?'

'Come on, man!' He lit a cigarette, blowing the smoke sideways. 'The whole of East Glasgow knows Joe Massey is a runner for your man Wheatley.'

Danny shook his head. 'Keep your voice down. Be careful what you say, Bobby Craig.'

'All right, act the innocent, Danny. D'you want to hear this or what?'

Danny lifted his beer glass and drank back the rest of it in one slug. 'Go on.'

'Then he started up about Vincent Skee.'

'The money-lender.' Danny knew what was coming next.

'Aye, the Spaniard told her about how Vinnie Skee would be chapping on their door if he wasn't good enough to give her his full pay-packet every Thursday.'

Danny shook his head. He could only picture the women opening their doors to Mary's husband with their dugs on show and smiles on their faces because they were going to dip into Mary's purse. 'What does that mean?'

'So the Spaniard goes on about how Vinnie Skee lends you ten bob and expects to get back a shilling a week for twelve weeks and woe betide a wife who misses a payment.'

'And he said Vinnie Skee is also part of my man's operation?'

'Aye, how Wheatley set Skee up and takes the lion's share of the profits. He called Wheatley a gangster.'

'What did she say?'

'Something about him being a good man, a socialist – a city councillor. You can imagine what William says to that – about the City Chambers being the house of corruption.'

'And then?'

'She screamed at him she didn't care and she would see Wheatley because all she wanted was to get out of the hovel they lived in. That's when I heard him moving close and I backed round the corner sharp. He came out slamming the door behind him with a bad look on his dark face. The baby started greetin'. I made myself scarce.'

Danny took his bad arm. 'Did he hit her, Bobby?'

Craig shook his head.

Much later that night Danny staggered up the hill to the Wheatley house from the tram stop in Shettleston Road. Darkness had descended, but he had set a drunkard's bearing and anything in his way would be kicked or elbowed away, be it one of the plane trees lining the street or the pillar box halfway up.

How much of what he had learned should he tell Wheatley? Need he know that Mary now had chapter and verse on his operations? Was now the time to tell his boss that Mary had been telling all the tenement womenfolk what a fine man he was? Danny decided he would not. JW was too self-absorbed to be concerned what people thought.

How much better off would Mary be with a man like Danny himself. She had a brutish husband who had a reputation with the ladies. She had an eye for a married man twice her age only because of his money. No, if anybody deserved to have Mary, it was Danny McAleer. He turned into the side ginnel that led to the alley. His shoulders careered off the brick walls on both sides like a ball-bearing in a tube as he made his way along. He counted the back entry gates and opened the one for the Wheatley house.

Inside the courtyard he made for the lavvie, eased the door open and stepped inside. He unbuttoned his flies. The rush of water from his bladder was immediate and strong enough to make him shudder with relief. 'Like a horse,' he said to himself. He finished, buttoned up and headed for the back door. He would flush it in the morning.

Four

It was a year before Bobby Craig sent a boy with another message for Danny to meet him in the Auld House bar. It had been a sombre week. Glasgow, being a port city, had been hit hard by the sinking of the Lusitania. Danny had heard Catherine Wheatley berating her husband about the monster Huns and their dastardly warfare, using torpedoes launched from a U-boat to sink a passenger liner. 'Over twelve hundred killed, John. Ninety-four of them children – thirty-one just bairns in their mothers' arms. Now you must persuade your pacifist friends we have to fight with all our might.' Danny had not waited to hear the answer.

This time the men found a corner table in the smoke-filled room and sat with their drinks in front of them. It was unseasonably warm outside and, with a fire roaring, the sweat on their brows mixed with the sulphur in the air and made their eyes sting. The glass of heavy was cool in Danny's hand.

Bobby's right jacket sleeve was empty and the cuff pinned to his shoulder.

'What's that about?' Danny said, pointing.

Bobby looked sheepish. 'When ma arm is in the sleeve I look like I'm fit enough for war. My hand is useless anyway so I don't miss it tucked inside. This way I look like a brave boy back frae the Front. No silly biddies will be troubling me with white feathers.'

'Look at us. We'd make one good soldier between us.' He hit his stiff leg. 'My leg and your wing, whit a pair, eh?'

They raised their glasses and laughed.

'So, what news?' Danny leaned forward.

'There's been another wean.'

'So soon?'

'Aye, a few weeks ago. I saw them out at the weekend, the Spaniard's wife and the babies top and tailed in a pram. The one before only a year old, they say.'

'What's this one?'

'Another girl, name of Millie.'

'And is all well?'

'Aye. But it's not the only news. I struck up a conversation with her. "I heard you had another one, Mary. Let's have a peek," I says.'

'What did she say?'

'Nothing'. So I peers inside. "I see you have another chip off the old block, right enough. There is no disguising those black eyes and the over-cooked look." Well, she puts her chin in the air and looks down her nose at me as if I was smelling stronger than the stink off the furnaces. "You keep your opinions to yourself," she says.'

Danny took a pull at his drink.

'So I says, "ye know I have to report back to Danny McAleer. He's still asking after you." She blushed, Danny. I swear she blushed like a twelve-year-old. And she comes back with, "You tell Mr Wheatley all is well with Mrs Mary Ireland." All hoity-toity like.'

'Have you got that right, Bobby. She said "tell Mr Wheatley"?'

'Aye.' Craig looked at him sharply. 'Whit's it to you, by th'way?'

Danny lit a cigarette. Didn't he count for anything in her eyes?

When Craig recognised that Danny wasn't going to answer he continued, 'No, it had to be the way I said because I says, "You don't think Wheatley would sully his suit bumping into the likes of me? No, I'll keep Danny McAleer up on your daily doings, like I have been." She ignored that one and tried to push past me.'

'Is that all?'

'Naw! To keep the banter goin' I says, like you do these days, "Shall I tell Danny that the Spaniard will be taking the King's shilling, by th'way?" She barged the pram straight at me and I got meself out of the road. "Tell him what you want," she says.'

'So what are you saying, is he joining up or not?'

Craig sat back with his palms up. 'Wait on, big man. I'm getting there. So later I'm talking to Lou – y'ken, the Spaniard's sister – while I'm waiting for Charley and I says, "wherever you go these days the recruiting sergeants are hounding us men giving out the shilling. I'm buggered if I'm interested. What about your Charley?" She says, "He's in no hurry to join up. He'll wait for the call. Not like his daft brother. That William has a rare fever for a smart uniform and a regular pay packet, especially now that the rents are going up all over Parkhead. He and Mary were thinking of moving to two rooms and a kitchen. Now I wouldn't be surprised to see him coming up that stair with the army's tartan breeches on his fat backside just so as the woman and her weans can stay in a single-end."'

Craig wiped a hand across his mouth, taking away the beer foam and leaving a leer in its place. 'So what will your Mr Wheatley want with the Spaniard's wife when he's away at the Front, Danny? She's going to be awfy lonely, by th'way.'

Danny had hardly heard the last remark. Something Bobby said earlier had stuck in his mind. 'What was that about rents?'

Craig offered up his empty glass with his left hand. He resumed talking only after Danny had returned with a replacement. Craig took a few deep swallows. 'Where've you been? The landlords are putting the rents up all over Glasgow. For the first time in years the men are getting a regular wage from their soldiering. The money's going straight from the War Office into the landlords' pockets.'

'The boss will be interested to know,' Danny said.

'He might also want to know that, according to Lou, your woman, the Spaniard's wife, is stirring them up against it. She's telling anybody who'll listen that it's not right for the landlords to be profiting out of the war. She's trying to get the women to stand up to the sheriff's men when they come to turf them out for not paying, not just in Parkhead and Shettleston but all over the East End.'

'But she has only now dropped a wean.'

'Aye, well, she dumps both of them with Lou and goes out agitating the women in the steamies an' the closes.'

Danny stood up. 'Time for me to get back to Shettleston. Thanks, Bobby.'

'Huh! You think Wheatley's going to be interested? The landlords are the same people he has to his Saturday night –' he put on a West Side accent '– bridge party soirées. The same people have taken the food out of the mouths of tenement weans for years. You think he wants to stop them?'

Danny hauled his straight leg on to the tram's platform and paid for his ticket to Shettleston. If Bobby was right and Mary was trying to agitate the women not to pay the rent increases, JW would want to know while he could still take the credit.

'I had already heard about the rent rises,' Wheatley said.

Danny had reported back, standing on the rug in front of Wheatley's desk. His boss sat behind it. The lenses of his spectacles and the papers in front of him glowed orange in the light from the desk lamp. 'We have a case here in Shettleston, Mrs McHugh. Her husband enlisted straight from the pit and now the factors want to turn her out because she owes rent. I'm writing an article for this week's *Forward*.'

He ran his hands over his hair and pulled at the points of his waistcoat. 'If we can get the Parkhead women out, who knows what we will be able to achieve? I think it's time we met with Mary Ireland again.'

Danny's blood surged like in the old fighting days. 'Do you want me to talk to her?'

'Aye. D'you think she will come to the house? No, on second thoughts, ask her when it will be convenient to come to the ILP rooms.'

'She has a wean only a few weeks old, according to Craig.'

'Well we shall have to find out whether she is fit enough for some action on behalf of her sisters on the tenements.'

Friday May 14, 1915

Danny had dressed in his smartest blue shirt under his Sunday jacket. His boots shone. But by the time he was by Mary's close his shoulders bore the black dust from the works and the back of his throat stung with the taste of it. He'd been in the cleaner air of Shettleston too long and his lungs were labouring from the thickness of the smog-soup he had once taken with his mother's milk.

He called out on the stair. 'Mary Ireland, are you there, woman?' Doors on each landing opened and the shadows of heads leaned into gaps. Some remembered the sight of Danny from the old days and quickly retreated, others kept an eye out.

'If you aren't the Ireland woman keep your nose out of her affairs,' Danny called. 'If you can tell me which landing she is on, give me a sign.'

One of the doors opened a crack more and the woman behind it waved him up. 'Next landing, Danny McAleer. I hope you're not collecting from the likes of her. She has two weans to feed, her man in the army an' aw.'

'Mind your blether, woman. I'm not on collecting business.' It would start tongues wagging but he didn't want to give Mary a bad name in the close. He trailed his leg up to the next landing.

One of the doors opened and a baby's cry sounded louder.

'Whisht! Who is it?'

'It's me, Danny McAleer.'

'Come in, Danny, come in.'

He looked round the single-end room. The cavity bed was closed and opposite it a girl in a vest and Terrycloth sat unsteadily by the open bottom drawer of the clothes press. The range gave out an oppressive heat. The doors to the presses for pots and food were both closed. The table was clear except for a cloth with a lace centre piece. This was a woman who took pride in her house. She wedged the door to the landing open behind him.

'Cup o'tea, Danny? Or something stronger? I can offer you a dram. Come sit down.' She wiped her hands on the skirt of her spotless pinafore.

'Tea would be nice.' He took a seat at the table and checked he could be seen from the landing.

Mary gave him a nod. 'So you remember what it's like to live in a tenement where all the tongues wag at the slightest excuse, Danny.'

He nodded. 'I ken what it's like.'

The kettle was whistling quietly and Mary busied herself with it and the teapot. She poured tea for both and handed Danny milk in a jug. She passed the sugar bowl. 'Be free with the sugar, Danny. Don't fret, we can spare it.'

It was what any tenement wife would say. Danny shook his head even though he preferred his tea sweet.

'Well, I didn't think I wid be seeing you until I came to ask for Mr Wheatley's help with the summer outing.'

'Canal trip to Easterhouse again this year?'

'The air is so pure there it makes their wee chests hurt, the poor bairns. They go dipping in the loch there. It's a rare treat for them. Did they no' have trips like that in your day, Danny?'

'Nothing like it. We didn't have women like you who would take on the organising.'

'Well, I wouldn't be able to without the Co-op and people like Mr Wheatley. Anyway, why are you here?'

Danny poured some tea into the saucer and blew on it. When it was cool enough, he took a sip. 'Grand tea.'

She nodded and crossed her legs. She trailed a hand behind her and took her elder daughter's hand. The baby in the drawer had gone quiet.

'I hear they're putting up the rents around here.'

'Aye, as soon as the men started joining up. Most of us have good money coming in the now. Beardmore's has gone over to munitions work so there's plenty of overtime to be had. My William's away in Liverpool training with the army and I go to the post office to collect his money. It's there every week regular as clockwork, better than when the men were home. The landlords know it, so are making money out of it. It's shameful, by th'way.'

'Well, Mr Wheatley wants to take action against the

landlords and their factors. Would you be able to chivvy the women hereabouts to back him up?'

She looked down into her teacup shaking her head. 'I've tried. They don't have much to do with politics round here. What have the politicians done for them? They don't know about the Labour movement. Most around here, men and women, can't read. All they know is that councils are full of the boss classes. Why would they take to the streets for a politician?'

'Why don't you meet with JW – Mr Wheatley – he'll explain it to you.'

Her head lifted and those wide pale-lidded eyes shone at him. 'I ken I will. Let us see what your grand Mr Wheatley has to say to get the women of Parkhead out for him.'

Danny left Mary the price of a tram ticket and laboured down the stairway and back to Shettleston. He cursed himself for not being more forward with her. If she didn't know how he felt about her how would she be able to respond in kind?

Five

Danny and Wheatley sat at the green-baize-covered table in the Independent Labour Party rooms off Shettleston High Street. Danny had made a pot of tea and sat sipping from the saucer and watching Wheatley while he read some council papers. Occasionally, Wheatley would shake his head vigorously or tut-tut and make a note in the margin with his fountain pen. Danny knew better than to speak.

They heard the main door open. Wheatley shuffled together his papers and nodded for Danny to go. He discovered Mary a step inside the door looking around the small plain-walled hall. Danny was conscious of the smell of dust that hung about the place and contrasted it with her neat, polished room in Parkhead. 'You found us, then, Mary,' he said.

Mary bustled up to him and offered a handshake. 'Well it's no distance from the tram.'

Danny led the way into the committee room and stood to one side. Mary approached the table, shrugged off her shawl and folded it over a chair back. She was still patting it into place when she spoke. 'Danny says you want to see me, Mr Wheatley.'

He stood and offered his hand. 'Straight to business, Mary. Yes. Thank you for coming. Sit down.' He gestured to a chair and waited for her to sit. Danny's eyes widened. He hadn't seen Wheatley do that for any woman other than his wife in all the years he'd worked for him.

'You'll have a cup of tea? We have a pot here.'

'Aye.'

'Danny?' Wheatley was smiling at her and tossed the word in Danny's direction as a bone to a dog. The younger man felt a shiver of irritation run down his good leg. JW always reserved his most dismissive behaviour for when Danny didn't want to be marked as a lackey.

Danny poured a third cup and passed across the milk and sugar.

Wheatley's jaw went slack as he watched Mary take three spoonfuls of sugar before stirring the heavy liquid vigorously. She put the cup to her lips. 'Ach! You make a fine cup o' tea, Danny. You'll make some lucky woman a fine husband.' She shook up her shoulders and Wheatley chuckled. Danny, still standing to one side behind her, pursed his lips and took a deep breath.

The colour was rising in Wheatley's cheeks. He took off his glasses and polished the lenses with a handkerchief. 'To business, Mary, to business. You are, if I may say, a rare example for the women of our city.'

It was her turn to blush and she gave her tea a second stir.

'No, I mean it. You have few of the advantages of many others, yet you have decided to act on behalf of your class, of your se– ah, kind.'

'I would do mair if you let me, Mr Wheatley.' She tapped a fingertip on the baize. 'Why is it I am not allowed to join the party, by th'way?' She leaned forward.

'Are you not?' He waved his hand in front of his face. 'It never occurred to me you couldn't. You don't have the vote, so –'

'Och! Don't fret yourself, Mr Wheatley. I do what I can with the Co-op. It does me.' She picked at a piece of loose cotton on her blouse; it was faded from washing.

'It's what you can do to mobilise the women of Parkhead I'm interested in, Mary. Can you turn them into an army?'

'Can you give them reason to step out of their closes?'

'I think I can. First I need to know you will help me. Are you prepared to take on the landlords and their factors over these rent increases?' His eyes were lifting her out of her seat.

She brought a fist, frail as a blackbird's claw, down onto the table top. 'I am, Mr Wheatley, I am. I will follow you.'

'Let me tell you about Mrs McHugh.' Wheatley said. He looped a thumb under the lapel of his jacket and raised his chin. 'I was at the Sheriff's Court yesterday to stand for her in the hearing of her eviction case. When I arrived I found at least fifty, probably a hundred, other women in the same straits as her; and all the officers of the court sitting around smiling while these women and their children were being ordered to be put on the streets. Even though the union offered to pay off her arrears, the Sheriff gave the factors their order. Mrs McHugh is to be out next month. All this is happening while her husband is in an English hospital bed recovering from injuries he received on the Western Front fighting for his country. What sort of gratitude is that?'

Mary shook her head her bottom lip turned down.

Wheatley continued. 'My comrades in the local party are organising the people of Shettleston to meet at the McHugh house next Wednesday week after work finishes. Would you try to get the women of Parkhead to join us?'

'I will do my best.'

'I can ask no more.' He unscrewed the top of his pen and it hovered over a fresh sheet of paper. 'Come now, Mary. We shall make a plan of campaign.'

Wednesday June 9, 1915
Wheatley had chosen the McHugh's as an example but it could as well have been any soldier's family in Shettleston, Tollcross, Parkhead, St Rollox, the infamous Garngad – anywhere in East Glasgow. But, that day, it was to Mrs McHugh's house that Danny limped alongside the twenty or so members of the Independent Labour Party. They could see something special was happening. Men drifted in to join them like tributaries feeding a river. It was if they were building a crowd for the football at Celtic Park. The men's boots sparked on the flags as they hurried down the Shettleston Road.

The top of William Street was a sight to behold. Danny had never seen so many women collected together in one place.

From their bonnets and shawls they were from the tenements. From the lowest 'hairy' to the highest 'doilie', they had marched down behind Mary.

Her shriek went up. 'That's him! Mr Wheatley!' And a high-pitched holler such as would be heard in hell came from them. The men, more used to being massed in a crowd, stood to one side watching as the women shook their fists and elbowed each other, all the time keeping up a flocking, mocking screech.

Wheatley put his hands up to silence them. 'It's good so many of you have come out in support of your sister, Mrs McHugh,' he shouted. 'If you will let me through to the front of the house, I can address the crowd and we shall make sure we send the landlords and their factors packing.'

They greeted this with another yell and the group parted. Mary took Wheatley by the arm and led him through to the front. Danny followed and felt the women's slaps on his back. There was steam coming off the huddle of them trailing a strange mixed smell of the Parkhead Forge, tobacco and sour whisky. It was good to get through them and to the small area where Wheatley stood in front of the cottage.

Mrs McHugh looked old enough to be Wheatley's mother but was probably fifteen years his junior. She had the look in her eyes as if Wheatley were a statue of Christ on the cross, tears streamed down her cheeks. She grasped his hand. 'It's wonderful what you are doing, Mr Wheatley.' Mary elbowed her aside and stood rigid alongside Wheatley as they turned to face the crowd. Her face was flushed and her eyes sparked with excitement.

Andrew Fleming came out of the house with a kitchen table and set it down. Mary and Danny helped Wheatley onto it. He turned to face the crowd and they fell quiet. Danny again marvelled at the magic of the man. Wheatley in front of a crowd was a man transformed. He mesmerised them into thinking he was the Messiah himself.

His voice was its usual high pitch and he went back to the language of his youth as he always did with a Glasgow crowd. Danny noticed how Mary stood proprietorially at the side of the table with her feet planted apart and her arms wide as if to hold back a crowd. She had the same look on her face as Mrs McHugh.

'Thank you for coming to this place, men and women of East Glasgow.' He looked at the women steaming in their shawls. 'I want to say a special welcome to the women of Parkhead –'

The rest of his sentence was drowned out by the women's soprano holler.

'This is an evening we will all remember. It's the first stirring of a movement. The working class movement!'

The cheers boomed out, this time from all sides.

'This is a fight on behalf of a poor woman, Mrs McHugh here.' He signalled Danny to push the woman forward. Mary nodded vigorously as if the McHugh woman was in the limelight at her behest. 'She's to be evicted tomorrow.'

The crowd surged forward with cries of, 'No!'

'She is one of us, one of you,' Wheatley shouted. 'The women of East Glasgow – no, the women of Parkhead–' He shouted the last word, knowing it would draw a high-pitched roar in response. He calmed them with a flutter of his raised hands before continuing. 'The women of Parkhead – the women of all East Glasgow are united against the unfair tactics of the landlords and their factors. Will you and the men gathered here let this woman be put out?'

The crowd surged forward, fists raised. 'No!'

'Will we let the landlords take more money out of the pockets of our brave fighting lads?'

'No!'

'Will you allow this eviction to happen?'

'No!'

Wheatley put his hand to his ears theatrically. 'I can't hear you.'

'No!' The sound of them was louder than would greet a Celtic goal.

Wheatley paused and the crowd hushed, waiting.

'Then you, the men and women of East Glasgow, must be the ones to stand in their way. Tomorrow you must be the ones to picket the house and turn the factors back. Will ye do it?'

'Aye!'

'Will ye?'

'Aye!'

'Will you give your names at the ILP rooms the night and pledge you will be here the morrow?'

'Aye! Aye! Aye!'

The sounds of the crowd's shouts reverberated in the heavy air. Danny caught John as he jumped down. Mary, too, held on to him and her face burned hot when he smiled at her and winked. The crowd swept the three of them up the street towards Shettleston.

Andrew Fleming and the rest of the ILP committee signed up more than five hundred men and women to come back the following day. As the last one left, Wheatley stood with Mary in the deserted hall. Danny could tell from the way she was shifting from foot to foot and hugging herself that she was overcome with the emotion of her first mass demonstration. He sensed she was holding herself back from throwing herself into Wheatley's arms to celebrate their achievement.

Was it only his presence holding her back? If it was, it was not out of any respect for his feelings. As far as Danny was concerned she had no inkling of how he felt for her. No, it was only propriety making her keep herself reined in – the fact of them both being married. Danny wondered how his boss would have reacted had she thrown herself at him and, at that moment, Wheatley reached out with both hands and, when she took them, flung her round in a reel. They threw their heads back and hooted and cackled like a couple of teuchters on Burns' Night as they spun round and round.

Thursday June 10, 1915

Shettleston was home to a revolution. The children gambolled round their mothers as they marched to the points of demonstration. William Street was thick with the Parkhead women led there by the diminutive Mary Ireland. No factor's men were going to reach the McHugh cottage with their dignity intact. A red flag flew protectively over it.

Wheatley led Danny to Mary as soon as they arrived. Danny's smile was as wide as the Clyde.

'You're looking pleased with yourself,' Mary said.

Danny was emboldened by her welcome. 'It's a fine sight, you leading all these women.'

Wheatley nodded. 'Indeed it is, comrade. It swells my heart to see the women out for their sister.'

'You're in danger of giving me a swelled head, Mr Wheatley,' Mary said seeming to ignore Danny's opening.

Danny gave her a wink. 'There's no danger of that, I have never met a woman with her feet more firmly on the ground.'

She blushed and then looked at Wheatley expectantly as if she needed him to validate his lackey's comment.

Wheatley waved his hand at the insignificance of what had gone before. 'To business, Mary. We won't keep this crowd happy by leaving them hanging around. We must give them some action.' He signalled to Patrick Dollan and Andrew Fleming to join them. Danny stepped back but Mary bustled into the group.

Danny heard their deliberations above the hubbub from the crowd. Wheatley spoke first. 'Comrades, I think Mary and I should lead the women to the factor's office in Shettleston Road. We can make our feelings known there. You keep the men here. If the police or the sheriff's men try to reach the house – well, I leave it up to you. Just make sure the men here are not the first to make trouble.'

Patrick frowned. 'They'll start drifting away if we can't promise them some action.'

Wheatley's face was set hard. 'Don't worry. If we can't keep the bailiffs occupied in the High Street, they'll be down here to turf Mrs McHugh out. The men will have their rammy.'

He turned to Mary. 'It's time for you to take command of your army of women and lead them into battle. Can you do it?'

She puffed up her chest and drew herself up to the rigid stance Danny remembered from that first sight of her in Anstruther Street. 'Aye,' she said, holding Wheatley's gaze as she spoke.

Wheatley paused a moment, as he looked back at Mary. Danny felt the tension and shifted from good leg to bad until Wheatley broke the silence.

'You had best let them know where we're taking them,' Wheatley said signalling a low wall for her to stand on. 'I've seen you in action, Mary Ireland, I have every confidence you can take this crowd with you.'

Her face was flushed and energy seemed to spark from her pores as she jumped on the wall and yelled a tenement holler to get their attention. The women knew it was a call for silence. As the noise from them dropped so the men stopped their blethering.

The crowd pressed in around him. Danny took a deep breath and could almost taste the fug of pressing humanity in his mouth. He wouldn't have believed it, even though he had seen Mary see off Bobby Craig and the gang, but now, with the sun breaking through on an East Glasgow morning, she looked calm, as if mercury flowed through her veins, as if being the dynamo at the hub of an engine of turbulence was her true place.

Her voice was high but it did not break. 'Listen up all of you. This is what's going to happen. The women here, my group from Parkhead and Mr John Wheatley's from Shettleston and Tollcross, will join forces and march to the factor's office where we will state our case against the rent rises.'

She had to stop because the women screeched and cried out in support. She put up her hand. 'The men will stay here with Mr Patrick Dollan and Mr Andrew Fleming in case the polis come with the bailiffs.'

She looked down at Patrick Dollan who was tugging at her shawl. 'I'll take over here, Mary. You join John and take the women away.'

Danny followed her through the crowd of women moving off in the direction of the High Street. He pushed a space through for Wheatley who was in his wake like a tug following a liner. All three emerged into the clear stretch of road at the same time. It was slightly uphill of the crowd. 'Mind all the women follow us.' Mary shouted and turned to Wheatley. Danny was to one side, watching. 'Are you ready, John?' It was the first time she had used his Christian name.

'It's an honour to be a comrade at your side, Mary,' he said and linked her arm in his as they started up the road.

Danny saw how tightly she hugged Wheatley's arm to her bosom. Was she so wound up in the excitement she had forgotten Wheatley was not her man? Or did she know well enough the effect such an embrace from a young woman of her age would have on the boss?

They led the crowd of over a hundred along the centre of Shettleston Road to the factor's office. On one side the horse traffic and occasional motor car had to pull over to allow the deluge to pass. The crowd streamed around the stranded trams as a torrent parts for the boulders in its path but rocks them with its power.

A group of five police officers was waiting outside the court building and Wheatley took their sergeant by the elbow and steered him away. Danny stuck close to his heels. 'Now, Sergeant,' he heard Wheatley say, 'we have to consider the best way to avoid a breach of the peace here, don't you think?'

The policeman removed his helmet, cradled it on his forearm and used his free hand to wipe the sweat off his brow with a handkerchief. Danny could barely see his lips move, hidden as they were by a heavy, grey moustache, stained yellow to one side by cigarettes. 'We have to uphold the law, Councillor, and ensure the sherrif's men can go about their duty,' he said.

'Of course, of course. But what purpose would be served by a confrontation today? You would end up taking women to the cells, depriving children of their mothers. How will that make their men folk react?'

The sergeant wiped his creased brow again and Wheatley, sensing his hesitation, pressed on.

'If you can delay the enforcement for twenty-four hours, I will see what I can do to get a satisfactory end to the dispute. In the meantime, I will vouch for their behaviour. If the court doesn't send in the men, I will make sure these good women keep the peace.'

The sergeant nodded, smoothing his helmet backwards over his head and adjusting it so the peak was low over his eyes. Then he shouldered his way through to the courthouse. A few minutes later he emerged and nodded to Wheatley over the heads of the crowd.

Wheatley shouted above the murmur. 'We have an assurance from the police that no action will be taken against Mrs McHugh today. Let us go back to her house, give her the good news and decide what our next action should be.' As they went back the way they had come, Danny noticed a group of the few men who had accompanied them break off down Kelton Street.

Friday June 11, 1915

The numbers had flagged. Most of the men who had been out the day before had returned to work, disappointed by the lack of action. After the assurance that Mrs McHugh was safe for at least another day Wheatley had stood them down. Many of them, with the unexpected bonus of a half day of leisure had spent it in the bars and Danny imagined that this morning their heads would be pounding as hard as the crashing presses and cutters they attended.

The Parkhead women were out in force and Wheatley acknowledged as much. 'It's good to see our comrades from Parkhead here again. My special thanks to Mrs Mary Ireland of the Co-op Guild who has done so much to help our cause.'

A cheer went up from the women and while Mary blushed they started a chorus of 'For she's a jolly good fellow...'

Wheatley shouted over them. 'Yesterday some of our men left the main group and broke windows in one of the factors' houses. We are not here to wreck homes but to prevent them being wrecked. While they were away, Mrs McHugh's house could have been taken over by the bailiffs.'

'We wouldn't have let them do that – not with five hundred women here!' It was Mary Ireland's shriek. The women laughed and Danny smiled.

'Aye,' Wheatley said. 'But burning effigies and breaking windows is a waste of our precious energies. I remember three years ago when your men – or the men of some of you – came to my house and threatened me. It didn't change me... I'm still here!'

'Aye, a bad smell is hard to get rid of!' It came from the back of the crowd and heads turned.

Wheatley hesitated for a second. Possibly Danny was the only one who noticed it. 'A bad smell, all right, and I get right up the noses of the boss class – the mine and factory owners and the landlords. It's they who are trying to get rid of me. Will I stand down?'

'No!'

'Our strike committee, myself and Patrick Dollan of the Independent Labour Party and Mrs Mary Ireland of the Co-operative Guild, made a plan yesterday and now we will act on it. The men are to stay here and guard the house. I will lead a deputation of the women to the Armaments Committee office in the city. We will demand that evictions cease. I want soldiers' wives, mothers, sisters and daughters to lead the march. Are you ready? Are you ready to march?'

'Aye!'

'When we get to the City Chambers I shall send a telegram to Lord Kitchener in London. I will make him take notice of what's happening on the streets of East Glasgow.'

'Hurrah!'

Wheatley, his face flushed and his breathing short, turned to Mary. 'Will you come with me to City Chambers? You deserve to be right where the action is.'

'What about here? Who will look after Mrs McHugh?'

'Find one of your women you can trust to mind her. The men will stop an eviction. I want you with me, Mary, to share our triumph.'

Mary broke away and held a quick discussion with a clutch of women who stood alongside her.

When she turned back she linked her arm into his and looking up at him, she said, 'They have it under control, Mr Wheatley. We shall go into the city and give Lord Kitchener hell.'

His pigeon chest puffed and it, rather than his belly, led the parade up William Street to the Shettleston Road. The march of over two hundred women, led by the sweating, suited figure of John Wheatley arm-in-arm with the striding Mary Ireland, turned west towards the city. Danny hop-skipped one step behind the leading couple driving his straight left leg as fast as it would go.

The mass of women marched along the Gallowgate, turned at St Enoch station into George Square and finally halted outside the City Chambers. Wheatley was puffing. Mary fanned her face with her free hand. Danny noticed how she leant her upper body into his boss. Her eyes were wide and her smile broad as whippet's.

Wheatley took off his bowler hat and took a handkerchief to his brow. He patted his companion on the hand and detached her from his arm. 'It's time for me to whip 'em up again.'

The women were looking round wondering what would happen next. Wheatley beckoned Danny closer. 'There's a stepladder behind the porter's station inside the door. Tell him I want to talk to the people. He'll understand.'

When Danny emerged with the steps, Wheatley motioned for him to set them up by an empty plinth alongside the door. The City Chamber had no steps leading to its double-height doors and members of the council were used to making impromptu speeches from the shoulder-high platform it gave them. Danny held the stepladder as Wheatley climbed it and shakily transferred to the ledge. His hands went up and the women stopped shuffling their feet. 'We first have to tell the good people of the City Council and the Armaments Committee who we are,' he shouted. 'Are you the wives and mothers, the sisters and daughters of soldiers?'

A crashing cry of exclamation sent the pigeons up as if a line of beaters was crossing the square.

'And are your men fighting the bosses' and landowners' war at the Front?'

'Aye!'

'And have the landlords put up your rents?'

'Aye!'

'Can you pay?'

'No!'

'Will you pay?'

'No!'

'Will you be evicted?'

'No!'

'Will you?' this time Wheatley held a cupped hand to his ear.

'No!' The howl of the women would have frightened the Kaiser's men. Mary was screaming louder than most, jinking up and down on her tiny shoes and waving to Wheatley as if she could have his attention all to herself. Danny watched her in her frenzy and, involuntarily, his head shook slowly from side to side.

'Will you?' Wheatley's high-pitched voice reached a crescendo.

'No!' This one was loud enough to reach their men in France.

'Then I will send a telegram to Lord Kitchener from these offices and I will tell him that your landlords are exploiting the war effort and that you will not pay the increases and you and your men deserve no less than the government's protection in this. Shall I send Kitchener your message?'

'Aye!'

'You have done your job here, good people of Parkhead, of St Rollox, of Shettleston, of Tollcross, of Baillieston. You can leave me and your representative Mary Ireland to negotiate on your behalf.'

Danny watched Mary straighten her back and jut her chin proudly before she stepped forward and stood below Wheatley. She turned to face the crowd. This was her calling. There was no trace of the shyness Danny had seen three years before. In front of Danny's eyes, Mary was emerging from the tenements on to a wider stage. The look of it lowered his spirits. It felt the same as when he stood on the dockside waving to his eldest sister who leaned, straining over the rail of the ship taking her to a new life in America.

He was jerked back to the present by his boss's voice. 'Hie ye back to your homes or to William Street. We shall meet again later outside the McHugh house. When, I confidently predict, we shall have won the day. You shall stay in your homes. You shall not pay the increases. You shall *not* be evicted!'

With each of the last sentences, Mary raised her clenched fist to the sky. The women cried out in response, spitting their anger at the Chambers building. Then they turned and, pulling their shawls about them and gossiping in groups, they drifted back east.

Wheatley signalled Danny to join him and Mary. Inside, a wide staircase hugged the veined-marble walls of the cavernous entrance. Wheatley and Mary stood on the first landing and waited for Danny to catch up. Wheatley was breathing hard and his eyes were alight. His voice was high and excited. 'I love this!' The sound echoed around the space. 'Right enough, we are helping the working people of this city, but it's what it does to my insides I do it for.' He held his pudgy fists in front of his chest and shook them at the others while gritting his teeth. 'It makes me feel so alive!'

He led them through a door into a large space dotted with leather club chairs and went across to one of the desks. Mary pirouetted slowly taking in the tapestries and oil paintings, each as huge as a side of the McHugh cottage. Here the ceilings were so far away you would need a fire company ladder to reach them. Highly-coloured men in armour chased women in shifts across the sky. Danny thought of the dark, single-end where his mother had raised him and his three sisters.

'John!' A tall, thin man strode across the room. He held up a bony hand connected to a frail wrist. 'Was it your people filling the square?' With his gaunt looks and curtain of hair flopping over his forehead, Jimmy Maxton was Glasgow's most recognisable Labour councillor.

Wheatley's voice took on a tone as if he was sharing a new discovery. 'This, Jimmy, is Mrs Mary Ireland, a new activist in my constituency. Mrs Ireland is from Parkhead. Her husband is fighting in France.'

Danny assumed Mary would tell them that William was still in training at Aintree but she set her lips firmly together and bowed her head, evidently thinking that the lie suited the moment better.

Maxton turned and took her hand. 'Welcome to the cause, Mrs Ireland. We need all the help we can get. If I had my way your man would be here at home – not fighting our German working class comrades.'

'You don't need to get on your soapbox with Mary, Jimmy. She's one of us.'

'What's your plan, John?' Maxton said.

'We shall send a telegram about the rent rises to Kitchener.'

Maxton's forehead was creased. He looked down at the paper on which Wheatley had made a few scribbles. 'So, let me help you. What do you intend to say?'

Wheatley turned to Danny and Mary. 'You two wait for me downstairs. Jimmy and I will work on the telegram.'

Mary led the way out. Danny could sense that she had been hurt by Wheatley's dismissal. 'You mustn't mind him when he has work in hand – he gives it his full attention. It's his way. It makes him what he is.'

She turned, five steps below him, her head at the height of the top of the calliper where it circled his upper thigh. 'Don't you stick up for him, Danny. I will not be treated like a toy he can throw out the pram when something shinier comes along.'

He negotiated the steps, sideways like a crab, left leg always leading. When he reached her he took her arm. 'He's a determined man, Mary. He has been since the early days. He's one of eight children. They were brought up in a single-room cottage in Ballieston. When you think how far he has come –'

'Aye and I'll wager he's trodden on a few bodies on the way up. Well he's not going to trample on me.' She swept on down to the bottom of the stairs, stopped and called out over her retreating shoulder. 'I shall take my women back to the McHugh house. Tell John I'll see him there.' She crossed the hallway, heels clacking and out into the sunshine.

A bleakness descended on Danny. If she was setting her cap at the boss, there would be no place for him.

Saturday June 12, 1915

The McHugh house was still under the protection of the demonstrators and the sheriff's men had not yet received orders to proceed with an eviction. Even if they had they would have baulked at taking on the people massed in front of the house. The front elevation of the cottage was hidden behind the ranks of women with their chests puffed up with the importance of their role. They looked like show birds at a country fair. The cocks prowling on the periphery were out-of-work men fresh from their wasted Saturday morning hour at the factory gate. They scraped their boots, eyed the women, smoked their precious stash of tobacco and spat in the gutter as they waited for action.

Andrew Fleming approached Wheatley and Danny as they surveyed the picket. 'John, it's bad news from the courts, Davey Hardie has been fined five pounds for what happened at the factor's house on Thursday.'

'Can he pay?' Wheatley's forehead was furrowed.

'No. The alternative is thirty days.'

'See comrade Fulton, we should have enough in the party funds to spring Davey out. If the committee doesn't ratify it, I shall pay it myself.'

Fleming tipped his hat and hurried away.

One of the women crowding round asked Wheatley whether he had heard from Kitchener. 'I am feart to tell you, he's not going to help.' He held up a hand. 'Have you seen Mary Ireland, by th'way?'

The woman pointed through the mass of bodies. 'She's over by the house.'

Wheatley and Danny scrimmaged through the bodies until they discovered Mary sitting on a wall at the end of the terrace, her knees spread apart under her skirts. She was soothing a baby wrapped in a shawl on her lap.

'That's a bonnie wean you have there, Mary,' said Wheatley. 'How old is she now?'

'Millie here, she's nigh on six weeks.'

Wheatley reached out a hand and touched the shawl.

The women close by drew nearer intent on where his hand would rest.

Wheatley, made suddenly aware of their presence, straightened up and raised his voice for the benefit of them all. 'You still have a good turnout, Mrs Ireland. You're a real organiser. I say it again, we need you and your like in the party.'

Mary's answer was equally forced. 'When we get the vote will be soon enough, Mr Wheatley.'

'Well, keep up the good work. When do you go home?'

'When it's dark.'

'I am sure Mrs McHugh is thankful for what you are doing.'

'We're not just doing it for her – it's for each of us who are not paying the rent increases. None of us can afford to be evicted with our men away.'

The women gave a faint hurrah.

He turned to the crowd beyond. 'Good women of East Glasgow.'

They responded with a weak cheer.

'Yesterday, I sent Lord Kitchener a telegram, asking for his protection for all the dependants of your bread-winners who are risking their lives in the service of his army. You should not be put out on the street for refusing to pay the rent increases you are suffering because of war-plundering landlords. His answer was that he would not increase your men's pay to meet the increases. He offered no protection. He said nothing of the exploitation of the war by the landlords.'

This was met with howls and boos.

'But our fight does not stop here. Many of you will know Jimmy Maxton. Jimmy and I will take on Mrs McHugh's case. The Independent Labour Party here on Clydeside, which Jimmy and I represent, will join forces with our comrades throughout Britain and we will force the government to give you that protection.'

Mary was first to raise her fist and holler her support. The women behind her followed.

'The fight is not over. You, the women of East Glasgow, have shown you are a force to be reckoned with. We shall need you again to fight for the cause of the working men and women of this city.'

Again Mary led the cheering.

'We have won this day. The sheriff's men will not dare to carry out evictions while the threat of your action hangs over them. If a call comes to support of one of our kind we shall do it. I need to know – if the call comes, will you be there?'

Mary raised her hand but, when she realised she was the only one to respond, dropped it quickly.

'Will ye do it?' Wheatley shouted.

This time the crowd shouted back.

'Until we good people meet again!'

As the crowd drifted away, Wheatley called to Mary. 'Mrs Ireland, may I have a word?'

She turned back, the baby slung in her shawl across her bosom. Danny stood close by.

Wheatley offered his hand. 'Mary, you have been a true comrade in this matter. Surely, with women proving themselves in all sorts of men's work while this war is on, it won't be long before there is equality at the ballot box. When that day comes, I hope you will be the first woman to join our party here in Shettleston.'

She smiled shyly. 'If it ever happens, I will knock on your door to be first in line,' she said. Their hands were clasped together. Danny recognised an intensity burning in Wheatley's eyes and wondered if she saw it too.

Finally, Wheatley let her hand go and straightened up. 'How is your husband coping with the training?'

'He can't write to tell me so I don't know. He will be at the Front before the year end.'

'Let's hope this war is over before that happens,' said Wheatley.

She nodded.

'Well, you had best be on your way.' He turned to his man. 'Danny, will you escort comrade Mary to her close?'

Mary spoke once they were seated on the tram. The baby slept in her arms. 'Do you think we gained anything, Danny?'

He shook his head. 'Not as far as I can tell, Mary. Not yet. Despite all your good work the rents stay the same. The factors will still enforce payments.'

She turned to face him and smiled though her eyes were wet with tears. 'It will not be so easy to get the women out again. Not unless I can show them a result. I'm going to tell my women that we are to strike. We will pay the old rate of rent not a penny more. This will be Parkhead's answer. I'll see whether I can get the women in other parts of the city to do likewise. We shall not leave it to the men.'

Six

Wednesday October 13, 1915

As the summer ended, even the politicians in London recognised the natural justice of what the women were asking for. Wheatley told Danny that a bill to take rents back to their pre-war levels was on the verge of enactment. 'Go see Mary Ireland,' he said, 'tell her the good news. She should hear it from us first. Tell her what she and her Parkhead women started is going to benefit women and their weans all through Great Britain.'

Mary had been busy. With the support of Wheatley, Dollan and other ILP leaders, she had helped create Women's Housing Associations across Glasgow whose members followed the pattern set in Shettleston. The women downed tools when they heard that one of their number was threatened with eviction and rang hand bells and bashed bin lids to call the women to cram the stairs of the closes and bar the way to the Sherriff's men. Gradually the strike gathered pace and moved south into England where Wheatley was called to speak to meetings and give evidence to a Committee of Inquiry in London. From time to time he instructed Danny to report his progress to the Spaniard's wife.

On these occasions Danny would take the tram to Parkhead and he and Mary would sit drinking tea in her single-end. When he arrived she would scoop up Ella and Millie and take them to Lou's two rooms on the same floor so the adults could talk alone. Her eyes shone when he told her of his travels and Wheatley's successes. It was very easy to lose himself in those wide, coal-dark eyes and her enthusiasm for their shared cause. Her energy and moral courage won his admiration, and her femininity and the vulnerability of her tiny form secured his gallant protection.

He could not admit to himself that he loved her. He had grown up knowing his limits. As a boy, after the polio, he knew he was never going to play for Glasgow Celtic but he found a different way of making his mark. While Mary was married and as long as she held JW in higher esteem, it would have to be enough for him to be a constant in her life. If he could stay alongside her, one day she might see how much he could mean to her.

On the afternoon that Danny went to see Mary to tell her of her impending victory, her face was already burning with the knowledge of it. 'You see, Danny,' she said. 'The world is changing because of this war. The working-class women of Glasgow are learning. Our place is not by the hearth but out in the streets forcing the men in power to think again.'

Mary poured the tea while Danny, sitting by the table in sight of the open door, passed on the rest of Wheatley's report. 'You should be very proud of what you have achieved, Mary. Maybe you should have the women in your Association out for a celebration.'

Mary leaned on the table. 'Och, Danny. I don't know whether I'm coming or going. I should be happy for the victory we have with the rents, of course I should. But how can I celebrate when the weans' father has gone to the war? He came home for embarkation leave at the weekend and he is in France by now. What shall I do?'

Danny had the urge to crush her in his arms, but stayed firm in his chair. 'What can you do? You can be proud of your man and pray for his safe return.'

'I want him safe, right enough.' She chuckled even though there were tears in her eyes. 'But he can stay away for the duration. I collect his money and we don't know what to do with it all without him drinking the bigger portion of it.'

'You don't mean that.'

'I do and I don't,' she said, twisting her cup on its saucer and smoothing down the skirt of her pinafore.

'Mr Wheatley will find things to keep you occupied. And I

don't mean knitting socks for the soldiers.' They both laughed.

'Mr Wheatley is such a fine man. To think he started out no more than a bog-Irish miner.'

'You can't help but admire him.'

She looked at him sharply. 'You dinnae sound as if you mean it, Danny. If he was a younger man... and single...' She smoothed her pinafore again.

He snorted and spluttered tea back into his cup. He put it down and wiped the front of his muffler. 'You're joking with me Mary. The man is twice your age and he hasnae a fine figure on him.'

She looked into the fire and smiled. 'It's a rich man's belly, right enough, but there's a fire in it, Danny. He's a man to change things.'

Danny topped up his saucer from the cup. 'His money gives him the freedom to do it and he didn't get that by treading the angel's path.'

She looked up from below her hooded eyelids. 'I do believe you're jealous of him, Danny McAleer.'

Danny blushed. 'Well, it's something when a fine woman such as yourself, married by th'way, talks like that about a man twice her age to a man of her own age. If it wasn't for this...' he clunked the heavy boot onto the floor.

She patted his arm. 'It's nothing to do with your leg and you know it. It's more to do with him being in his place – money, vitality and power to change things and me being in mine. Although I can see he's a bit sweet on me.'

'Listen to you. You are a wife with two weans and you are talking to me as if I was scrubbing clothes with you in a steamie.'

She put up her hand. 'You're right, Danny. I'm sorry. Perhaps I'm maudlin because my man is gone. You must put out of your mind everything I've said.'

Danny slid his cup across the tablecloth to be filled again. 'I will. Anyways, we should be celebrating the Rent Restriction Bill.'

'I'm not after having a celebration.' Her eyes were focused on pouring the tea. 'The government is only giving us our due,

Danny. I would rather we didn't have this war. It's no' a fight started by working men but it's working men dying in it. I would rather have my man here safe.'

Danny took his time stirring his tea.

Mary sighed and straightened in her chair. 'Could you ask Mr Wheatley for a favour for me Danny?'

'What would that be?'

'The Co-op Guild Christmas party. Do you think Mr Wheatley would make a personal donation to the fund for presents? I mean as well as what we get from his company. With most of the men away the children there will have nothing except what we can give them.'

Danny nodded, pushing the chair back noisily as he rose to leave.

Sunday December 19, 1915

Mary had sweet-talked Wheatley into giving more than money and after lunch on the day of the Christmas party Wheatley and Danny walked up Shettleston Road. The wind blasted into their unprotected faces dragging tears from Danny's eyes. His cheekbones stung as minute daggers of ice, carried on the wind, stabbed deep into his pores.

His toes were numb as they climbed the iron stairway behind the Co-operative store. They bustled through the door into the porch. Upon opening the inner door, they were assaulted by ear-piercing shrieks from the children and Danny imagined their absent fathers cringing under a bombardment of screeching shells. He made more of his limp as they entered the kitchen; he didn't want the women there to think he was a shirker.

Mary came away from a group by the water boiler as the men took off their hats and unbuttoned their coats. She carried a brown enamel teapot, a handle for each hand, her wrists showing no strain from its weight. The other women watched keenly as she spoke. They would have noticed Danny more had he been Wheatley's dog.

'Welcome Mr Wheatley. Right on time.' She turned to Danny. 'Will you be Mr Wheatley's helper?'

He nodded. 'As long as I don't have to wear a costume.'

Mary pointed to the red coat on a table by the door to the hall. 'You get ready, Mr Wheatley, and I'll tell them to prepare the children.'

When she came back, Wheatley was dressed. 'Don't go in until they are quiet,' she said reaching up to adjust Wheatley's beard, looping one of the earpieces more closely. Her fingers touched the side of his face. Danny sensed a tremor of interest surge through the women behind him. 'Can you see without the spectacles, Mr Wheatley?' Mary asked.

'Not sufficiently well to see the children's faces and read the labels.'

'Keep them on then,' she said. She placed her hands on his shoulders. For a second Danny thought she was going to lean forward and kiss him and he heard a communal intake of breath behind. But she merely turned him to face the door. She kept her hands lightly on his shoulders as they listened to the introductions. A man's voice called for quiet.

There was silence.

Mary leaned past Wheatley to open the door and her upper body came in contact with his arm. Danny picked up the Hessian sack. It was heavier than he expected.

As they walked in, the children leapt to their feet. They started cheering and waving their hands in the air. The sound was sharp in Danny's ears, but he was more marked by the heart-bursting sight of the glowing, dirt-smeared faces as he followed Wheatley to the small raised area where a chair waited.

Wheatley sat down in his place and held up a hand. The noise stopped. 'Are you ready for Christmas, children?'

They answered with a roar, jiggling on their backsides and waving their hands.

'Have you been good?'

The response was less confident.

'Well, let us see if I have something for you in my sack.'

As he called the names, the children stepped forward shaking with anticipation. For the most part, the girls wore dresses faded and patched. They bore signs of hems having been let down, or seams re-sewn. The boys were more raggedy in darned woollen sweaters above knickerbockers to below the knee. None of these children's bellies would not be as full again until the winter was finished. For many, the meagre gift from the Guild – a painted top or a few coloured pencils – would be the only present they would see until the next Christmas party.

Seven

Saturday December 25, 1915

On Christmas morning the Wheatley family attended Mass as usual while Danny helped his mother prepare the dinner. Her eyes were on him as he peeled and cut the vegetables and she sighed as she fussed into his place to take over the task and finish it properly.

'I don't see much of you, these days, son,' she said as she plucked the leaves from the Brussels sprouts.

He looked down at the quarry-tiled floor and, extending his left leg straight out behind him, bent to pick up a dropped potato peeling. 'I've been busy, Ma. There's twice as much to do these days what with the business and the politicking.'

'I wish you could settle down. Get a job away from here. With the war on there's opportunities for men like you who can't join up.'

'I like working for JW. Remember, he took me on when it looked like I'd spend my life hanging roon' on street corners.'

She sighed. 'Aye. He did and we have to be grateful for it. But you should take advantage of the situation. God knows I didn't want you to have the polio but if it keeps you from being killed. I have to be thankful for it. There's many a man coming back with his body smashed up far worse than you. I'm sure you could find a nice wee girl –'

'Ma.' He put his hand on her forearm. 'I'm fine as I am. There's time enough for me to find someone. I'm no' getting into rucks any more. Better I stick with JW than look for something new and have it all fall apart when the war's over and the men come home.

She shook her head. '*If* this war ever ends.'

After the McAleers had cleared the celebration dinner things away and Danny's mother had been dismissed, it was time for Wheatley to leave for a demonstration against conscription. The organisers knew that holding it on a day when many workers had a holiday would increase the turnout. Naturally, he expected Danny to go with him.

They were on the tram heading towards the city before Wheatley spoke. 'I hope we have a good turnout the day. We would have preferred to hold the meeting out of the cold in St Andrew's Hall. The less committed will now stay at home by their fires.'

'What happened with the Hall?'

'The usual. When the St Andrew's people heard we're pacifists they turned us down. Jimmy and I tried to book Glasgow Green but the council denied it to as well – so much for the People's Palace.'

'So it's in the street.'

'Aye – we have to make sure it's not going to look good for the council in the papers tomorrow – banishing working men to the streets.'

The tram was stopped at George Square by the number of men crossing the road and heading north. There were hundreds of them, the mist from their bodies and the cigarette smoke knitting together a cloud that hung above them like a Zeppelin. Their flat-capped heads bobbed stiffly as, shoulders hunched against the cold, they hopped to avoid the traffic.

When Danny stepped down, all he could see was a crush of bodies blocking the street. Wheatley put his hand on top of his bowler and lowered his neck into his scarf as he started up the street. The older man's lips were blue with cold despite his heavy overcoat. Most of the men, like Danny, had their jackets buttoned with the collars turned up and wore woollen scarves as well as mufflers or neckerchiefs.

Wheatley spotted a familiar face. 'Davey!'

A stocky man in his early thirties turned. His face was pale and square, adorned by a straight moustache. He wore a trilby. 'John! It's good to see you, man.'

Wheatley took off a glove and they shook hands vigorously. David Kirkwood gave a cursory nod of the head towards Danny.

'I hear you told Lloyd George what we think of him, Davey.'

'Aye, well whit made him think he could come tae Glasgow and get us to accept de-skilling of the workforce?'

'Dilution, Davey, you have to use the right terminology, you ken?'

'Whatever you call it, it's taking money out my members' pockets. The Clyde Workers' Committee sent him on his way.'

'I hear you as good as called him a slaver.'

Kirkwood smiled. 'I did no such thing. I telt him we would listen to him patiently and weigh his words carefully because every act associated with him has the taint of slavery about it. A completely different kettle o'fish.'

'Aye, I cannae think of a better way to get him to listen to your point of view. I doubt he's here today?'

'There was talk of him staying when it was St Andrew's Hall, but no, he's gone south with his tail between his legs.'

'So who is here then?'

Kirkwood took Wheatley by the arm and they started jostling through the crowd. Danny followed taking in the mixed smells of booze, cigarettes, coal dust, engineering oil, sulphur or any of the other scents that betrayed a man's habits or workplace.

Kirkwood was talking and Danny strained forward to hear. 'Manny Shinwell is up first for the seamen and then the running order is John Maclean, Jimmy Maxton and Willie Gallacher.'

'That should stir things up.' Wheatley said.

'Aye, well it's mostly to tell the men what happened with Lloyd George but we're also making the point that the working-class has to stand solid against this capitalist war. When the authorities are trying to shut us up we have to make ourselves heard. Will you want to say anything, John? We can always find room for your educated point of view.'

Wheatley stopped their progress and held up his gloved hand. 'This is your show, Davey. I would be out of place.'

Kirkwood shrugged. 'Suit yourself.'

They had reached the front of the crowd where a flatbed steam-truck was parked. Men set up a ladder on the back and Manny Shinwell climbed nimbly to the platform. He took the first of a row of four chairs. The ghost-like Maxton followed him then the others. Shinwell stood and held up his hand. The crowd went quiet.

'Comrades! It's good of so many of you to forego your firesides to be with us today.' His voice soared between the high buildings and over the heads of the men. There was a scraping of hundreds of boots as the men at the back shuffled forward. 'We have been told there are over two thousand men here today. It's a clear demonstration –'

Danny felt a movement to his side and realised that Wheatley was making his way through the crowd. Danny followed. A small woman was crossing from Kyle Street, where the road was empty, towards the lorry. It was Mary. Wheatley met her by the rear of the lorry and took her arm. She had a black coat on under her shawl and judging by the discolourations on the frayed sleeves where they showed, the coat had spent far longer in Parkhead's foul atmosphere than Mary had.

Danny stood a couple of paces back from them, but could still hear Wheatley's gushing. 'It's so good to see you, Mary.' He took his bowler hat completely off his head – not just tipping it – and looked around. 'Let us take a position as near to the stage as possible so you don't get crushed.'

He steered her back to where they had been and Danny took up a place a few feet to one side. Wheatley and Mary nodded to Kirkwood who nodded back and then all three turned and looked up to watch Shinwell. Mary's back was stiff and her eyes focused on the makeshift stage. She linked her left hand behind Wheatley's arm and pulled it against her body. From time to time one turned to the other and pressed a mouth close to an ear to whisper some commentary on the proceedings.

The speakers changed but the sentiment stayed the same. All the while a line of policemen formed along the east side of the street.

When Maxton came on, the crowd were ready for warming up again and he gave them fire and brimstone. The lanks of his hair flailed against the sky like a cat o'nine tails as he flung his head this way and that, spitting spume against the boss classes who had taken them into war and were responsible for making widows on Clydeside and other working-class enclaves far removed from Westminster. He finished to a huge roar.

Wheatley, Mary still clinging to his side, turned to Danny. 'This lass is cold. We're going for a cup of tea.' He took out his watch and flipped it open. 'It's three-thirty now. It will soon be dark and this will break up. What say you come to the apartment at six-thirty? Then you can escort Mary back to Parkhead.'

They only had to go back down the street a short distance before cutting through to Ingram Street where Wheatley rented two rooms for those nights he and Danny were kept in the city by late night council sittings.

As Danny listened to Willie Gallagher's rousing speech, he wondered what Mary would make of the apartment with its own bathroom and a gas copper so you could have a hot bath every day if you chose. He imagined her eyes popping as she realised just how much of a class apart Wheatley was from the man she had married. Would it be the start? Mary wasn't the first tenement woman to fall for someone from the boss class and betray her marriage vows. Danny shivered, not just from the cold; he couldn't stand to think of what Mary and JW would be doing.

The police moved in once the speeches were over and the crowd drifted away. There was scuffle as the four speakers were taken into custody. A policeman commandeered the steam wagon and drove the leaders away, each man shackled to another as they sat on the flat bed.

Much later, after spending the rest of the afternoon loitering over a tot of whisky in a lock-in at the Stag bar in Candleriggs, Danny climbed the steps to the apartment and twisted the bell. Wheatley opened the door and nodded him in. He led the way up the further flight to the wide landing with the butler's sink, gas stove and Danny's fold-down bed propped against the banister. The door to the bedroom was closed. Danny made sure his eyes didn't settle on it as he passed.

A blast of heat hit Danny when Wheatley opened the door

to the main room. Mary sat on the couch. There were two empty teacups on the side table next to the teapot and a plate with the remains of a bought cake. Danny was suddenly aware of the sourness of the whisky in his stomach.

Mary was already in her shawl and she stood up, her hand held to her bosom. 'This is very good of you, Danny.' she said. 'It's only a fifteen-minute walk for me from here. It really isn't –'

Wheatley interrupted. 'No, I insist. Danny will take you. It's no trouble. I have some work to keep me busy here for a while –' He pointed to some council papers on the low table next to the armchair. 'Danny and I will make our separate ways back to Shettleston.'

Danny nodded and held the door open.

'Wait outside for a second, Danny, will you?' Wheatley said.

Danny went through the door, closed it behind him and stood on the landing. It opened again only ten seconds later. Mary came through with her head bowed and her hand still clasped to her shawl.

They walked side by side in the light of the street lamps without speaking. As they reached her close Danny turned to her. She silenced him with a look. 'I ken whit you're thinking, Danny McAleer. You need say nothing.' With that she turned and, as she dropped her hand to lift her skirt for the step, he caught sight of a new pin in her shawl. It was made up of silver bars with leaves hanging from them and in the centre there was a rose set with a cairngorm that glinted in the street light.

Eight

Thursday February 3, 1916

In the weeks following Christmas Day, Wheatley and Danny took the tram into the city two afternoons a week on the pretext of council business. Danny would alight at Parkhead Cross where Mary would be waiting by the stop. He would walk her on down Castle Street, past the infirmary to Ingram Street, where he would see her up the stair to the door that Wheatley would leave ajar for her. Mary would nod as Danny turned away. All this was conducted in silence.

Then some busybody talked.

The first Danny heard of it was when a boy came from Bobby Craig to the house in Shettleston. He went to the Auld House in Parkhead that same Thursday night. Bobby was leaning by the pumps holding his pint in his left hand. The folded right sleeve of his jacket was pinned to his shoulder with a kilt pin. He looked every inch the veteran.

'Still hiding your arm, I see.' Danny said.

'I don't need some bizzom giving me whit for.' He waved his pint towards Danny's leg. 'I see your limp is worse these days. And, by th'way, I'll wager it's no more painful today than it was the day before war started.'

'Aye, right enough. What's your poison?'

Bobby indicated a table and took his drink to it while Danny waited for the two pints of heavy to pour. When he took them over Craig's pint glass was empty.

'Are you having trouble with an advertiser?' Danny asked.

Craig put down his glass and wiped the foam from his top lip. He looked out furtively from beneath his heavy forehead.

'Nae, nothing like it. They're all behaving fine. It's your boss's personal business that's the subject for discussion the day.'

'What does that mean?' Danny gave him the look. Craig should know he wasn't interested in loose talk.

'Whoa! I'm not looking for trouble, big man. It's something your boss should know and it's no' my job to tell him, is it?'

Danny put his hands palm down on the table top. 'Right enough, Bobby. On you go.'

'There's talk of the way yon Mary, the Spaniard's wife, is spending her afternoons. She's leaving her weans with her sister-in-law and disappearing for hours.'

'So? What has this got to do with Mr Wheatley?'

Craig leaned forward. 'You've been seen, Danny-boy. Meeting at the tram stop and stepping off west together.' He took a slurp of his drink. 'All respect, big man.' He put down his glass and tapped Danny's leg. 'She's not going to be looking at you for a bit on the side, is she, by th'way?'

A pain shot through Danny's chest at the truth of it. 'So what are they saying?'

'That your man Wheatley has a love nest in the city and she's seeing him there.'

Danny shook his head. 'Well, if you hear anybody saying anything you can tell them it's a boatload of shite. I may have seen Mary once when I got off the tram while I was doing a collection. We may have had a brief conversation – she likes to be kept up to date with party business – but they're taking two and two and making five of it.' Danny banged his pint glass down on the table angrily, sending splatters of froth across the two men.

Friday February 4, 1916

The morning was cold as Danny laid and lit the fires before the rest of the house stirred. He let Maggie, the daily, in and she set about making the family's breakfast. They heard the post drop on the mat and Maggie went to collect it and take it into the dining room.

The raised voices started almost straight away. Maggie and Danny could only catch a few words in every sentence but it was clear Mrs Wheatley had received a letter giving her unwelcome news. Danny's stomach churned. If it was what he thought, how much better prepared would Wheatley have been if he had said something rather than sleeping on it?

'Thank the Lord the children are at school... don't have to hear... their father...' was all he heard of Mrs Wheatley.

Wheatley was quieter. 'Catherine... deny it... council... Danny...'

'Danny? That pimp!'

Maggie smiled and shifted her thin frame in her chair. 'Looks as if you're in the bad books, Danny.' She took a sip of her tea. 'Seems like the master of the house has been taking his business elsewhere. Why's that your fault then?'

'Hold your tongue, girl.' He as much wanted her to be quiet so he could hear what was being said as to observe some propriety. She pursed her lips.

JW's voice had taken on a low, placatory tone while Mrs Wheatley's had lost none of its shrill energy. 'What do you take me for? Do you think I'm stupid?'

Danny couldn't make out Wheatley's response but he could imagine Mrs Wheatley standing at the mantelpiece as she spat at her husband, 'This time you've really done it John. You can't pretend there's no baby.'

Danny's breakfast lurched to the back of his throat. A baby? Who knew about it? Who had written the letter?

Mrs Wheatley's voice lowered ominously. 'I need time to think about what I'm going to do. Leave me alone. Get out! Go to your apartment and stay there for all I care.'

Danny heard the door open and then light footsteps on the stairs. Mrs Wheatley had left the room.

There was silence for a minute or so while Maggie and Danny did no more than look at each other. Finally there was a shout from the dining room. 'Danny!'

He went in. The table was still laden with the half-eaten breakfast. There was a letter on blue paper in Mrs Wheatley's place.

'JW?' Danny said.

Wheatley was slumped in his chair. His eyes were narrow

behind the spectacles and he worried at his lower lip with a fist. He flicked his other hand across the table in the direction of the letter. 'Know anything about that?'

Danny knew better than to say he hadn't been listening. 'Nothing, boss.'

Wheatley sighed. 'It's anonymous of course.' He stood up and looked at the envelope. 'Posted yesterday in the city. Could be from anybody in Parkhead.'

'What does it say?'

'Read it.'

Danny hesitated.

'Go on, man.'

Danny picked it up. It was in black ink: 'YOU SHUD NOW YOR HUSBAND IS SLEEPING WITH A WIFE FROM THE TEMNENTS AND SHES HAVING HIS WEAN.' Danny replaced it on the table.

Wheatley straightened his back and drew in a breath. 'I want you to go straight over to Parkhead. See Mary. Check how she is. By the time you get back here I will have packed some clothes and we shall move into the city apartment until things calm down.'

Danny wearily climbed the stairs to Mary's single-end and knocked in the usual way, this time more aware of the ears that would be pressed against each of the front doors he passed.

Mary was wiping her hands on her pinny when she opened the door. 'Och, Danny! It's awfy early for you to call. Come in. I'll make a fresh pot.'

He looked around the room. 'Where are the girls?'

'Playing next door with their cousins. Sit down.'

Danny sat at the table and looked out through the open door onto the landing. Mary filled a kettle. He heard a toilet flush and a neighbour passed the opening glancing in. Danny raised a hand from the table.

'What's this about, Danny?' she asked.

'Some busybody frae round here has taken it upon themselves to do a charitable act.'

Her brow furrowed as she placed the kettle on the range. 'What do you mean?'

'Mrs Wheatley has received a letter.'

She groaned and eased herself into the chair across the table from her visitor. 'The meddling bizzom –'

'You know who wrote it?'

She waved her hand about her face as if throwing off a fly. 'No! But it will be a woman – some wifey who can't bear to see another grasping at a bit o' happiness.'

'But it said you are expecting.'

'Fuck!' She spat it out with such force he could almost see the word shattering as it hit the table top. He jerked back. He couldn't remember when or if he had ever heard a woman say that.

She shook her head. 'I'm sorry, Danny. It's just... you can't keep anything to yourself round here.'

'So is it true?'

'Aye. I only just worked it out myself in the last few days. I havnae had...' She examined and picked at the lace centre of the tablecloth. '...you know, since my man left. I thought it was the worry of him being away. It's not as if...' The kettle started to sing.

Mary went about making the tea with her mouth tight shut. Danny could think of nothing to say in response. What was she trying to tell him?

When the cups were poured and in front of them, Mary crossed and closed the door to the landing. She saw his look. 'Don't worry. It's not as if I have a reputation to protect any more. Let me tell you this,' she sat down. 'I may be having a baby, it's true. But Mr Wheatley doesn't have to worry. It isn't his.'

'Are you sure?'

She sighed. 'I can't afford to see a doctor can I? But I'm beginning to show and William had embarkation leave in October before he went to France. The dates make sense'

'So you think he may have left you a wee present.'

She smiled. 'Aye. That's a good way of putting it, Danny. Things are happening too fast for it to be anything to do with Mr Wheatley.'

'So I should tell him that?'

'Aye.'

'How many people know?'

'I told Lou last week. She won't have kept it to herself. The news must have reached somebody with an axe to grind against me, or William, or even Mr Wheatley. They heard the two stories and drew the wrong conclusion.'

'And a letter goes to Mrs Wheatley,' Danny said.

'Aye'.

They sipped their tea in unison.

'What were you going to say – when it became obvious?'

'I've hardly had time to think, but I would have to stop seeing him, wouldn't I? It wouldnae be fair.'

'Fair to who?'

She put her head in her hands. 'None of them... all of them... I don't know.' She looked across the table, drawing tears from her eyes as she rubbed her palms down her cheeks. 'I have to put a stop to it. You're here, Mr high-and-mighty-go-between, so you might as well tell him. There'll be no more visits to his posh flat in Ingram Street for me. Aye, tell him that.'

When Danny arrived in Anstruther Street, there was a motor taxi parked outside with the driver waiting. Maggie opened the door and told him that Mrs Wheatley had said he was to go straight up to the attic room and clear out his things. She told him Mrs Wheatley would be moving a maid into his room as soon as the space was free. Evidently she enjoyed being the bearer of bad news.

It took him only a few minutes to pack his belongings into a small cardboard suitcase, which he put in the hall alongside Wheatley's large valise. He knocked on Wheatley's study door.

'Come on then, Danny. Let's be on our way.'

They talked in whispers in the taxi. 'What did she have to say, Danny?'

'The letter is right. She is... in a condition.'

'Don't be so touchy, Danny. She's going to have a baby, yes?'

'Yes, but not yours, she says. She's almost certain it's a leaving present from the Spaniard – from his embarkation leave.'

Wheatley let out a sigh of relief. 'Thank God for that, Danny. When the baby is born with the Spaniard's colouring, everybody will see it's nothing to do with me. Perhaps then I shall be able to persuade Catherine to take me back.'

'Mary says there will be no more visits to Ingram Street. It's all over.'

'I ken that already.' Wheatley turned away and studied the shop fronts along Gallowgate and they passed the rest of the journey in silence.

Nine

Thursday May 18, 1916

At the Shettleston Independent Labour Party constituency meeting some three months later, John Wheatley proposed a motion to admit women members. It was carried. At the same meeting, with ill-concealed vindictiveness, Andrew Fleming, now vice-chairman, presented Wheatley with a letter from the committee offering sympathy for his continuing domestic troubles.

Afterwards, on the way back to Ingram Street, Wheatley turned to Danny. 'You must get over to Parkhead tomorrow and see Mary. It's important she becomes our first woman member as I promised.'

Danny furrowed his brow. 'What about Mrs Wheatley? Will she no' be expecting it?'

'Leave the thinking to me, Danny. I promised it to Mary Ireland and she shall have it.'

Danny contemplated the prospect of visiting Mary the next day. It would be the first time since he and his boss had moved out of Anstruther Street. He had tracked the approach of spring as each dawn swept into the skylight above his cot on the landing at Ingram Street. He skivvied for the pair of them. He was first up, strapped on his calliper and made a fire in the main room. Then he would go down to the bathroom on the half-landing and light the gas under the copper so Wheatley had hot water for his shave and wash.

While Wheatley was in the bathroom, Danny would collect bread and milk and make a breakfast of porridge and bread with jam. Some weekends he would cook a fry-up. They ate out in the evenings at the Lyons Corner House, Kate Cranston's Tea Room, or the dining room in the City Halls round the corner. They both put on weight and Danny noticed how his skin suffered from the rich food they were eating.

Wheatley went home every Sunday to attend mass because, as he put it, they were still a family in the eyes of God. Wheatley had used these opportunities to collect more of his things until his entire wardrobe was at Ingram Street. Danny wondered if Mr Wheatley would ever return to the family home.

If Wheatley was depressed at not being able to see his wife or the children, Patrick and Lizzie, he didn't show it. He never mentioned Mary either. He focused initially on the usual round of business as City Councillor and making speeches for the Labour Party. Then, after Wheatley had read about Sir Roger Casement's arrest in Ireland on the Good Friday, he became immersed in events there. 'It's my birthplace, Danny,' he had said while reading aloud descriptions of the siege at the Dublin GPO.

The executions had started on the 3rd of May and Wheatley had cried when he told Danny about each new atrocity culminating with the firing-squad execution of James Connolly while he sat in a chair. 'He was a good socialist,' Wheatley had said, tears shining on his cheeks. 'Did you know he once lived in Glasgow? I might have met him and not even known it. He was a true hero, dying a martyr's death for his country. For his sake and for people like him in Ireland and Scotland we have to fight harder to turn out the ruling classes.'

Danny wondered whether, at times like these, JW thought either of Mary or his wife. It seemed he sought his comfort only in his politics. Whereas, for him, every day that went by, a vision of Mary would pop unbidden into his mind as he pulled the blankets around him in the narrow bed or when he set about his chores.

Friday May 19, 1916
Next afternoon there was a commotion as Danny limped up the stairs in Mary's close. The nearer he came to her single-end the more it became apparent it was the centre of the storm.

A broad woman barred his progress at the top step on Mary's landing.

'You will go no further, Mr McAleer,' she said, folding her arms under her bolstered bosom.

'What's happening?'

'She has started. The midwife is here. We have no need of a man.'

Danny made his way to Craib's bar on the corner. He took a hof n'a hof, chasing each swallow of heavy with a sip of whisky. The woman, whom he had assumed to be Mary's sister-in-law, Lou, had said it all, 'we have no need of a man'. Danny was twenty-five years old and it seemed he would spend the rest of his days waiting on Wheatley. What was it Mrs Wheatley had called him – a pimp? He ordered a second round of drinks.

There was Mary squeezing out her third wean while the Spaniard was fighting the Hun. Did he stand a chance now Wheatley was out of the picture? Did he have to hope the Spaniard would join the growing list of Highland Light Infantry mortalities? Was it his only chance for happiness to take up with the Spaniard's widow and two – no three – weans?

Bobby Craig had told him that, to keep the job in the family, Mary had taken over the milk round. Despite being in the early months of another pregnancy, she had, first thing every morning, left the depot hauling the handcart, ladled out the customers' milk and tallied their cans. The only thing she couldn't do was load the full churns onto the bed of the cart at the start of the day. She relied on one of the boys in the depot to help her.

Danny imagined the young wives who had previously dodged payment realising the new 'roundsman' was not to be charmed into ladling out a little extra or taking payment in kind. Now she would be relying on a boy to stand in to keep the round going until she was fit to start again.

Nobody disturbed Danny as the bar closed its doors for the stay-behind and he switched to pints so as to make his drinks last. Finally, as the last regulars left, he staggered back to the Spaniard's close.

All was quiet on the stairs and he knocked at Mary's door.

The large woman opened it.

'So you're back, then,' she said.

'The original bad penny,' he said and gave her what he thought to be a winning smile.

She flinched and he realised that the stench of his night's drinking had wafted across on his breath.

He tried to look past her bulk into the room but she stepped into his view.

'I'm only trying to look, woman. Has the wean been born?'

'Aye Mary has had a bonny bairn. A fine big boy with a shock of black hair, the picture of his father.'

'A boy, then.' Danny tried to pull himself straight and his arm slipped on the door jamb.

'A boy,' she said. 'Thomas William.'

Danny turned away and clomped back down the stairs. He limped the mile or so to Ingram Street and dragged himself up the three flights to the apartment. He let himself in with his own key. Wheatley was nursing a whisky in the main room.

'Come in, Danny. Come in.'

'I've had a belly full, JW. It's best I –' He turned back to the landing where his fold-up bed waited.

'No. Stay with me for one, Danny.' He poured a second glass.

'I only came to tell you that Mary has had the baby. A big boy by all accounts, shares his dad's dark looks. She's calling it Thomas. It seems she did the sums right.'

'I never doubted it, Danny, but it's good to get the confirmation right enough. Now come in and have that drink.'

Danny still held on to the door handle. 'I don't know...'

'Come in and have a drink, Danny, *please*.' He took out his fob watch and studied the face. 'We have only now passed midnight on May 19th – the end of my birthday. You can at least share a drink with a man on the day after his birthday. We can celebrate mine and young Thomas's – for we share the same day.'

Ten

Thursday May 25, 1916
'They all know by now the wean is not mine,' Wheatley said. He was telling Danny what had happened at the meeting he had attended earlier as they strolled up Anstruther Street at the end of the night. The meeting had been called by a specially constituted disciplinary sub-committee. 'It was born inside the nine months since Mary's man was away and it has a shock of black hair like a Hottentot according to all reports.'

Danny pushed his left leg along as fast as he could to keep up.

'So why do they busybodies have to concern themselves in my private affairs? I have a good mind to leave them to their tin-pot politicking.' Wheatley turned to Danny for an answer.

'What happened?' Danny asked.

'Och! For public consumption they are going to send me another fraternal letter wishing me well now my domestic difficulties are over. In private, wee Andrew Fleming told me – told *me* – I should look to my future behaviour if I wanted their continued confidence as prospective Parliamentary candidate.'

Danny knew better than to comment.

'As if Shettleston Independent Labour Party would be anything without me at its head. Bloody upstarts. It's the trouble with town politics; little men sprout ideas above their station.'

He became silent as they approached the house. They had been together nigh on seven years and Danny knew when a storm was brewing.

Wheatley stopped at the gate of his house and turned to face Danny. 'You should go to Mary's and ask her to be at next week's meeting. I want to make good my promise to enrol her as our first member.'

Danny touched the peak of his cap. 'I'll do what I can to get her there, JW. But she's only just had the child.'

'Aye, well, see what you can do.' He leaned over the gate to release the latch. 'Now you go on to the Ingram Street flat. I'm going to try to make my peace here now I can tell Catherine I have a clean sheet. If I'm out on my ear, she'll still let me spend the night on the couch. Either way, there's now a bonnie young housekeeper tucked up in your bed so there is no room for you at the inn.'

They said their goodnights and Danny headed back down towards Shettleston Road and the city tram.

Friday May 26, 1916

Danny was up early and headed out into the rising sun towards Parkhead Cross. The air steadily thickened. The acid bitterness of the devil's powder sparred in his nostrils with the stench of bad eggs, both fighting to overpower the other and leave him incapable of drawing breath. Young Tommy would grow up with powerful lungs, he thought, or he would die trying.

Mary greeted Danny at the door to her room with the babe wrapped to her chest inside her shawl. The boy could have been at the breast for all Danny could see before he averted his eyes. Tommy made not a sound.

'Looks like you've got a good one there,' Danny said, nodding towards the dark head.

She kept up a swaying motion. 'Young Tommy Atkins here is a good'un all right. Let us hope his father lives to see him.'

Danny sat down while Mary fussed with the tea things. 'Where are the others?' he asked.

'Across the landing with Lou,' she said smiling. 'But let's not beat about the bush today, eh? What brings you here?' She smiled and sat down all the while encircling the back of the dark head with her hand.

'JW – Mr Wheatley – was asking for you.'

She wiped the back of her hand across her mouth as if to wipe the smile away. 'Nae doot he was mightily relieved the bairn came too early and too dark to be his.'

'He would have stood by you. Done the honourable thing,' Danny said. 'He's a good Christian.'

'Some will say not Christian enough to keep it to himself, though.'

'Tongues have been wagging.'

'Well they should know he was always a gentlemen with me. It was my fault he went astray.' She studied the pattern on the lace table centre, nudging the fibres into place with a fingertip. 'He has to go back to his wife and bairns. I understand that.' She nudged a knuckle along her cheekbone. 'There never was going to be anything in it. I was always more a distraction than anything real to him.'

Danny put his hand across the table towards her. 'You know I'm here if you need anything.'

She didn't move her hand to touch his. 'I know it, Danny. But we must both go back to our own.'

'He has been torn. He's a good Catholic.'

She drew herself up in the chair. 'He's a better socialist than he is a Catholic and that's all I'll say on the matter.' She blew her nose on the piece of cotton that lay across her shoulder. 'In any case whit are you doing sticking up for him? He wouldnae do the same for you.'

A darkness fell behind Danny's eyes. 'He's been good to me and I'm loyal to him in turn. If I thought there was a chance with you for me –'

She held up her hand. 'Whisht! You'll wake the baby with your prattle. Best say what it was you came to say.'

Danny told her Wheatley had asked for her to enrol into the party at the next meeting.

She shook her head, smiling wistfully. 'He'll not see me at the Labour rooms any time soon. The tongues wag enough round here without me spreading it to Shettleston. You can tell Mr Wheatley that I won't set foot in those rooms or the Co-operative Guild until the war is over, my man is home and I can keep it respectable.'

She was good to her word. For the next two years Mary stayed away from the Co-operative Hall and the party. From time to time, Danny saw Bobby Craig in his pinned-up jacket. Craig filled him in on Mary's news and how the children were progressing.

She continued with the Spaniard's milk round and business thrived. Most of the local women were better off through Wheatley's intervention on rents and because they could collect their men's wages if they were soldiers or find unskilled work themselves.

Those with husbands in reserved occupations – the pitmen, dockers and munitions workers – benefited from the excessive overtime hours. There simply wasn't enough non-working time left to spend the wage, especially with stricter enforcement of licensing hours. The lot of the average working family in the tenements improved.

Danny's duties took him away from the tenements. Wheatley bought a Wolseley saloon motor car which its previous owner could no longer afford and Danny learned to drive it using a linked metal device to depress the clutch pedal with his right hand. It took him many weeks to master double-declutching without crunching the gears. The steering wheel was left to its own devices when he had one hand on the clutch handle and the other on the gear lever. Danny's driving position was open to the elements and Wheatley sat in the fully upholstered rear section listening to the cogs crashing inside the gearbox. 'Don't leave the gears in the road, Danny,' he would shout from the back seat.

When Danny paid a rare visit to Mary and told her that JW had bought and moved into a swish big house in Sandyhills, alongside the golf course south of Shettleston, all she offered was, 'Perhaps he's not even a good socialist, these days.'

So Danny moved into a room over the garage in what used to be the stable block, behind the big house. His duties now were to drive the boss to his meetings and make sure he looked like handy muscle for when anybody took exception to what JW said.

The Armistice was signed in November 1918 and Lloyd George called the General Election within the week.

Eleven

Tuesday November 19, 1918

Wheatley summoned Danny to his study using the telephone system that linked all the main rooms in the house and the stable block. Wheatley's new desk, even bigger than the one in Anstruther Street, commanded the room. 'I'm appealing for help from all like-minded constituents, Danny. What do you think my chances are of mobilising Mary Ireland to the cause?'

'If she was keen to help wouldn't they find work for her in the Parkhead ward?'

'Don't answer my question with another question.'

Danny looked down at the plush carpet. 'I'm not sure, boss. Last time I spoke to her, she wasn't impressed with you moving into the big house.'

Wheatley chuckled. 'She's a good class-warrior.' He took off his spectacles, huffed on the lenses in turn, before polishing them on the paisley handkerchief he kept in his top pocket for the purpose. 'I would have said the same in her position.' He pointed to the chair. 'Sit down, Danny. You're making the place untidy.'

Danny sat and fiddled with the metal joint of the calliper at his knee.

Wheatley spread his hands. 'What does she expect? Things have moved on for us, haven't they? Now I'm running the *East Glasgow Observer* I'm totally legitimate. I don't need you out there on the streets anymore, do I?'

Danny knew he wasn't meant to answer. There was still some coercion involved in the advertising, but it was no longer his concern.

Wheatley twisted his head as if a new thought occurred to him. 'What's Bobby Craig doing these days, by th'way?'

Danny shrugged. 'Don't mind him. There's always work for muscle – even one-armed muscle – if the hirer is not too careful about which side of the law he's on'.

'Aye, good. But as for Mary, what can I do?' He stood up and faced the window, which looked out over the garden. 'I'm a legitimate publisher. I have ambitions to take the working-class fight to London. In this constituency I have to look like a successful tradesman. I'm a model for the class I'm seeking to represent. In other constituencies we have candidates who are shop-floor workers, skilled tradesmen – Jimmy Maxton's a teacher – I am no less of a socialist than any of them. Can you persuade her?'

'I don't know.'

Wheatley came to Danny's side of the desk and perched his backside on the corner. A less substantial piece of furniture would have tilted under the weight of him. 'You don't live on top of us now, Danny. You don't know how it is.'

Danny continued fussing with the joint on his leg. He would have liked to stretch it out but Wheatley's polished black shoes were in the way.

'Mrs Wheatley and I ... we have separate bedrooms here. She has never forgiven me for what happened with Mary, if you know what I mean.'

Danny grasped behind his knee with both hands and pulled his leg straight even though he risked kicking his boss.

'Aye, I ken. It's more than you need to know. But I want you to contact her for me. Do you know when her man returns from the Front?'

'I don't.'

'Well, can you at least talk to her? I am sincere in this. I would like her to be at my side for the campaign.'

'I'll see what I can do.'

'Aye.' He straightened up and returned to his chair. The ladder back extended high above his head. 'Do what you can, Danny, as a friend to both of us, me *and* Mary.' He reached across to a small box filled with business cards and riffled through them his lips pursed. He selected one and offered it to Danny. 'This may help sway her. It's her Independent Labour Party membership card. I enrolled her as Shettleston's, maybe even Scotland's, first woman member two years ago. Tell her I honoured my promise.'

Danny went back to his room. He had no desire for JW and Mary to be back together again. With the war over, the Spaniard would return, dashing Danny's hopes of saving Mary from widowhood. Why should Wheatley's money mean that he, a fat pig of a man, should have her in his bed?

Later the same day, Danny trudged up the dark stairway to Mary's landing and knocked at her door. The brass of the doorplate shone as bright as ever.

She didn't look surprised when she opened the door. Danny's presence in the road had probably been passed to her even before he stepped into her close. 'Come in, Danny. It's been a long time.' She had a dark-haired boy clinging to her leg. Danny recognised his shirt as the top half of one of Millie's dresses. It barely covered his bulging nappy.

'So this is Tommy,' Danny said. He bent from the waist to put his head on the same level as the boy's, but his straight leg meant he hadn't the flexibility to stoop low enough.

The boy drew back and pulled a fold of Mary's skirt in front of his face.

'Two years old and never seen his father yet,' she said.

'Any news from France?'

'I know he's alive and I know he's coming back but they don't seem to know when. We are at the bottom of the heap as always.'

Danny felt the familiar lurch in his chest. There was something in her chippiness that excited him. He wondered whether he would ever lose the feeling.

'How is he?' Mary sounded offhand.

'Who?'

'You know very well, John – Mr Wheatley.'

'That's why I'm here. You know he's standing for Independent Labour in Shettleston. He wants you to work for him.'

'Could he no' come here himself?'

'You ken he couldn't.'

She took a deep breath. 'Aye.' She straightened her back and tried to manhandle the boy to the side of her. 'Where are my manners, Danny? Will you take a cup of tea? I'll put the kettle on.'

Mary moved to the range with Tom still attached to her skirt and poured some boiling water into a waiting pot.

'Do you know anybody here in the Parkhead ward?' Danny asked.

She shook her head.

'You haven't joined the party here, I hope.'

'How could I? I've had my hands full with the bairns. Anyway, why would I? I don't qualify for the vote.'

Danny thought about this. 'You are not thirty yet, Mary?'

'Not until next year – but it's not material. I would have to be a house owner as well.'

Danny rubbed his forehead. 'Right, it's never straightforward. You think women have made a big advance because of what they did in the war but it's not for the working woman.'

'Listen to you, Danny! The regular suffragette. Anyway, what will you do with your vote? Your first time.'

Danny grimaced. 'It would be my neck if I voted for anyone other than the boss.'

'He wouldn't know.'

'Oh, he would find out. I have nae doubt of it.'

They both chuckled. Mary brought the pot to the table and asked Danny to sit. She came back with the cups and milk and sugar. 'You are probably right enough, Danny. Anyway I hadn't thought to join in yet. Maybe when William is back and the bairns are older.'

Danny pulled out the card with red edging. He passed it across to her. 'JW wants you to know he honoured his promise. He enrolled you in Shettleston two years ago. You were the first woman member in his constituency, maybe in Scotland.'

She shot Danny a glance.

'Aye, even before Mrs Wheatley,' he said. 'He wants you to come to next week's meeting. I could pick you up in a motor.'

She laughed. 'Not here you couldn't.'

'At the Cross, then. I'll pick you up there and bring you back. I'm sure they'll find work for you to do.'

'Aye, making the tea and handing out the oat cakes.'

'That's not the way JW is thinking.'

'But what about the rest of them? They'll know why I am there, won't they?'

'Not if it's all in the past, Mary.' He could tell by the way her teacup trembled as she brought it to her lips, it was not what she was thinking.

Friday December 13, 1918

On the evening before the day of the election in the new parliamentary division of Shettleston, Mary, Wheatley and Danny stood at the campaign table in the committee room watching the local party chairman collate the last of the canvassing returns.

'How's it looking, Fred?' said Wheatley.

Fred Cooke shook his head. 'It's too close to call.'

'If we could only be sure of the tenement men, John,' Mary said. She used his Christian name naturally now, even in company, and Wheatley accepted it without protest. 'Many of them didn't register and those that did may prefer to stay at home or in a bar.'

In the three weeks since Danny's visit, Mary had become a fully integrated activist in the election committee. It was she who had pinpointed that they had to mobilise the new working class voters if Wheatley was to win against the Coalition Conservatives' local man, Rear Admiral Adair, who had an enviable war record.

Mary and Wheatley were inseparable and seemed unaware of the glances they attracted from the others when they left the party hall together in the Wolseley with Danny at the wheel. The daily plan hardly varied. Danny would drive the car to a street corner where Wheatley and Mary would set up stall. Wheatley would take a loud hailer and start haranguing a growing crowd while Mary would move amongst them handing out leaflets.

Danny's job was to stay behind the wheel ready to move

off in case somebody took exception to his boss's rhetoric or Mary's supportive comments.

If any working man had the temerity to question Mary's role and ask why she wasn't in her place in the kitchen she would launch into a tirade about the value of that man's vote and though she would use *her* vote wisely if she had one, she couldn't vouch for him as he was clearly a man with nothing but a head full of old-fashioned prejudices. Often her voice would carry over Wheatley's less rambunctious exhortations.

It was Mary who drew up the plan to persuade the tenement men out for Labour and, as the 14th of December approached, the Wolseley, with the two campaigners and a pile of leaflets aboard, would stop by pubs at their most popular times. On these occasions the roles reversed and Mary would shout through the loud hailer while Wheatley gave out leaflets. Wheatley would then be subject of some joshing as the men asked him who his boss was. Some of it was less good-natured, for many of the Parkhead people knew what had gone before and Wheatley had to turn a deaf ear to the more ribald insults that came his way.

Danny drove the car between stops while Wheatley and Mary talked excitedly about their last encounter with the constituents and their minor successes at converting new voters to the cause.

As the campaign drew to a close, the atmosphere in the committee room was tense. Andrew Fleming ignored Mary's contribution and addressed his remarks directly to the candidate. 'Those men were always a doubt, John. It was a tactical error to go for them. Our returns show that many will vote for the Coalition out of patriotism or because it was them that gave them the vote. They see it as a betrayal to vote for anyone else.'

Mary drew a breath and seemed ready to explode. Wheatley laid a restraining hand on her arm. 'You may be correct, Andrew. But we were right to go where our natural support lies – in the tenements. It's the direction Mary took us and I think she was right.'

'We will see whether *Mrs* Ireland was right or not tomorrow,' said Fleming and Cooke nodded with a knowing sneer.

Saturday December 14, 1918

On election day, the committee room was a hive of activity. Runners brought in the voter returns from the polling stations and Cooke and Fleming crossed off the names from the canvassing returns. As the day progressed, Danny and Mary and other party members in motors or on bicycles would go out to known Labour supporters who had not yet voted and chivvy them to the polling station.

Mary would jump out of the car as it slowed in front of the entrances to the closes and Danny listened as she hollered through the building exhorting the men out. Then she would leap back in the car and give Danny his next direction. He worked the hand clutch, the car would lurch forward with a crashing of gears and they would head off in a pall of blue smoke. 'Don't leave them in the road, Danny!' she would echo, her eyes afire with enthusiasm for the battle. And Danny would smile into the mirror, shake his head and feel again the hollow in his chest that he knew would live with him as long as he found himself in her company.

Finally, with the polling stations closing, Danny ferried the team to the count and drove out to Braehead House to pick up Mrs Wheatley. She kept him waiting outside before finally appearing, wrapped in a fur coat.

'So is he going to win, Danny?' she asked as she settled in the seat.

'It's very close according to the returns, Mrs Wheatley.'

'Why didn't you come to get my vote out, Danny? I had to order a cab.'

'I'm sorry, Mrs Wheatley, Mr Wheatley didn't say to –'

'No, he wouldn't have done. He knew I was going to vote for Rear Admiral Adair.'

Danny stayed silent.

'Does that shock you, Danny McAleer? Does it shock you that I should vote to keep my husband away from London?'

Danny concentrated on changing gears without flinging his passenger forward. No it didn't shock him. Given all that had happened it didn't shock him at all.

It was a close thing. There was a recount and Wheatley was defeated by seventy-four votes. They later discovered that this was the smallest victory margin in Britain that year. Mr Wheatley smiled alongside his wife on the stage as the returning officer gave the result. Danny could see that only Mrs Wheatley's satisfaction was genuine.

Danny took the defeated candidate and his wife home first and then returned for Mary. Her eyes were red. He pulled her to him and her head lay against his chest.

'Och, Danny! Seventy-four! If I could have got round to ten more closes we could have won.'

'It's not your fault, Mary.' He patted the back of her shoulder and kissed her lightly on the forehead. 'You couldn't have done any more.'

'It's not how Andrew Fleming will see it.'

'Aye, well, what does he know? Come on. I'll take you back to Parkhead Cross in the motor.'

She pulled away from him. 'You're a good man, Danny.'

'I know,' he said. But not good enough, he thought, as he helped her into the back of the car.

Twelve

Saturday January 18, 1919

Wheatley sat slouched in his upholstered office chair with his back to the room and looked out across the ha-ha at the bottom of the garden to the golf course beyond. It was deserted. A cold rain was falling in swathes as if God's hand was painting the sheets of grey wash this way and that with a mighty paintbrush.

Danny shivered as he sat in the lower visitor's chair facing the desk. The cuffs of his trousers were soaked from the short walk up to the house from the garage, and the fire hadn't yet warmed the room. He wondered what his boss was thinking.

The Bolsheviks had assumed power in Russia and there were many in Glasgow who saw Britain going the same way. One of Glasgow's leading anti-war agitators, the communist John Maclean, had been pardoned and released from gaol weeks before. Straight away, he had set about bringing revolution to the streets where the workers were competing for their jobs with demobilised soldiers.

Trade Union leaders, principally Willie Gallagher, Davey Kirkwood and Manny Shinwell, drew up plans to press for a reduction in the working week from fifty-four to forty hours. This would create jobs for the returning soldiers.

Jimmy Maxton, who, like Wheatley, believed passionately in the democratic route to socialism, also failed in his run for parliament in the previous month's election and found common cause with Maclean's Clyde Workers' Committee.

The narrowness of Wheatley's defeat should have established him as a hero of the left but he was viewed with suspicion by all his peers except Maxton, who, being from the intellectual tradition of the left, sympathised with Wheatley's cerebral approach.

Others saw Wheatley's route out of poverty as a betrayal of his class. They believed the rumours about Wheatley's advertising racket and his occasional forays into money-lending and were openly hostile. For Maclean, Gallagher, Kirkwood, Shinwell and others, Wheatley was a well-fed cuckoo in the Red Clydeside nest.

Danny had seen the recently issued CWC handbills calling for a General Strike in support of the 40-hour week. It was scheduled to start on the last Monday in the month. He guessed his boss was pondering which position to take.

Wheatley swung round. 'I have to be seen to support the strike, Danny. God knows I don't want to tramp the streets in this weather but...' His voice trailed off.

Danny sat patiently, still unaware of why he had been summoned.

'We had our best success when we persuaded the women out back in '15.'

Danny knew he was expected to stay silent.

'But with their men back in the closes, demobbed or out of work, I am not sure they'll do it. What if I try to get them out and they don't come?'

Danny turned to the fire, rubbed his hands and faced his palms to the glowing embers.

'Put some more coal on, Danny. Let's have some heat in here.'

Danny shook the brass coal scuttle and two lumps of anthracite each the size of his boot tumbled out. Almost immediately, they bubbled tar and spat jets of flame as the trapped gas was released.

'No, I shall merely have to offer my services to Kirkwood and the others. I shall telephone the CWC and say I will address workers' rallies here in Shettleston. If I can keep the extremists out of my constituency, at least my people will only hear my version of "a land fit for heroes".'

Danny stood up. He sensed he was about to be dismissed.

'You go and warm up the motor. I have a feeling we shall be on the stump outside the factories again.'

Saturday January 25, 1919
In the days leading up to the strike, Danny and Wheatley toured the factories in Shettleston. On this Saturday, as on every day that week, Wheatley stepped down from the car as the factory hooter sounded. Standing in his bowler and overcoat, as the rain foamed and steamed with chemical reactions around his feet, he exhorted the workers to stay off in support of the forty-hours movement on the following Monday. He urged them instead to attend the meeting at the city's St Andrew's Hall and the subsequent march to George Square.

Climbing back into the car he took off his gloves and rubbed his hands together. 'I'll catch my death doing this, Danny. And what for? The betterment of the Worker's Committee. Maclean and his workers' revolt!'

Danny had left the engine running. 'Is that it for the day, JW?'

Wheatley blew into his cupped hands as he leaned forward to speak though the open window behind Danny's back. 'Aye. Let's see what's for my supper back home. Cold shoulder and tongue, I havnae doubt.'

As the car sloshed through Shettleston's streets, Wheatley took out his fountain pen and writing pad. 'What about this, Danny?' He had left the window to the passenger compartment open and was calling out enough to be heard over the sound of the engine. '"*Though a popular revolt is morally justified, I fail to see how it could be successful in Scotland where power is held by the capitalist.*"'

'Very good, JW. For *Forward*?' Danny half-turned so his boss could hear.

'Yes, and this, "*the Independent Labour policy should rely on brains not bullets?*"'

'That's good too, JW. Aye, brains not bullets.'

Wheatley took off his glasses and rubbed his eyes. They shone blue in the small electric light illuminating the back of the motor. His tongue protruded slightly as he wrote. 'This, listen Danny, this is good, "*when the smoke of revolution clears we will see the debris not of the capitalist system but the ruins of the socialist movement*". Aye, that will stir them up.'

'Maclean and his cronies are not going to like it, JW'

'They are part of the problem, Danny. It's Jimmy Maxton and me – we are the coming men. We're the ones the people of Glasgow will vote for.'

Wednesday January 29, 1919

It was the third day of the strike. Danny parked the motor near the apartment house in Ingram Street and opened the door for Wheatley. Their breath clouded in front of their noses. Wheatley's bowler was already on his head and Danny quickly donned his cap.

The street was crowded with working men heading west, flat-capped heads sunk into the upturned collars of their jackets. Their boots crunched on the street and the steel blue of cigarette smoke hung over the small groups as they joshed their way along. The fibres of the working clothes gave up the metallic sharpness of molten iron, of steel plate being worked. The air carried the taste of sulphur to the back of Danny's throat.

Nudging elbows prompted one of their number to look up from time to time to study Wheatley in their midst. His heavy overcoat and gloves made him out to be one of the boss class on a spying mission. On occasion, Danny would have to step in the way of a carefully angled swinging arm or a bustling shoulder. As they walked along St Vincent Street and were joined by others from south of the river, it became clear there would be very few factories operating in Glasgow that day.

Early that morning, Wheatley's motor, with Danny at the wheel, had toured the Shettleston constituency to make sure that the pickets were in place and the strike was solid. The only factory they missed was Beardmore's, the massive foundry in Parkhead, not because it took them near Mary Ireland's close, but because it was sure to be silent. Davey Kirkwood was Chief Shop Steward there and Wheatley's appearance at the gates would only antagonise him. But, if the Shettleston experience was replicated elsewhere, and the signs were good, the strike would be a success.

The blackened columns of St Andrew's Hall seemed to be at one with the heavy grey sky. They supported a pediment from which eight caryatids looked down pitilessly on the steaming mass of men collecting at the entrance. A few policemen were trying to make them form two queues, one to each side of the door.

Wheatley led Danny up Granville Street. 'Follow me. We'll find a way in at the stage door.'

The man in the cubicle at the performers' entrance had lost his right arm and was scarred down the side of his face. His grey hair clung precariously in small clusters on one side but grew luxuriously on the other. Danny limped in behind Wheatley and gave the man the wounded veteran's nod that he had learned over the previous four years.

Wheatley bounced with unnatural bonhomie. 'I see you haven't seen fit to join the strike.'

The concierge responded gruffly. 'Aye, and if I had who wid open the place up for yon wasters.'

Wheatley chuckled. 'We've come to see the Workers' Committee people who have booked the hall. Gallagher? Shinwell? Kirkwood?'

The man flicked a thumb down the corridor. 'Follow your nose. Last time I saw them they were behind the rostrum. I will say to you whit I said to them, an' aw. Touch anything to do with the organ and you will be oot. And that goes for your comrades in the hall, by th'way.'

Wheatley nodded and went through. Danny followed, making sure the clump of his boot could be heard above the din coming from the hall.

At the end of the corridor after two right hand turns that took them past the dressing room doors, they came across a gaggle of men collected behind the screen like wifies at the tap. Here the men, who filled the auditorium to bursting, braying about the success of the day so far, drowned out normal conversation.

After a brief huddle with the committee Wheatley returned

to Danny. 'They are going to address the men but only for a short time because there are as many locked out as are inside.'

Danny bent his head nearer to Wheatley's mouth.

'They have reserved seats in the front row and they will save one for me. I was looking for Jimmy Maxton but he's not here. Anyway, you go back to the car. The committee will lead the men from here to George Square for a bigger rally with speeches. I shall get up in front of them then. I'll come back to the car when it's over.'

'Are you sure you'll be all right?'

Wheatley made a shooing motion. 'On you go.'

When Danny was back in the car he contemplated the alternatives. He could sit in the cold, sheltered by the awning and wrapped up in a rug while he waited for the boss. He could find a tea room somewhere. The third option was to drive two miles out to Parkhead Cross, park the Wolseley near the football ground and walk to Duke Street where he hoped Mary would provide the tea for free. It was over a month since election night and she might even be pleased to see him. He was clambering out of the car with the starting handle in his hand almost before he realised he had made the decision.

'Och! It's good to see you, Danny. Come away in. I'll make a pot.'

Mary was bustling in the house with the young Tom clinging to her skirts. The two older girls studied Danny solemnly with dark eyes beneath fringes of black hair cut to meld into their heavy brows.

'It's not so cold now, Ella, Millie, put on your heavy coats, take the boy and play in the court while Mr McAleer is here.'

The girls took the coats that hung behind the main door and put them on all the while watching Danny.

'Come on now, close your mouths or you'll be catching flies,' said Mary as she fussed them through the door and called after them. 'Do Tommy's coat on the stair – before you go outside.'

She turned back to Danny. 'So tell me. How is the strike looking? There's not been a sound from Beardmore's so far this day, by th'way.'

'It's rock solid in all the Shettleston wards, Mary.'

'Aye. I heard you and John were out and about.'

'They're all in the city. The Workers' Committee will be whipping them up in George Square by now.'

'And John?'

'Aye, he's there with them. He will have his turn on the rostrum.'

Mary started pouring the tea. 'Well I have some good news. My man has had his demob papers. He's down south but he's on his way home. He'll be here next month.'

Danny felt as if he had a knife twisting in his side. Mary was handing him a cup and saucer and he focused on taking it from her. 'He'll come back to all this strike –'

'He has the milk round – he can pick up where he left off.'

'Only because you kept it going.'

'It was good to have it to do –'

'And raising the weans –'

'I've had my hands full.'

They were both silent. Danny knew she was thinking about Wheatley.

She placed a plate with a slice of barn brack on it in front of him. 'I would like to see him. Before...'

Danny took a bite. 'This is a rare fine cake, Mary. Thank you.'

'Where could I see him?' She held her hand to her shawl touching the silver pin with the cairngorm.

'He's going to be busy over the next few days, with the strike and all.'

'Come on, Danny. It's me you're speaking to.'

Danny sighed. 'It all depends on what happens today. The committee are meeting with the Lord Provost. They're going to ask him to tell the bosses in Glasgow they have to go to a forty-hour week. If it happens, the strike will be over and you shall see JW before the week is out.'

She set her jaw firm. 'What are the chances? Sir James Stewart!' She spat out the Lord Provost's name like a swearword. 'He spends more time in The Merchants' House than he does in the Council Chamber. Whose side do you think he is on?'

'He has to take notice of a General Strike, Mary. Glasgow will not produce another nail until it's over.'

'But who has time on their side, Danny? The working man with a family that needs to be fed or the bosses in their mansions with their bank vaults bulging?'

Danny looked at the clock on the mantel. 'I'd best be getting back to collect the boss.'

The streets that took Danny to the city were thronged with men trudging back to their homes. There was no light-hearted joshing – they had more the look of men attending a wake.

Wheatley was waiting in the Ingram Street flat. He made a point of consulting his pocket watch as Danny opened the door.

'Sorry, JW. I went to visit Mary Ireland.'

Wheatley's features softened. 'How is she?'

'She has news –'

'Not another wean?'

'No. It's her man. He's coming back next week. Demobbed. A hero from the Front.'

Wheatley didn't react.

'She wants to see you, JW. She's hoping you may have time if the strike is over. Did the Lord Provost agree to do what the committee asked?'

Wheatley shook his head. 'I'll tell you about it in the car.' He led the way downstairs and on to the street.

On the road out to Shettleston Wheatley pulled the partition aside to speak to Danny. 'Stewart has said he will talk to his colleagues on the Council before agreeing to intervene. He's buying time. He asked the strike committee to come back on Friday for his answer.'

'Buying time? What for?'

Wheatley shook his head. 'Who knows? But if the government wants to break the strike, they're the ones with time on their side.'

'That's what Mary said.'

'She has a better head for politics than some in the

Committee. Davey Kirkwood and Manny Shinwell are both hot-headed. They have no idea of strategy. They are not even aware that they're having their strings pulled by Maclean and Gallagher.'

'So what happens next?'

'We stay on the side of the angels and try to keep Shettleston solidly behind the strike at least until Friday.'

'When the Provost gives his answer?'

'Kirkwood and Maclean told the men to come back to George Square on Friday to hear what Stewart has to say on behalf of the bosses. The committee wants an even bigger turnout than today. They plan to halt the city centre. They have asked the Provost to serve a notice to stop the trams in the city so they are not causing a danger. What with the men being whipped up by Kirkwood, Shinwell and the other trade union leaders, if this was all happening in the summer I would fear for the city.'

'What about Mary?'

'Let's see what happens on Friday. But you had best tell her to keep out of the city that day.'

Thirteen

Friday January 31, 1919

There was a mist that morning. It pulled the smoke out of the air and pushed it against Danny's nose and mouth like a cold flannel. He sat in the front of the Wolseley, driving Wheatley round the factories to check the pickets were in place and the strike was still solid. As before, he parked the car in Ingram Street, a short walk from George Square.

They heard the crowd before they saw it; the noise of thousands of conversations going on at the same time, escalating and falling in an ebb and flow of voices. As if providing a line of melody above the bass, chants broke out. They called into question the parentage of specific factory bosses. They pleaded for the forty-hour week. They shouted for the Lord Provost Stewart's neck.

The square was an ocean of flat-capped, bobbing heads. A haze of mist and cigarette smoke hung over them, interspersed with the occasional blood-red flag. Here and there a man had taken the vantage point of a lamp-post and clung to it as if it was the only thing stopping him from drowning in the sea of cloth caps.

Danny jostled a path along the wall of the City Chambers building and in past two policemen who were standing outside the entrance door. He wondered what they would do if the mob decided to ransack the building.

The Workers' Committee had taken up a station through the first portico beside the broad staircase. The hall was warm and the gaslights gave a glow to the gold-streaked marble walls.

It was Maxton who detached himself and shook Wheatley's

112

hand. 'John, we need you here. Your cool counsel. If we're not careful, things could get out of hand.'

'What is it?'

Maxton drew Wheatley away to a corner and, while there heads were together in conversation, Danny sauntered through to the main entrance hall.

It was easy to distinguish the two sides of the day's dispute. The Committee, Maclean's men, were in heavy woollen double-breasted overcoats, open to show shirts under knitted waistcoats. The paper collars on those that had them were soft and worn, folded over plaid ties. Those with no collars had mufflers tucked in. Their thick serge trousers telescoped above heavy work boots. Some carried trilby hats and others had flat caps stuffed in their coat pockets. Manny Shinwell's pipe was puffing smoke like the Royal Scot. These men formed one group.

Their political opponents were evidently collected somewhere else in the building but every now and then Danny would see one of their number passing through the entrance hall. They wore day suits of dark worsted, with sharp-creased trousers above polished brogues. Their collars shone brilliantly under the chandelier. Their dark ties were knotted with a flourish and the ends pinned with a jewel.

Danny imagined a row of bowler hats that must exist in the building somewhere so that these cocks could cover their heads on the few steps from the entrance to their motor cars. The air was heavy with the scent of their cologne and brilliantine, and Danny imagined them to be better placed in a Georgian court rather than an industrial dispute in Britain's second city.

He was brought out of this reverie by Wheatley's approach. Danny was struck by how his boss, from his shining brogues to the bowler hat he held in his right hand, was in the colours of the opposing team.

'Danny, we're going to need your help. These men –' he signalled over his shoulder, '– have no idea what to do. Stewart has told them he's still talking to the representatives of the bosses. They're over at The Merchant's House.'

Danny nodded.

Wheatley's speech had taken on a breathy quality. His face was flushed. 'Kirkwood and Shinwell reckon there are ten thousand or more men out there. They're waiting for somebody to tell them something. I don't know how long they'll stay like that. The magistrates have not stopped the trams – I don't know whether the Provost even asked them. It's all coming to a head.'

'What do you want me to do?'

'Shinwell has had a look out one of the windows but he can't see anything because of the crowd. From what he can see, the police are building up a force at the far end of the square – Queen Street. D'you think you could get out there and see what's happening? If they try and clear the square... ' He shook his head. 'Just see if you can find out what the polis are up to and report back.'

Danny crossed the yard or so of flagstones that separated the building from the crowd. He jostled his way into the scrum. The smell of cigarette smoke, stale booze, factory and foundry, sweat and body fug, settled around him. He lowered his head into it and dived forward elbowing and barging into the mass. From time to time he would lift his head like a swimmer to check his progress, then he pushed forward again. For the most part the men stepped out of his way, with the occasional, 'What's the rush, Jimmy?' or a 'You're heading the wrong way, big man,' before going back to their business. It would take a particularly foolish, drunk or brave man to step into Danny's way. When one or other chancer tried, Danny found it worked to stamp on the barring man's foot. That way he maintained his progress with the least effort.

He looked over the top of the mass and saw he was only ten or so yards from the Queen Street end of the square. As he hunched down, he became aware of a flow of bodies around him. There was some sort of exchange happening.

Danny felt a hand on his shoulder and looked up. He saw first the chest and then the grand moustache of a man who had all the hallmarks of a regimental sergeant major.

'Aye, you'll do. You come forward,'

'What's going on?' Danny shouted above the din.

'We're pulling the old sweats to the front here. Anybody who can't look after himself if things get rough is being sent back.'

'Why?'

'The polis have been reinforcing along Queen Street. There was only a row of them at first. See?'

Danny was now close enough to the front row to view the ranks of blue four deep on the Queen Street pavement only a few yards from the expanding crowd of men.

The 'sergeant major' shouted over his shoulder, 'They're pouring in from St Vincent Street. There's a row of trams down there. I think they want to clear a way for them to get through the square.' He went back to managing the flow of ex-servicemen to the front of the crowd.

Danny looked along the front of the two facing armies. The police were organised in ranks, standing to attention with their truncheons drawn in their right hands. At regular intervals sergeants carried long nightsticks and tapped them on the ground like fighting bulls pawing the dust.

The men in the front row of the crowd yelled abuse. Occasionally, a chancer broke ranks and, feet moving like a boxer, extended his hands at waist level, palms upward and fingers twitching, to invite an adversary to take him on – 'if you're hard enough'. The taunts were met by the impassive stares of the policemen, but Danny could tell they were ready for action.

He turned and retraced his steps. Now, as he approached the front of the City Chambers, he was aware once again of the exchange of bodies. The fighters were being drafted to outer rows of the massive scrimmage of men covering the whole of the square.

When he reached the entrance, he saw why. A cordon of blue was now drawn up in front of the building. They must have infiltrated the same way he and Wheatley had earlier by following the building wall from Ingram Street to the south or from George Street to the north. It looked as if they intended to clear the square by advancing on the crowd from both the east and west at the same time, squeezing the demonstrators out along North Hanover Street to one side and Hanover Street on the other.

Danny spied Manny Shinwell standing on one of the pediments alongside the entrance to the Chambers and pointing with his pipe to a part of the crowd on the north side of the square. He seemed to be giving instructions to someone below but the surging crowd blocked Danny's view. At that moment a whistle sounded. It was answered by a chorus. The police sergeants had their cheeks puffed out producing a shrill descant. It was countered by a low rumble as the ranks of policemen growled in their throats and started to move forward.

Danny felt the compression as the first rank of protestors stepped back. The police only had five paces to advance before they were on them. They took the last two at a rush and then leapt indiscriminately upon individuals, dealing out blows to heads and shoulders. They shouted and Danny could make out only fragments, 'Clear the Square!' 'Rioters!' 'Move on, now, move on!'

The roar of men in conflict rose to the fury of a hundred steam engines. The advance had started in the centre directly opposite the entrance to the Council Chambers and now the line split as if to sweep the strikers to both north and south. Scuffles broke out where the ex-soldiers fought back. But it was bare fists against truncheons and as, the centre line cleared, Danny could see the bodies of fallen strikers littering the space.

The line in front of Danny broke for a second and he took the opportunity to run for the doorway as best he could with his one unbending knee.

Inside he found the committee grouped around Shinwell. His voice was pitched high. 'They say they read the Riot Act! I saw Sherriff MacKenzie over by the Merchant's House. I think somebody snatched it away.'

Davey Kirkwood's chest was heaving and his whole frame was tense as a boxer waiting for the referee's signal, 'I'm going out there,' he announced.

'What good will it do?' Wheatley said. There was a sheen of sweat on his brow.

'We have to know whit's happening to our men. Give them our support.'

Maclean leaned in and prodded Wheatley on the lapel. 'Aye, those may not be your kind out there, Wheatley, but they're my comrades, every man-jack of them.'

Wheatley stepped back shaking his head.

Maxton took Danny by the arm and pointed up at his face. 'You're bleeding, man. What's going on?'

Danny touched his cheek and felt the cut. He looked at his fingers smeared with blood. He must have taken a cosh and not noticed. 'It's nothing. It looks to me as if the polis have a plan. They have moved in down the middle and are driving the men away north and south. There was no warning. Some are fighting back but getting cracked heads for their troubles.'

Maxton spoke quickly. 'If there are men injured we must clear them from the square. Will you help me, Danny?'

'We don't want the men dispersed all over the city. We have to call them together again.' shouted Kirkwood. 'Come with me, Willie. We shall pass the word to meet up again on Glasgow Green. We'll regroup there for our next move.'

'I'll help,' Manny Shinwell said. 'We shall split up and spread the word, meet on Glasgow Green.'

The three of them made for the door but as soon as they were in the open four policemen set upon Kirkwood and Gallagher. Both went down. At least one police boot went in. Shinwell put his hands up and was pinned against the wall.

Danny made as if to go after them but Maxton tugged his sleeve. 'Over here, Danny. These men need our help.'

There were about fifty men left in the square which was now surrounded on all sides by lines of policemen facing outwards. Some were staggering, holding their heads, others sitting dazed and more lying prone. Maxton went to the nearest of these and turned him over. His face was smeared with blood that was still escaping from a gash above his eye. 'Take him inside. Let's hope they can find some bandages.'

As they dragged the man along, his boots trailing on the flags, Danny saw a small dark figure carrying a bundle of packages scurrying into the City Chambers. It was Mary Ireland.

The entrance hall became a first aid station. Danny and Maxton dragged and led the injured men in and Wheatley and Mary sat them down and bandaged their wounds with strips torn from the sheets Mary had carried into the building.

The square was clear but those inside could hear the noise of conflict around its perimeter where the police and the strikers were still facing off against each other.

Danny sat and rested his leg watching Mary winding bandages around the heads of those who had been battered. Two men were still out cold lying prone on the floor and Wheatley had sent a messenger up the hill to the infirmary for it to send an ambulance for them. A group of men with broken arms or wrists sat sullenly, smoking and waiting to be told it was safe for them to trudge up to the infirmary without fear of arrest.

As soon as all the men were inside, Maxton had left by a side entrance. He said he would pass word to the men to make their way to Glasgow Green. He hoped that using word-of-mouth the whole mass of men – they reckoned about thirty-five thousand in all – would leave the confrontation and collect in the riverside park where it was more difficult for the police to form any sort of cordon.

The ambulance men came in carrying two stretchers and took the two unconscious men away. One of them reported to Wheatley that the north side of the square was now clear of demonstrators. It was safe for the walking wounded to leave. When Maxton returned, Danny, Wheatley and Mary must have looked a bedraggled group. Their clothes and hands were smeared with blood and their faces were pale with the reaction of what had happened around them. None of them was a trade unionist; none had an official role as far as the strike was concerned.

Maxton clapped Wheatley on the back. 'It looks as if it's up to you and me in Glasgow Green, John.'

Wheatley smiled wearily. 'Aye, but I'm not the sort who can whip them up to take on the police.'

'I know what John Maclean would have us do –'

'Maclean! He'd be storming Maryhill Barracks like it was

the Winter Palace, taking the guns and marching on London.'

Mary spoke quietly. 'The men are ready for it, ye ken. They have come back to nothing. No toil. No home fit for heroes. Nothing. They're in the mood for revolution.'

'And the troops in Maryhill – who are the very men Mary's talking about – most of them are waiting to be demobbed. They'd happily hand over their guns and join in.' Maxton said.

'Whoa!' Wheatley held up a hand. 'You are surely not telling me you are up for a fight, Jimmy?'

'We are both out of the same mould, John, always will be.' Maxton sounded disappointed with himself. 'We say it's change frae the ballot box or no change at all. But Mary's right, by th'way. The men who've been in the square this day will now be even hungrier for a fight.'

'We have to steady the ship.' Wheatley said. 'The pickets must stay in and the workers stay out until Davey and Willie are bailed out. Then we hand the reins back to them. So it's you and me on Glasgow Green, Jimmy.' He turned to Mary. 'Will you join us?'

She nodded. Her eyes shone like jet.

'I remember you from the rent strike, Mrs Ireland.' Maxton loomed over her. 'You are the activist John is always blethering about.'

Mary blushed. 'Aye, well we weren't going to stand idly by with the landlords exploiting the war and our men oot the way.'

'And Mr Ireland, has he returned?' Maxton's eyes flitted between her and Wheatley as he spoke.

She studied the graining in the sheet of marble at her feet. 'No, Mr Maxton. But he has survived, thank God. He's down south. He'll be back in Glasgow next week.'

'I am not sure that God has had much to do with it, Mary.'

Wheatley interrupted. 'Wisht, Jimmy, we will have none of your atheist blether. Come on, we have a job to do.'

Fourteen

The four of them hurried across the Saltmarket and on to Glasgow Green. They had their first sight of the Clyde to their right, fast-flowing and thick brown, reflecting the leaden sky. In front of them and way into the distance the grass of the park was obliterated by the dark mass of milling strikers.

One man detached himself from a fringe group of about ten who were under the massive stone arch which signified the start of the People's Park. 'Is it you, Mr Maxton?' he said.

Maxton nodded and swept the hair back from his forehead. 'And you are?'

'Jimmy Auld. I'm on the sub-committee for the strike. The rest of them, the ones not in the infirmary or gaol, are over there.'

'What happened after George Square?'

'The polis pincer movement took us by surprise – there was no warning. I ended up on the south side but there were as many to the north. Fights broke out along the line and they hauled a good number of us off to the cells. They'll be on the wrong end of a good beating there, an' aw.'

'But you still heard to meet here –'

'We saw our men on the far side moving away along George Street and guessed they would be heading for Glasgow Cross. When we met up there they told us about the plan to regroup here. But the polis were waiting for us. This time we chased them off. We made a mess of the railings, though.'

Danny surveyed the scene. There was rubble all across Saltmarket and the road on to Albert Bridge. The fence around

120

the Green had been torn down in places. The strikers guarding the park entrance held lengths of metal like spears slackly in their hands. He pictured the men using them like bayoneted rifles prodding at the policemen until they gave way.

'Where are they now, the polis?' Wheatley said.

'Over the other side of the bridge.' Auld laughed. 'But I don't fancy they'll stay in the Gorbals for longer than necessary. I wouldn't like having those goons behind me.'

The men smiled.

'Will you address the men, Mr Maxton?'

Maxton nodded.

'Mr Wheatley will want to say something as well, won't you John?' Mary said. Danny looked for Maxton's reaction. The tall man turned away as if searching the crowd for someone he knew.

Auld led the group to the western bandstand and Maxton and Wheatley mounted the steps. Danny stood alongside Mary and Auld turned back to his colleagues on the committee.

'It's been an exciting day, Danny,' she said without taking her eyes off Wheatley.

'It has, Mary. What made you come, by th'way? I warned you not to. In all these thousands of men there must be no more than a hundred women.'

'You said the Lord Provost would be telling the men they had their forty hours. I didn't want to miss it.'

'I said he would come back with an answer. I didn't ken it would be to provoke a bloody riot.'

'When I came along George Street I saw the Sherriff reading from his paper. I guessed it was the Riot Act. I saw them take it from him and tear it up. That's when the police signal went up. The first row of police went in smashing heads and I could see there would be injuries. So I ran back to get some bed sheets from the first store I came across in Buchanan Street. I had to spend a week's money.'

'Don't worry, I'll make sure JW sorts it out,' he whispered, hoping his boss wouldn't overhear.

The crowd erupted into noise. The men had been listening quietly while Auld introduced the two speakers and now greeted Jimmy Maxton as a brother.

He leant forward, the parapet of the bandstand cutting into the front of his thighs. The breeze caught the lank of hair that hung down across his eyebrow and he brushed it back and punched his fist into the air. 'Tens of thousands of working men have withdrawn their labour this week. The foundries and shipbuilding yards, the factories and the steelyards, all are silent. Glasgow industry is silent. But Glasgow's working man is not silent!'

The men all around the bandstand in the fading light roared in response.

'You have shown this week that you are a force to be reckoned with. On Monday, the first day of the General Strike in Glasgow, the Clyde Workers' Committee estimated that forty thousand men withdrew their labour.'

There were more cheers.

'By Wednesday, when five thousand or more of you marched from St Andrews Hall to George Square over seventy thousand men were out. And today, this Bloody Friday –'

The crowd went wild. They cheered and shook their fists, the ones with railing-spears brandished them over their heads like Zulu warriors.

'Aye, this Bloody Friday, when honest working men were beaten to the ground by the police, we have won the day –'

The cheers rose up again and subsided. Danny could feel a tension in the air. The men were waiting for the next order, an order to take the fight forward.

'The battle goes on. The strike must stay in place. We have not won a promise for forty hours from the Lord Provost. Our peaceful protest has been met with violence. We will not stop here!'

Maxton's voice had reached a crescendo almost screaming the last words. This time the response was muted. Danny could feel the coil of frustration in the men winding tight and waiting for release.

Maxton had stepped back and now it was Wheatley's turn. He took off his bowler hat and passed it back to Auld. Then he smoothed his hair back over his head. He gripped one lapel of his coat. Then he took that hand away and clapped it knuckles down into the palm of the other. He licked his lips.

Danny realised his boss was actually nervous. He had never spoken to a crowd of this size before and it was a daunting sight.

'Comrades!' It came out strangled and high-pitched. Wheatley paused and took a deep breath. 'Comrades!' It was still high-pitched but no more than usual. 'Many of you have served your country in the war to end all wars. Am I right?'

There was a hurrah from a few voices and then laughter.

Wheatley looked down smiling and pushed his glasses back up his nose. He raised his head.

'Where is your "home fit for heroes"? Tell me that. Where is your job?'

This time there was a reaction in the crowd.

'Do you want to put another man out of a job so you may work?'

A lone voice from the crowd piped up, 'Aye, I do, thank you very much!' It was followed by laughter.

Danny saw electricity surge through his boss. 'You there! You have no place here. This is a place for working-class solidarity. Where one working man looks out for his brother. Where we are all comrades. As you looked out for your comrades on the Front, so we look out for each other here. If we get the forty-hour week there is enough work for all.'

The crowd was surging now, a new energy flowing through it.

'Every man here is his neighbour's comrade. It's the bosses who want to set worker against worker. Our weapon is our solidarity. Our weapon is resolve. Together you cleared this People's Park of those who wished to deny you the right to protest. You are the army of the workers. You can win this battle with the ruling classes. It's won at the negotiating table when your representatives know you are solid behind them. It's won at the ballot box when you vote for Labour candidates, men like you, to take the battle to London. It's a battle of the minds. It's a battle of wills!'

Wheatley allowed the shouts of approval and the clapping

to die down. Danny could hear the ripple of the river coursing under the bridge a hundred yards away. It was nearly dark.

Wheatley began again in almost a whisper. 'You have shown this week that you have the resolve to fight this battle. You have shown today that you have the solidarity, working-class soldier and working-class worker, to stand side-by-side against the forces of the ruling classes.' Wheatley paused for effect, tapping a single finger of one hand into the palm of the other. 'But do you have the will?'

The crowd came back, 'Aye!'

Now he tapped two fingers. 'It will mean another week without work, without a wage. Do you have the will?'

They came back louder, 'Aye!'

Now he brandished three fingers. 'The pickets stay in – the workers stay out – until you have forty hours.' Wheatley's voice was now as loud as Danny had ever heard it. Flecks of saliva spat out. Wheatley closed his palm and held it up shaking as if he held their resolve in his hand. 'Do you have the will? Do you *have* the will?'

'Aye! Aye! Aye!' The cheering continued long after Wheatley had opened the hand and held it up to ask for their silence.

He looked up and his glasses flashed in a streetlamp light. 'This day is over. This day will be remembered as Bloody Friday. It's your victory. Now away to your homes and conserve your energies for the trials ahead.'

As the crowd cheered, Wheatley shook hands with Maxton and Auld and the three of them left the bandstand to be engulfed in surge of back-slapping congratulation. Mary left Danny's side, ran to Wheatley and attached herself to his arm. Over the next few minutes the crowd thinned and Maxton and Auld went off to join the others who had led the men to the park. Wheatley and Mary hugged. 'You have never done better, John. The strike will stay strong.'

'As long as we can keep the hotheads like Maclean under control,' Wheatley said. 'He will try to whip together an uprising. I shall have to spring Shinwell and Kirkwood tomorrow in the hope their cooler heads prevail.'

He pulled Mary to him. 'But that's for tomorrow, my little

Mary. Have you eaten today?'

'Nothing since breakfast.'

Wheatley turned to Danny. 'You find yourself something to eat. I shall take Mary here for the slap-up tea she deserves. She was the hero of the hour, a veritable Florence Nightingale. After tea, she and I will go back to Ingram Street and we can meet up with you there. You can then escort Mrs Ireland home.' He took out his watch. 'It's a few minutes past five o'clock. Be at Ingram Street at nine-thirty ready to take Mary home. How does that sound?'

Danny grunted.

Wheatley beamed at Mary. 'Is that acceptable to you, young lady? Will your weans be looked after?'

'The bairns are with my sister-in-law. It will be no trouble for her to look after them until I'm back.'

'That's settled then. Sauchiehall Street for you and I. What about you, Danny?'

'Och! I'll have a fish supper and a couple of pints and be at Ingram Street in good time.'

'Very well then.' With a wave of his bowler Wheatley stepped away with Mary on his arm.

Danny watched the dispersing crowd file out of the park towards The Saltmarket to the right and Albert Bridge to the left. The last of those going south over the bridge stopped and turned back. Some of them began to run, waving away the stragglers who had yet to reach it.

A rumble of noise sounded from across the river. It was the roar of petrol engines mixed with the banshee squeal of metal tearing against metal. The few remaining men in the park cocked their heads, listening. Some who, perhaps, had heard the noise before turned, faces pale, eyes staring, shouted a warning. The roar, the sound of a hundred factories in motion, vibrated even through the sole of Danny's great boot.

The noise was coming from the bridge as if the structure was wrenching itself apart before being swept away down river. But it stood firm. And then, silhouetted against the sky's dusk light, over the brow, a thin snout appeared. It traversed left and right sniffing the air before moving forward. Then came the flat-topped disc of a turret and finally the great bulk with steel tracks screeching and scrunching on the tarmacadam. It was the first of the British Army tanks.

As the last of the stragglers fled, Danny ducked behind the cover of the bandstand. He counted a column of four tanks and at least ten truckloads of troops crossing the River Clyde from the Gorbals and heading towards the city centre, before he left the scene and made off east along the river bank.

Fifteen

Sunday March 21, 1920

It was Danny's thirtieth birthday and it coincided with a Sunday, which should have been his evening off. He was at a lock-in at The Old College Bar, round the corner from Ingram Street, nursing a pint.

He had spent a good number of his evenings since January the previous year waiting on the boss while he dallied with Mary in the Ingram Street apartment. Wheatley was away from home at least two evenings a week on the pretext of conducting council and party business. This continued even after William Ireland returned. Danny knew well enough that in the tenements a cuckolded husband often tacitly accepted the intrusion of a 'fancy man'.

From Bobby Craig, Danny had heard how the Spaniard had let the milk round go, considering the work beneath a hero from the Front. With the head of the house out of work and three weans to feed, the 'gifts' the wife brought back from her assignations were what kept the children's bellies full and him in drink and tobacco. It was not to be turned down.

Staring into the bottom of his glass, Danny was only dimly aware of the waves of conversation swelling and swirling around him like the waters of the Clyde when they came upon one of the buttresses of the nearby Albert Bridge. His mind filled again with the picture of the British army tank's gun-barrel as it came over the crest of the road.

He had taken JW to the courthouse the next day, for the appearances of Shinwell, Kirkwood and Gallagher, and Wheatley had stood bail for all three. The Clyde Workers' Committee reconvened on the Sunday and the strike remained solid. The British Army maintained guard over key points in the city and its inhabitants became used to seeing the sight of the Tommies with their fixed bayonets and cockney accents on the steps of municipal buildings. Remembering the Dublin uprising only three years earlier, the army made a special point of manning the post office. There were tanks at all the main junctions.

The strikers had returned to work two weeks after Bloody Friday on the promise of a forty-seven hour week. It was a seven hour reduction but still seven hours away from their target. The Committee, its work done for the moment, split up. The British Army drifted away and Glasgow settled back to normality, which for the working people meant six back-breaking days of toil each week, often in extremes of temperature, working in treacherous conditions with life-threatening materials or machinery. At the end of the day, they returned home through more poisonous air to overcrowded and unsanitary homes.

Someone jostled Danny's arm and he cast his eyes up slowly as he planted the base of his pint in the centre of the beer mat. The man had the look of someone who had spent all weekend drinking through a week's wage. 'You're Wheatley's man, by th'way?' he slurred.

Danny nodded curtly and reached into his jacket pocket for a newspaper, which he unfolded corner by corner as if to do it faster would tear the delicate newsprint.

'Don't be like that, big man. I remember you frae George Square.' The man pushed his cap back revealing a scar that ran from his eyebrow and into his scalp. 'It was over a year ago but I mind it like it was yesterday. Fifteen stitches: they hurt like buggery going in I can tell ye.'

'You were taken into the City Chambers?'

'Aye. You dragged me there with Maxton.'

'I remember.' He said it in the hope that the man would move off.

'And that wee lass with the brown eyes – very tasty. She bandaged me up and looked out for us until they took me to the infirmary.'

'And they put the stitches in.'

'I still went to Glasgow Green, mind. Saw your man make his fine speech, an'aw.' He hawked and spat on the floor.

The barman was on him straight away. 'You! Any more o' that and you are oot.'

The man held up his hand and, making an effort to straighten up, focused his eyes on Danny. 'Yer man and Maxton, the revolution was there for the taking and they just bleated like baa-lambs.'

'What d'you mean?'

'John Maclean has said it since. If he had been there, we would have taken over the city. All we needed was to march down to Maryhill, by th'way. There were enough ex-servicemen in Glasgow Green to have taken on those kids frae down south. The army men in Maryhill, ken – they were all Scots, all working men. They would never have used their arms against their own kith and kin. They would've been on our side. That's why Lloyd George didn't turn them out – no' from Maryhill. The city would have been ours – yet all yon politicians did was talk.'

Danny sighed, 'Aye, well that's all they know.'

'True enough, big man.' He paused to belch and Danny had to move his head to escape the stink of old beer and haggis suppers. 'Aye, true enough. Mark this, big man, we could have taken the city. The poor people of Glasgow should always remember Bloody Friday – the day we missed our chance to do whit they did in Russia.'

Danny wiped the flecks of spittle from his lapel. He put his hands up to keep the man at distance. 'You're beginning to annoy me now, pal.'

'Ooh! The big man is annoyed.' He waggled his head. 'We can't annoy the big man now, can we, everybody?'

He made the mistake of looking round to make sure he had an audience. In a split second, Danny slipped off his stool to free his leg. He saw that stamping on the man's steel-capped toe would be fruitless so kicked him in the shin.

'Ow!' The man went down on one knee as if to genuflect and the last thing he felt for some time was the caress of Danny's boot as it rammed into his solar plexus. Danny stepped carefully to avoid the contents of the man's stomach that were emptying onto the sawdust, and limped out of the door. On the way to Ingram Street, he wondered why he was so short-tempered these days.

Thursday April 24, 1920
It was a bright evening in the middle of April before Mary spoke to Danny other than to say 'good evening' or 'goodnight.' Since Bloody Friday, Wheatley had told Danny during the day whether his services would be needed. If there was to be an assignation, Danny collected Mary from Parkhead in the early evening and drove her in silence to Ingram Street. In the few hours he was alone he went to The Old College Bar until he was barred after the fight, then he gave his custom to Morrison's Bar in Duke Street. At nine-thirty in the evening Mary would step into the back of the car for the return journey, back to the same Parkhead corner. The evening ended with a terse 'goodnight' from both sides.

But on that bright evening in the middle of April, Mary spoke hesitantly. 'Danny?'

Danny's right foot hovered over the brake and he grabbed the handle controlling the clutch. He looked into the mirror sharply. 'What is it, hen?'

'There is something John should know and I don't think I can tell him.'

'Is it the Spaniard? If he's –'

'No, it's nothing like that. Can you stop the motor, Danny? I need to talk to someone or I'm going to burst.' She started to cry. 'I need to talk to you.'

Danny pulled the motor to the side of the road and stopped the engine. He stepped into the back and sat alongside Mary on the calfskin seat. She slid away from him. It was warm and the small windows made it like a cocoon. He was conscious of how close she was in such a confined space.

'Och, Danny. I've made a rare mess of things.'

'What is it, Mary? You couldn't have done anything that makes me feel badly about you. You know that.'

She shook her head as if his feeling were an irrelevance and Danny felt the familiar empty feeling building in his chest.

'What is it then?'

'I have fallen for a baby. I'm going to have another bairn. I think I'm three months gone.'

Danny looked up at the ceiling. He wondered whether to turn on the interior light.

'Aren't you going to say anything?'

The obvious question seemed to be sucking the air out of the space between them. 'Does the Spaniard know?'

'William? Not yet. He hasn't been the same since he came back from France. I don't know what happened over there. He won't talk about it. But he's different – very different.'

'How so?'

'He liked a pint but he wasn't a big drinker, Danny. You know that. Now he spends everything on it. When he comes home –'

Danny clenched his fists. 'If he's violent –'

She put her hand on his arm and it reminded him of how close she was. He could smell her perfume. It was a French one that JW had bought her.

'Oh, Danny. You'll always be my protector, won't you? Always looking out for me. If only –'

Danny prayed for her to finish. What did she mean? Was she holding out some hope for him? But there was silence.

When it became too much he blurted it out. 'Are you saying the Spaniard can't be the father? Is that it? Because if it isn't his... you know I'll step in for you. I would do anything for you.'

Her hand was still on his arm and she patted it. 'It's very sweet of you, Danny. But it's not the answer. You know the way of the tenements when this sort of thing happens. John will have to acknowledge the baby is his and face up to his responsibilities. You wouldn't expect any less from him, would you?'

Danny shook his head, a leaden sadness in the pit of his stomach.

'You have to talk to him for me, Danny. Please. You have to be our go-between.'

Danny stopped the motor outside the Ingram Street building. It was normal for him to wait anything up to an hour for the boss to emerge for the return to Braehead House. Danny considered the news. His one hope was for JW to refuse to do the decent thing. In those circumstances, the Spaniard would be within his rights to put Mary out. She would then come to him. He wished he were higher in her pecking order but he understood he would be her last resort. He could live with it if she could.

'Is everything all right?' Danny asked as the door opened and Wheatley stepped in.

'Shouldn't it be?'

'Mary hasn't said anything?'

'Sweet, Mary.' Wheatley smiled as if remembering an intimacy. Danny drove from his mind any thought of what it might be. 'Why would she?'

He decided it would be better to broach the subject now while he was driving. The occasional glance in the mirror gave him more control than having JW opposite him, interrogating with those owl-like eyes. 'Mary stopped the car on the way to Ingram Street the night. She had something to tell me – us.'

A glance in the rear view mirror told Danny that Wheatley had lifted his head, his brow furrowed. 'What would that be?' He spoke haltingly as if he knew what was coming.

Danny kept his eyes firmly fixed on the road. They were in the Gallowgate with Beardmore's huge forgeworks to the left. He could hear the booming and crashing of industry even through the closed windows. He could taste the iron dust in the air. Plumes of smoke and steam rose above them placing a dark screen between their scuttling motor and the stars. 'She's going to have a baby.'

Wheatley's eyes narrowed. 'So?'

'She telt me... she wanted you to know... it's not the Spaniard's child.'

Wheatley sighed and his right hand brushed from his forehead backwards over his thinning, brilliantined hair. 'And why would she tell *you* this?' Danny could hear again the JW he first knew, the collector of subscriptions, the lender of money, the hard-hearted chancer who had used Danny's boot to get results.

'I'm a tenement man, JW. I know the form when this happens.

It's not the first time and it won't be the last. Many a tenement family has relied on gifts from –'

'Be careful what you say, Danny. You may think you know everything there is to know about me. But I can be pressed too far. I can break you as easily as I can break a kindling stick.'

Danny adjusted the muffler at his neck. 'I ken that, JW. What I'm trying to say is there's a code, a way of doing things – for this kind of situation.'

'And she is saying the wean is mine? When's it due?'

'Aye, she's saying that she and the Spaniard... they haven't... not since he came back. He's no' the same man as went away. She says she is three months gone.' He glanced up at the mirror to catch Wheatley's reaction.

Wheatley touched the fingers from one gloved hand on the other. 'September or October, then.' He leaned forward, his eyes fixed in the mirror. 'So what's this code?'

'You'll accept the baby is yours?'

'Aye. I shall take Mary at her word.'

'Then there's compensation for seduction to pay.'

Wheatley snorted. 'What did you call it?'

The lights of the motor swung across the redstone fronts of the buildings lining the corner as Danny turned into Wellshot Road heading towards Sandyhills.

'Pull over here, Danny. We will settle this before we get to Braehead House.'

Danny swung over and parked the car opposite the closed wrought iron gates of Tollcross Park. The lodge building was a dark shape flat against the ground like a sleeping dog. Gloom hung in a dark curtain from the shimmering treetops.

'Give me the code again.'

'Compensation for seduction.'

'Grand words but what exactly do they mean?'

'It's a one-off payment. For the wean. The things the family needs. The wean will be accepted as part of the family.'

'But my child, Danny...' He said it as a statement of fact, a claim of rights.

'Not once the payment is made. You'll have no call on the child or the family. It's the way it's done. Better for all.'

'And how much is this payment?' Wheatley's spectacle lenses glinted in the mirror, reflecting the beam of an approaching motor.

'The family will be on nae more than ten shillings a week – when it's a good week and the Spaniard can pick up some casual work. He no longer takes work frae his brother. So I reckon thirty pounds –'

'Thirty. It's a good number, Danny. To a body who knows their bible, like me.'

'More than a year's money, JW. It's the right amount.'

'And what happens next?'

'I will go see the Spaniard and we will sort it out. He won't be any trouble.'

'And what about the future, Danny? What does the code of the tenements say about that?'

'In what way, JW?'

'Don't act as stupid as you look, Danny.' His teeth showed like a terrier's guarding a close. 'What about me and Mary...?'

'There's nothing to say you can't...' Danny ground to a halt.

Wheatley spoke through tight lips. 'Carry on as before?'

'Aye. Before and after the wean is born.'

'It's comforting to know I have the permission of my voters in the tenements of Parkhead. Go ahead. Sort it out.'

Danny nodded at the mirror. He used the handle to depress the clutch and moved his other hand to the gear lever.

'Hold on! " Wheatley's voice was stern. 'There's one more thing to clear up. What about Mrs Wheatley? What will she hear of this compensation?'

'She doesn't hear anything. As long as there are no more anonymous letters.'

'You'll have to put word about that I'd take a dim view if it happened again and I found out who it was. Now let's go home with no more said.'

Monday July 5, 1920
They sat in the parlour of a two-roomed apartment in the same building as Mary's old single-end. Danny sat opposite William. They were both in bed-chairs pulled up to the hearth. A fire

had been lit in Danny's honour. The room was stifling but both Danny and the brooding figure in the second chair wore jackets. The clatter of Mary fussing with the tea things sounded through the open door to the kitchen.

It was a Monday evening. Danny had originally arranged it for the Sunday but, when he told Wheatley, his boss had said they should not conduct such business on the Lord's day.

Danny studied the dark man. His head was hunkered down in his shoulders and his thick brows overhung black eyes. He looked for all the world like a soot-monkey, so dark was his skin. His lower face was smudged by the shadow of a beard that started beneath his eyes and went down into his collar. Danny had seen men like him in the baths. They wore their body hair like overcoats. He smoked a made cigarette which he tapped nervously against the rim of the upturned top from a marmalade jar.

Mary waddled in. Danny leapt to his feet and ushered her through the door, holding out both hands and offering to take the tray but only succeeding in guiding it into place on the small table between the chairs. Mary sat on a straight-backed kitchen chair next to the table.

'Tea? It's mashed.'

Her husband grunted. Danny couldn't decide whether this was his usual mood or he was this way because of the subject of the meeting.

William slurped some of the tea from his saucer. 'Let's hear what you have to say, McAleer.'

Danny took a sip and cleared his throat. 'In view of the events, Mr Wheatley is prepared to offer you compensation, Mr Ireland.'

'How much?'

'I'll come to that but first I need to establish the conditions.'

'Conditions!' The Spaniard slurred the word and waved a hand airily.

Danny sensed Mary shifting in her chair. He wiped his sweaty palms down his thighs. 'The payment will be made on the basis you accept the child into your family equally as the brother or sister to the other –' He looked questioningly at Mary.

'Three.' she said. 'Ella, Millie and Tom.'

'Of course,' Danny said. 'A true brother or sister to the other three children in the family. For his part, Mr Wheatley gives up all his rights in relation to the child. He has no call on you and you have none on him. Is that understood?'

'Aye, get on with it. How much?'

'The sum Mr Wheatley is prepared to offer is thirty pounds. Take it or leave it.' Danny saw, at the edge of his vision, Mary's face turn towards him when she heard the amount.

William whistled. 'It's a fair sum. I'll take it.'

'Mr Wheatley will have papers drawn up and I'll bring them for you to sign. The money will be paid over once the child is born.'

William nodded and looked up. 'Can you no' find yer way to make a wee advance? We've already had expenses, by th'way.'

Danny looked round at the large room which bore the imprint of Mary's neatness. The furniture appeared new. This and the larger accommodation would have set them back.

Danny peeled four ten shilling notes from the bundle in his inside jacket pocket. 'Here is two pound. You'll receive twenty-eight when the bairn is born. There'll be no interest.'

The Spaniard took the money and it disappeared into his top pocket. 'You'll be on your way –'

'William! Where are your manners?' Mary said.

'His business is finished.'

Danny held up his hands. 'I have to be somewhere.'

'I'll see you out,' Mary said.

Danny shook the Spaniard's hand. 'I'll see you at the end of the year.'

As they crossed the parlour, Danny noticed how Mary's back arched and pushed the bulge of the baby out before her. 'Where are the other weans?' he asked.

'With my sister-in-law. On our old landing.'

'I remember,' Danny said. 'You look well set up here.'

Mary opened the door and spoke lower. 'Thirty pounds! That's nigh on twice the going rate.'

'I ken but JW doesn't know it. I wanted to be sure he looked after you. Will you be all right, hen?' Danny put his hand on her arm.

'You're a good man, so y'are. I will be fine. He's a miserable bugger these days but he's no' bad to us.'

'JW asked to be remembered to you.'

'Aye.' She patted her stomach. 'I doubt he will be wanting to see me until this is oot the way.'

There was a shout from inside the house. 'Mary! Stop yer mithering and get inside.'

'You be on your way, Danny,' she said pushing him through the door. It clicked shut behind him.

The baby was born on the 7th of September. They called him Ronald. He came before his time and Danny saw him at about three weeks old. He had fair hair and blue eyes. Mary told Danny how the midwife had looked at her, William and the three other children and confidently predicted that the boy's eyes would change to brown within a month. The poor wee wean couldn't help it but it was obvious his colouring would be no comfort to the Spaniard.

Sixteen

Wednesday March 9, 1921

There was a thin layer of snow illuminated green-white in the headlamps of the Wolseley when Mary gave Danny the first intimation that all was not well.

Mary and Wheatley had been back in each other's arms by Christmas with the baby only three months old. It was much as before with Danny collecting Mary in Parkhead, taking her to the apartment in Ingram Street and driving her back. He heard that William customarily spent his evenings in a bar drinking away his compensation, so Mary would leave the four children with her sister-in-law.

That evening she bundled into the back of the car and settled down on the seats unbuttoning her coat. 'It's a lovely warm motor you have here, Danny.'

'Not in the front, Mary. The servants don't need protection from the cold.'

'I wondered why you kept that huge coat on with the heater belting out hot air.'

'There's enough of it in the back of this motor when I'm driving JW around.'

She gave a short laugh. 'You're a sharp one, Danny.'

Something in her voice made him look in the rear-view mirror. 'What's wrong, hen?'

'It's that worthless man of mine.'

He swallowed back the words 'which one?' and waited for her to continue.

'He's drinking us out of the little money we have left and he's losing more that we haven't on the horses.'

Danny wondered where William was placing his bets. Odds-on the money was finding its way back into JW's pocket.

'Did you no manage to get your hands on some of it for the weans?'

'No. "It's *my* compensation," he said. "Why should you get your dirty hands on it?" He's right but what about the bairns?'

'How is the boy?'

Her sad smile made Danny's heart lurch. 'He cannae help having blue eyes and fair hair, the wee scrap. The older ones adore him. Ella is the perfect little mother for him. But William, well, he just ignores him.'

'But is he behaving – William?'

'He is a bit of a brawler when he has a drink but he hasnae brought it home. Not yet.'

Danny pulled the motor up outside the flat and they both felt the wheels lock and slide forward. The kerb stopped them with a jolt.

'You let me know if he steps out of line.'

Thursday August 10, 1922
For the rest of 1921 and into the following year, all Danny and Mary's conversations were conducted through the rear-view mirror of the Wolseley. They spent half an hour together every two weeks or so watching the seasons change through the windows. All the while, the grime from the forges, the pressing plants, the shipbuilders and the factories settled over the buildings lining the road from Parkhead Cross to Glasgow Cross, through Candleriggs to Ingram Street and back again.

Were it not for the tarmacadam, the wheels would have deep-rutted the route, sloshing axle deep in the spring, testing the suspension on compacted ridges in the summer and crunching through the snow in winter. In this jungle of crag-sided, soot-smeared buildings and the sulphured hell of the machines of production, there were no leaves to cushion the route in the autumn. Glasgow Green to the south and the Necropolis to the north were the only breaks in the industrial wasteland of East Glasgow. They offered shelter to sickly trees too weak to throw their leaves beyond their boundaries.

Mary stepped lightly out of Parkhead's feeble sunshine into the motor with a distracted look.

'How is the boy?' It was Danny's regular opening question. 'He must be getting on for his second birthday.'

'He's fine.' Her voice carried no conviction.

'What does that mean, Mary? "He's fine".' He mimicked her flat tone.

She laughed. 'You're good for me, Danny. You can always make me smile.'

Danny mumbled under his breath. 'And that's all I am good for.'

'What did you say?'

'Nothing. Is everything fine, really?'

She sighed and slapping her hands flat down on the handbag in her lap. 'It's William. Every time he looks at Ronald… the wee thing can do nothing right.'

'Does he hit the boy?'

She hesitated. 'No.'

Does he, Mary? Tell me.'

She answered louder but her voice was unnaturally high. 'No. But he…'

'What?'

She nodded towards the road ahead. 'We're nearly there. It can wait.'

'Tell me, Mary.'

'He calls him the little bastard,' she blurted. 'Even when he's petting him, never Ronald, or Ronny, always "you little bastard".'

'And does he raise his hand?'

'No more than… I don't know. He was at the Front when the others were Ronny's age. I don't know–'

'Leave it to me.'

'Danny, don't –'

He pulled on the handbrake and turned. 'Don't you be feart. I will have a word. That's all.'

Sunday August 13, 1922

Three days later, on an evening off, Danny limped though

140

Parkhead tracking the Spaniard through the bars that were holding lock-ins. He eventually caught up with him in Craib's in Westmuir Street leaning against the counter with a half of heavy in his hand, another on the bar and matching whisky chasers. One of his drinking pals was in the middle of a joke as Danny dragged his leg to join them. He saw they had all read his calling card but wasn't sure if his reputation still had any currency. It was ten years since he and Bobby Craig had fought outside this very bar.

The man telling the joke paused and cast a puzzled look in the Spaniard's direction.

'William!' Danny laid a hand on the shorter man's shoulder.

'Big man,' William said. 'Will you take a drink with me?'

Danny nodded. 'A hof n'a hof, like yourself.' He glanced at the three goons who had been talking to William. They turned away. Evidently they didn't want to be part of the business that was to be done between the Spaniard and this stranger.

'That's a nice suit you have there, William. It's not often you see a man out of work in matching jacket and trousers, an'aw.'

The dark eyes were brighter than Danny remembered and there was a new swagger about the man. He ran a finger along his lapel. 'You have to make an effort...' He put out his lower lip and shrugged his shoulders before turning back to the bar and passing Danny his beer.

Danny reached across and took the smaller glass that was still on the bar. 'I will take the chaser first if you don't mind. I don't want to waste it.' He knocked the whisky back in one and made to replace the drink on the bar. As he did his arm brushed against William and made his beer spill over the side of his glass. An extra nudge sent the liquid back over the Spaniard's jacket and waistcoat so it cascaded down his front leaving a darkening stain in the wool of his pleated trouser front.

'Why you!' William jerked himself upright.

Danny smiled. 'Oops!' he said.

'You think you're such a big man. You are no better than a pimp.' William hissed.

Billy Craib, his prize-fighter's face crimson and hard as

granite, banged the bar top with his nightstick making the glasses rattle. 'You's two – ootside. You, with the gammy leg, you're no' welcome here again. Settle your battles ootside ma bar.' He flicked his thumb. 'Git!'

Danny led the way and turned as William followed him through the door. He grabbed the smaller man by the throat and dragged him to the outside wall not caring that the smaller man's head cracked against the sandstone. 'I have something to tell you that I didnae want the rest of Billy's bar to hear. When you took the money that has turned you into such a fancy piece, you said you would look after the wean as your own. Now if you don't start doing what you said, you'll have me to think about.' He gave him a tap on the shin with his boot. 'Don't think I've forgotten how to break bones, William the Spaniard, because I havnae.'

He loosened his grip and pretended to dust down William's lapels. 'Now get back to your drinking pals and I don't want to hear any more aboot it.'

Thursday October 19, 1922
Mary had a black eye when she stepped into the back of the motor. She had tried to hide it behind the veil attached to her bonnet but the presence of the veil and the shadow of a blue smudge behind it was enough for Danny. 'How did it happen, Mary? And don't tell me you walked into a door.'

'Och! He's come back so different. He won't talk about his war. When he's sober he closes himself off to me and, in the drink, he goes over all the ways I've been bad to him. Over and over.'

'Does he –?'

'I know I've not been a good wife. But he's been no saint. He thinks it's different for him.' She pointed at the eye. 'This one was my own fault. I asked for it. I should know better than answer him back.'

'It doesn't matter what you said, he shouldn't have...' Danny's knuckles were white as he gripped the wheel. 'Do I have to see him again?'

'No, please don't, Danny. I don't think he'll do it again. He

142

was so sorry afterwards. The poor man was weeping all over me.'

But at the end of the evening, it was Wheatley who raised the subject. 'Did you see Mary's eye?'

Danny flicked a glance into the rear-view mirror. 'Aye.'

'Did she tell you how she got it?'

'She didn't try to persuade me she walked into a door, if that's what you mean.'

'I think you should have a word.'

'I already did.'

'When?'

'A couple of months back when Mary told me about how the Spaniard disnae call the wean by his name.'

'What do you mean?' Wheatley's eyes narrowed.

'It's sorted JW, you don't need to know.'

'I do need to know if he's knocking Mary about. I do need to know if that young boy is getting battered.' He banged the knuckles of one hand into the palm of the other as if he was at a lectern. 'Be careful you don't get above your station doing stuff without my say-so, Danny boy. You work for me, remember.'

Danny grunted.

Wheatley sat back in the seat and looked out of the window. Danny concentrated on the road. It was starting to rain. He turned on the windscreen wiper and squinted through the murk where the single blade flattened the water droplets and spread them round leaving a smear to peer through.

After a few minutes, Wheatley spoke. 'I don't suppose you keep up with what is happening in Westminster, Danny?'

He shook his head.

'The Coalition is breaking up. Baldwin and his people will see Bonar Law off and the Unionists will leave Lloyd George stranded. He will have to call a General Election before the year's end.'

Danny tried to piece together how this related to the previous conversation. Perhaps it was JW's way of making peace.

Wheatley's back jerked straight and his chest puffed forward. 'As prospective Independent Labour Party candidate for the Glasgow division of Shettleston, I can't afford a hint of scandal. I can't afford to have you, my well-known associate, seen in the tenements cracking heads. Is Bobby Craig still around? It's time for you to have a sit down with him, I think. He can make sure William Ireland behaves himself.'

'If you say so, boss.'

'I do say so.'

'And does this mean you will no' be seeing Mary for a while?' Danny smiled into the mirror.

The face that looked back puffed up red and the lips drew back tight across his teeth. 'Damn your impertinence, Danny McAleer. You're forgetting yourself. I shall bloody well see Mary, of course I shall. And I shall have no more cheek from the likes of you.'

Danny beat a rhythm on the steering wheel with the palms of his hands.

Monday November 13, 1922

It was a few days before the election, and Wheatley felt they deserved a break from vote-hunting. As he had predicted, the previous month, Lloyd George had been cornered into calling an election and he designated the polling day to be the 15th of November.

In the few weeks they had for campaigning, the routine was much the same as the strike leading up to Bloody Friday. Danny drove Wheatley around the constituency from factory gate to factory gate to coincide with the hooter. The workers swarmed around the car, the shifts flowing in and out stranding it as effectively as if it had been at the confluence of an incoming tide and the Clyde's seaward flow. The outgoing workers trailed with them the pollution at the end of each shift: the soot of the foundry fire, the dust from flaming ore, the slurry from steel cutting and grinding, all to be washed off in the communal bath house at the end of the week.

All the while, Wheatley harangued them with his story: how he was one of them, how the party formed for them would improve working conditions, how, if he had his way, each worker would live in a low-rent cottage where their money would go into building communities not making landlords rich.

When Wheatley suggested a break from this routine, he ordered Danny to drive into the city and they went to Kate Cranston's tearooms in Sauchiehall Street.

'I can't decide whether this is a late lunch or an early tea,' Wheatley said as he took a bite from his sandwich. He wiped fragments of egg from his tie leaving a pale smear.

'You can relax, boss,' said Danny. 'It's in the bag. What with Aldred not campaigning and the Liberals on the run. You have nothing to fear.'

'Guy Aldred's the dark horse, Danny. The communists haven't put him up against me by accident. They hope the workers will see the difference between him and me with my fine house in Sandyhills. If he dropped his anti-parliamentary antics and stood against me properly, he would be a real danger. As it is we don't know the effect of all this smear and gossip about me.'

'Do you ken that he's behind it?'

'I'm sure he isn't. He's a principled man. He served most of the war doing hard labour because of his beliefs. No, it's not him. It will be the Liberals. No doubt they're hoping it will split the left and push our votes Aldred's way. We have to make sure our vote stays solid.'

Wednesday November 15, 1922
Come the night of the election, the Labour vote held up. Wheatley's majority over the Liberal Ramsey was near enough five thousand and Aldred lost his deposit. Danny saw that Mary was in the audience cheering as Wheatley, with Catherine by his side, made his acceptance speech.

As Wheatley finished, Danny stomped through the mass of people and intercepted Mary at the door. 'Stay, Mary. I'd like to talk.' He steered her to a quieter area behind where the officials were packing the ballots into cardboard boxes.

'Aye, it's a night to remember.'

'I don't want to talk about the election.'

'What then?'

'You ken what this means?'

She nodded. 'John will spend most of his time in London.'
'Yes.'

'It's no' what I wanted but...'

'He never made a secret of his ambition...'

Mary took out a handkerchief and blew her nose. Her eyes were moist. Danny wanted to sweep the small body up against him and hold her in his arms. 'Right enough,' she said. 'It's what he always wanted.'

'What about you, Mary?' He took her hand. He picked absentmindedly at the frayed threads on her gloved fingers.

She pulled her hand away. 'I have my family. I have my man.'

'But I won't be able to look out for you, you and Ronald. Not if I go to London as well.'

She looked up sharply. 'Will you?'

'He wants me to.'

'And...?'

Danny drew himself up to his full height and breathed deeply. He took her hand again. His chest hurt with the crush of feeling that he had for her at that moment. 'Not if you don't want me to. Not if you say to stay.'

'Stay, how?' Her forehead creased and the colour seemed to drain from her cheeks.

'You've known how I have felt about you. From the very start when I took you home after Anstruther Street. You had to see how it has hurt me so to see you waste yourself on him.'

There was a question in the look she gave him.

'Aye JW, him – but now the Spaniard as well. You can't stay with him. Not the way he is. Let me –'

'What are you trying to say?'

'Let me look after you. You and the weans. I have some money put by. I've been saving – it's more than enough for us to start over. We could get away from here. The five of us. Leave the Spaniard behind. Leave JW. We could go west to the coast. A wee cottage, a healthy place for the weans. And I wid treat them properly. You too.'

'Live as man and wife, you mean?'

'There are plenty doing it after the war. Widows with

children being looked after by men like me.'

'But I'm not a widow, Danny. I have a husband.'

'He's no good for you. I've seen him, remember. I know what he does to you and Ronny. He has gambled and drunk what money he had. I have saved ten times that. It would give us a good start, Mary. Come with me.' The tears streamed down his face and he looked around to check they weren't being watched.

She was crying openly as well. She shook her head. 'I can't do it. I can't leave him. The Spaniard. In sickness and in health.'

Danny slammed his hand against the thigh of his callipered leg. 'If it wasn't for this –'

She grasped his hand. 'You mustn't say it, Danny. The leg has made you what you are. Not "The Boot of Garngad", I don't mean that. Being the way you are has made you the kindest man I know.'

'Then why don't you do it?' He cast a look around the emptying hall. 'Leave all this behind?'

She put her head to one side and used a voice as if she were telling Ronny a goodnight story. 'Sometimes, Danny, being kind, being the best man, isn't good enough. A woman is looking for less than that.'

'I don't understand –' he said.

'Aye. And that is the problem, for a lesser man would.' She slipped her hand out of his grasp and tugged at the belt of her coat. 'Now I have to get back to my man and you have to get back to John. Tell him, a job well done from me, by th'way.' The click-clack of her shoes echoed around the room as she walked to the door, through it, and away.

He looked round. As far as he could tell through his blurred vision nobody had taken any notice of them. He wiped his eyes. His left leg felt unusually heavy as if the boot on the end of it was twice its usual weight. His life force was leaking through it, draining him, turning him into a useless lummox with no right to take up space. He bowed his head and a fresh tear dripped from his nose to splash on the shiny blackened leather that encased his withered foot. If she would not have him then what was the point of it all?

The clatter of the post-count commotion in the main body of the hall broke his thoughts. He wiped the back of his hand across his mouth and pushed his thumb and forefinger against his eyeballs to stop any more tears. He squinted against the pressure so as to double the pain. He stumbled back into the cleared central area of the hall and looked towards the platform. Wheatley was still there leaning down to take congratulations from his supporters. Mrs Wheatley stood behind him her hand resting on his shoulder.

Wheatley's spectacles flashed a beckoning signal as he lifted his head. Danny's chest was hollowed-out and aching, his throat constricted, and it was, perhaps, this that made the sound of his boot thud so heavily as he crossed the varnished floorboards towards his boss.

One

Sunday November 19, 1922

On the Sunday following the election, the ten new Glasgow MPs strode at the head of a swarm of hundreds of working men and their women who had come to give them a send off. An even larger assembly had gathered in front of St Enoch's station, the men and women clapping, stomping and hollering.

The new members shouldered their way through the crowd. John Wheatley was distinguished by his heavy coat and bowler hat, while the others were in belted raincoats and trilbies. The men and women around them thumped their representatives' arms and backs and shouted cries of encouragement. John detected an air of envy. These men were taking the fight to London and being paid £400 a year for the privilege!

He absorbed all this as he was swept through the station entrance and towards the London platform. And there she

149

was: Mary Ireland. Her dark eyes wide and bright beneath a black bonnet and her gloved hands clutched to her chest. They acknowledged each other with the briefest flick of the eyelids but still John's heart swelled and his breathing shortened. Then he was pushed forward and past her to where Danny McAleer waited alongside his cases.

The MPs had gathered for dinner earlier that evening at the Blytheswood Hotel. John's new colleagues had walked there but he rode in the back of the Wolseley. 'You know what to do, Danny. Cases to the station, motor back to Braehead House and cab into town. Be sure you don't miss the train.'

Danny tipped a finger to his forehead and, with a crunching of gears, drove the Wolseley away. It was a cold night and John was glad of his heavy coat and muffler for the few steps into the hotel. The staff directed him to a first-floor, private dining-room booming with triumphant male voices. Jimmy Maxton broke away from the group as John entered, took his hand and held it up like a referee awarding a fight to Jack Dempsey. The room hushed. 'Gentlemen, I give you the new member for Glasgow Shettleston, John Wheatley!'

The others, eyes sparkling in the light from the electric chandelier, shouted a hurrah, punching the air with their fists. Jimmy took John by the arm and leant his head in close, speaking quietly. 'Why are you always last to arrive, John? You shouldn't give these men reason to think you're too grand for them. Why, we could have a Clydesider leading the party before long! But you have to win round those closest to you first.'

Despite Maxton's misgivings, the others held back when they were asked to take their seats for dinner. They gestured for John to take the head of the table. Maxton sat on his right with Geordie Buchanan to his left. The three men represented the East Glasgow powerbases: Wheatley's Shettleston, Maxton for Bridgeton and Buchanan for the Gorbals. Campbell Stephen, who held the seat of Camlachie, which bordered both Bridgeton and Shettleston, was next in the pecking order. The others, representing outlying divisions, deferred naturally to the members in the city's socialist strongholds.

John looked to the man on each side and, for an instant, saw the three of them through the eyes of a stranger. His portliness was set between the short, slight, boy-faced Buchanan and the tall, stooping, emaciated Maxton. He smiled to himself. They had the look of a music hall comedy trio.

His blood ran fast as he watched the animated faces of the new MPs discussing the changes they were going to make when they reached London. The consensus was to put a socialist fire under the backside of the Conservative administration and have it burn so hot the government would eventually relinquish power. On all sides, his colleagues argued which of the two candidates they would vote for at the Labour Party's leadership meeting the next day: the conformist current leader, John Clynes, or the more radical Scot, Ramsay MacDonald.

At the end of the feast, with their chairs pushed back and cigarette and pipe smoke curling to the high ceiling, they listened as Maxton held the floor. 'Had our comrades won the 1918 general election they would have refused to take their seats in Westminster. They would have left the people who voted for them without representation and continued fomenting strikes and promising revolution. That's one way for Socialism. I call it the Russian way.

'On the opposite extreme, we have the Clynes doctrine, which is the constitutional way, the parliamentary way. But it's slow and cannot be effective while Labour is in opposition.

'The new Clydeside model is the third way, allying direct action to parliamentary representation. Ramsay MacDonald does not have the patience of Clynes and he is our best bet in the short term. But let me tell you this, fellow Clydesiders, fellow *red* Clydesiders' – this drew a cheer from the nine men – 'there is a body in our midst who is better equipped than anybody to lead the party along the third way. Nobody exemplifies the third way better than John here.' He swept a hand to his left. 'John Wheatley stepped into the breach on Bloody Friday and kept the strike solid in the face of British Army tanks.'

John blinked behind his glasses.

'He was there leading direct action and now here he is, leading us as we take our fight to London. I wager Ramsay

MacDonald will be Leader of the Opposition this time tomorrow and I tell you this, lads, if he has not enough fire in his belly to lead us into extra-parliamentary action, we shall put one of us in his place. What say you?'

Eight fists thrust into the air and the Red Clydesiders roared a shout that drifted out through the gaps in the sash windows and fell on the ears of the people of the city who had gathered outside to demonstrate their support. The crowd took up the deep-throated rumble, not knowing where or why it started, and a hundred voices shouted into the night.

John acknowledged the cheers with a nod of his head, his face burning. He took out his pocket watch. 'We had best be on our way if we are walking to the station.'

John could not put the fleeting glimpse of Mary out of his mind. Should he have stopped and acknowledged her? He would have loved to have been free to embrace her. Could he have allowed free rein to the instinct to take her in his arms? Would he have been able to stop himself from whispering urgently in her ear, come with me?

A voice cleared the tumbling thoughts from his head. It was Kirkwood speaking while theatrically pushing his trilby back and scratching his forehead. 'We are going to London to represent the working man, John, the one with patches in his breeks and holes in his boots. Did you need to bring your entire wardrobe?' He waved his hand across the matching cases at their feet.

John smiled and shook his head.

Shinwell shouted from further back in his reedy voice. 'There won't be room for all that, John. We've reserved only two compartments.'

John laughed. 'You know fine well these will go in the guard's van up by First Class, which is where I shall be, by th'way. I have this infirmity.' He patted his stomach. 'You are not going to make me sleep sitting in a third-class seat, surely?'

The others laughed.

'No, I shall be in a sleeper. McAleer will travel with you boys.' He took Danny by the arm. 'Call a porter and get these bags shifted,' he hissed.

Maxton smiled, nodding. 'Come on, boys, let's not forget, while most of us were no more than twinkles in our father's eyes, comrade Wheatley was a pit-boy doing a man's full shifts.' He led the eight men off. Each carried a single cardboard suitcase.

Up in First Class, John settled in his bunk, his feet beginning to warm the cold, starched sheets. He sipped from a glass of whisky brought with a nod and a wink by the steward. He sighed contentedly. ILP meetings were such drab affairs with the insistence on being teetotal. He was sure he was not the only member who took a tipple even though he had signed the pledge.

He recalled his leave-taking from Braehead House. Only his daughter, Elizabeth, now twenty-two, had seemed genuinely upset. 'Daddy, take care down there among all those tricksters,' she had said, her eyes brimming over.

'I will, sweet Lizzie, and you look out for your mother, mind.'

She nodded and they had separated so he could turn to Patrick, who, in the last year of his teens, towered over his father. They had shaken hands without a word. Finally, he had hugged Catherine and told her he would return, not the first weekend, because he would still be settling into his digs, but the second.

'Aye, well, take your time,' she had said. 'We shall see you when you can.'

'I have to come back for constituency business,' he had said and could have bitten off his tongue.

'Oh. Well we shall be sure to see you, then.'

How different it had been when he had the merest glimpse of sweet Mary. The look they shared had been charged with so much more. How would he live down there without her?

He tucked the blanket around. He recalled her bright eyes and the way they emptied of life when she was experiencing the spasms of ecstasy. He had seen no other woman transported, as she was, into another plane of existence by God's act of love.

How he would miss his passionate, fiery Mary.

He flicked the switch to turn off the electric light and recalled his nights with her in the apartment in Ingram Street, while his train, like a monstrous mechanical insect, tunnelled its way through the thick mud of smoggy night to London and the dawning of a radical age.

Monday November 20, 1922

When the train pulled into Euston, John, who had been up and shaved even before the steward brought his pot of tea, stepped down into the November smog. It caught in his throat and he was surprised to find that London's air was even more noxious than if he had been standing outside the forge at Parkhead. He pulled up his scarf to cover his mouth and nose. A whooshing exhaust from the engine made him turn and he peered forward to watch the dark form exhaling smoke and steam into the thick air. He heard his name called and turned back to watch his colleagues emerge from the mist. They were a ragtaggle band, faces gaunt from lack of sleep and jowls dark with stubble.

'Good morning lads. You look like you need to freshen up before today's meeting.'

Maxton gave him a sharp look. The men shivered as the mist swirled around them. There was a quick discussion while each of them outlined his plans for the morning and they checked the time and place of the party meeting. When everything was clear, the group hefted their suitcases as one and trudged to the ticket barrier leaving only the muscled bulk of Danny standing beside John.

'Morning, JW,' he said. 'Sleep well?'

'Like a baby, Danny. Now run to reserve us a cab and I shall organise a porter for this luggage. I shall meet you at the exit.'

Their destination was the Cosmo Residential Hotel in Marylebone. John had chosen it because it offered a cheap single room for Danny in the topmost floor, while his room lower down had its own full services. It was from here he would conduct his parliamentary business. He planned that he and Danny would stay in the hotel four days a week, returning to Glasgow on Fridays for constituency work over the weekend. While he stayed in Braehead House, also catching up on business affairs with his brother Patrick and Catherine's brother, Paddy, John intended for Danny to meet Bobby Craig in Parkhead. That way he would keep up with what was happening in the Ireland household.

Thursday November 23, 1922
Ignoring the tradition that new members of the house should take time to settle in before attempting to make their mark, the Clydesiders gave their maiden speeches during the first debate of the session. Kirkwood was most anxious to be first to put fear into the government and spoke passionately but intemperately about the conditions in his constituency.

Ramsay MacDonald, who had been voted leader of the parliamentary party on the day of the Glaswegians arrival in London, watched with growing irritation as Maxton, Buchanan and Stephen in turn gave firebrand speeches addressing the benches opposite as if they were a hostile crowd on Glasgow Green.

Only John, employing the guile he had learned on the City Council, gave a speech in keeping with the tradition of the House and made greater impact as a result. He ensured that it was his speech that was featured in the *Glasgow Eastern Standard*, a newspaper he was in the act of buying as part of the expanding Hoxton & Walsh publishing empire.

This is not to say John craved acceptance into the Westminster establishment. Despite his crisp white collars, fine suits and corpulent figure, he never forgot his one-roomed first home in Baillieston. When London's temptations beckoned him he forced himself to recall the village of winding wheels and slag heaps. He remembered well the privations of a coal miner, spending three hundred and more days each year in the damp, dark seams. He was there when fellow miners died hideous deaths in accidents caused by pressure from the owner to cut corners and maintain production. He had witnessed the demise of family members hastened by the insanitary conditions in which they lived. The Wheatleys had shared an ash privy with twelve other families, all with as many children or more. The only fresh water was drawn from a well over a hundred yards from their hovel.

He was fiercely proud that Baillieston's coal, glistening with the sweat of his labour, was transported by narrow-boat into the maw of the city's forging, plating and metal-bashing industry that spewed out the ships and railway engines which transported Britain's exports throughout the Commonwealth and the New World.

But that pride in production, in output, was poor payment for the hardship of life as an Irish Catholic immigrant in Glasgow. John was no friend of the landlords, factory owners and pit owners who sat on the government benches.

Tuesday July 24, 1923
Seven months later, Wheatley and Maxton were back in Glasgow having been suspended from the House of Commons.

The disgrace in Westminster that made him a hero in Glasgow came a month before, when a minister, Walter Elliot, had stood in the House to announce reductions in health budgets for Scotland. The Clydesiders were outraged and Maxton spoke for them first. He had only recently lost his wife. She had nursed their dying infant and then died herself from complications following its birth. Maxton spoke with cold fury about how much better even the poorest of English people fared compared to their Scottish counterparts.

When Sir Frederick Banbury, Member for the City of London, interrupted in support of the status quo, Maxton lost his head and, making the case that a reduction in the budget would result in the withdrawal of free milk from Scotland's most needy infants, described as 'murderers' those who supported the motion. He was invited to withdraw the word but refused.

In the midst of the commotion, John rose and, his face flushed, literally spitting his anger, said, 'If a person does an act calculated to kill anyone, even though he did not intend to commit murder, that person is a murderer. In that sense I believe the Right Honourable Member for the City of London is a murderer, and I repeat it. Bring back the lives of our Scottish infants and I will withdraw.'

The Deputy Speaker asked both Maxton and Wheatley to withdraw but they refused. They were suspended from the House and, in the melee as they left to the sound of baying from the government and cheers from the opposition, both Stephen and Buchanan shouted the offending word at the benches opposite and they too were suspended.

At one of the packed meetings in Glasgow, John had taken Maxton by the arm and whispered to him that the fracas had been a huge success for the left wing of the party. 'Westminster is the best broadcasting station in the world, Jimmy. We can use it for our message more effectively than any other agency.'

But all the professional success at the start of his Westminster career could not mask the ache of Mary's absence. Stifling in the back of the Wolseley, with the windows tight shut to stem the invasion of poisonous air, John could keep his silence no more. He put down the papers he was trying to read and slid the partition aside. 'Do you have any news of Mary, Danny?'

Danny nodded. 'Aye, JW.' He swung the wheel in a wide arc. 'Bobby Craig thinks there are problems in the Ireland house.'

John watched Danny's eyes. 'How so?' He leaned forward to better hear the answer.

'The Spaniard is now taking drink for his breakfast, dinner and tea. He's killing himself with the booze. There are rows in the house every night. He's roaring drunk, shouting obscenities at his wife and the boy.'

'Is there violence?'

'Nobody hears any and there are no marks on them people can see. When the Spaniard comes home, the older children can scuttle out of his way and stay in the house across the landing, but Ronny is only a wean. He's in the firing line.'

John felt his collar tightening and sensed the blood surging through arteries in his neck. 'And is the boy the cause of it all in the Spaniard's eyes?'

'That is whit Bobby says.'

'Where does he get the money for his drink?'

'Mary works and brings home a little. She has a job as a cashier at Templeton's. He takes the money from her. From what Bobby says most of her earnings go over the bar or to a bookie's runner.'

'One of ours, I hope.'

Danny's eyes turned back to the road and his voice took on a weary tone. 'Aye, JW, if it's happening in East Glasgow, of course it will be one of yours. But it's not the main point here.'

John pushed the driver's shoulder. 'Don't get above yourself, Danny. I know right enough what the main point is. Can you arrange to meet her without the Spaniard knowing?'

'He's either sleeping it off or blind drunk most of every day. I can arrange to meet her from Templeton's one evening. We can talk on the tram to Parkhead.'

'Well, you do that, Danny, and soon. See what she wants. Tell her I can look after her and the boy. But she has to make a clean break.'

Two

The heavy curtains were drawn back so any visitor to John's study would see out over the grounds towards the sun which, despite the late hour, was still a few hours away from the horizon. Beyond the ha-ha, a group of golfers laboured up the slope towards the eighteenth hole. The pale sandstone walls of the clubhouse glowed golden. It was the only building visible among the green of the tree-lined fairways that stretched away down the escarpment to the London Road. The room lights were out and John knew he appeared only in silhouette to his brother-in-law. He had chosen this room to be his study and positioned the desk to make the most of this effect.

Paddy Meechan was giving the weekly report on the businesses he had taken over progressively as John became more embroiled in politics. Paddy ran the hidden aspects of John's activities which had funded his early political career and latterly the acquisition of his legitimate publishing concerns. The money-lending business was now run totally at arm's length. The network of 'bankers' paid a cash tithe to Paddy for bankrolling them. They had similarly distanced the race-betting operations from the Wheatley name.

John's percentage take had reduced substantially by appointing Paddy and putting middlemen in place but the size of the operation had increased to cover all East Glasgow so it was still a lucrative business. Of course, the network had to be controlled even more closely than had the newssheet subscription business of the early days and this was where Bobby Craig's network of heavies came in. Any operative who neglected to 'volunteer' the correct share of his takings through the various layers of management would find an iron bar was every bit as effective at breaking limbs or shattering joints as Danny's boot had been over ten years before.

John's brother, Patrick, was in day-to-day control of the legitimate publishing business, Hoxton & Walsh, but again, each business in the empire: the printing firms in Glasgow and London, the political publishing, and the *Glasgow Eastern Standard*, virtually ran themselves.

Once their discussions had concluded, John dismissed Paddy and seconds later heard the telltale clump announcing Danny at the door. There was a knock and Danny's bulk filled the doorway.

'What is it? Do you have news of Mary?'

'Aye, JW. I met her from work like we said. I walked her home so we could talk. I don't think she had the money for the tram, anyway. That bastard takes every penny she earns –'

'Danny!'

'Sorry, boss. Bobby has it right. The Spaniard knows better than to hit her or the boy but she is at her wits' end. The boy is frightened of his own father. The Spaniard is on the edge and will go on the rampage sooner or later. She fears for herself and the boy.'

'Then I have to do something. Do you think she will take the boy to London?'

'She's desperate but I don't think she'll leave the other weans.'

'How old are they?'

'The eldest, Ella, is just ten. The two others –' he shook his head, 'maybe seven, eight?'

'And the boy is coming up three...' He steepled his fingers under his chin. 'Can you get word to her that we shall meet her from work in the Wolseley?'

Monday July 30, 1923
Two days later Mary stepped into the back of the motor and sat straight-backed and stiff alongside John.

He leaned forward. 'Take us the long way to Parkhead,

Danny. We shall need some time here. I shall knock when we are ready to go back.' He slid the glass partition into place.

He turned to the diminutive figure who jerked even further upright. 'It's good to see you again, Mary. You don't know how much I have missed you.'

She pulled a handkerchief from her bag and blew her nose. 'You have your own life to lead and so do I. We made our own beds. We knew as soon as you became an MP you wouldn't have time for me.'

'It's not a matter of time and you know it. I have no life outside politics. It isn't what I want but we have to make sacrifices for the cause.'

She shook her head slowly. 'You in your grand house in Sandyhills and your swanky hotel in London – such sacrifices.'

'Danny has been keeping you up to date with my doings, I see.'

'Danny cares enough for me to make time to see me at weekends. It's not as if I have a husband who cares what I am doing.'

He cursed Danny under his breath. Danny had been spinning a line about using Bobby Craig. He'd been dealing with Mary first hand. 'I care, Mary, I do. You have no life here in Glasgow. Danny tells me you and the boy are in danger from the Spaniard. We've reached a time when something has to give. Me being in London offers us a way out. You could join me there.'

'Oh, yes? And how would that work? Would you get a divorce? Of course you wouldnae. Even if you wanted it, you couldn't live with the guilt. Your Pope would have you flung oot the church. Start talking sense!'

He took her gloved hand but knew better than to interrupt.

She snatched her arm back. 'So would we live over the brush? You supporting me and the four weans? Something you would have to confess to your priest every day of the week. Not even thinking about what your fellow MPs would say. You would be flung oot the party, too! There's no future for us, John.' Tears started flowing.

He took her hand again and this time she let it rest in his

palm. 'You're right in every detail, Mary. I wouldn't do anything, I couldn't do anything, to jeopardise my position in the church or in the party. You ken only too well what they mean to me. But I have thought of a way – a way that works for both of us and protects the boy – my boy.'

She shook her head and he felt a hot tear land on the back of his hand. 'Your boy? You bought off your conscience as far as Ronny was concerned when you handed over the compensation to William. He was his boy from that moment on, even if the wee thing feeds his anger just by breathing.'

John bowed his head. 'I know. I was wrong but I can start putting things right. I can set you and Ronny at the heart of things in London. Think of it, Mary. He can get a proper education, go to fine schools in London. I can sort out a house for you both. It's the least I can do.'

She looked up into his eyes. 'I have *four* children, John. Not one.'

He paused before answering quietly, 'I know that, Mary, but I can only be responsible for one of them.'

'I can't leave them, John.' She was crying openly, her eyelids red. She blew her nose again.

'Think of the youngest. What sort of life will he have with that man hounding him at every turn? Your man has nothing against Thomas and the girls. They are used to his ways. Things will quieten down when Ronny is not there to provoke him. They'll be better off with Ronny away.'

'But I'm their mother,' she wailed, as if she understood well enough the power of his argument.

'You are but if it serves them better...'

She took her head in her hands as if she meant to squeeze the life out of herself. 'No. No!'

It was all or nothing. 'I have it worked out, Mary. You and the boy will have every comfort. I need a new base down there. I can't stay in a hotel for the rest of my political life. You shall keep house. I shall be your lodger. If you want a job I'll get you something in the printing firm I have down there.'

He turned to look into her eyes and took her hands from her face. They were wet with tears. As he swivelled on the seat his right knee slipped down and was nearly on the Wolseley's carpet. 'But I don't want you to work, Mary. I want you to help me with *my* work. Remember the Rent Strike? Remember how we worked together, back then? Remember Bloody Friday, when we fought on the front line for what we both believe in?'

Her eyes drew in and focused on him. He was reaching her. 'When I have a place down there, the Clydesiders, Maxton, Kirkwood, Buchanan, Stephen, others maybe, will meet there to plan how we deliver a socialist state to our people. You could be at the centre of things as we turn the old order upside down. You will be part of it, Mary. You and Ronny. Please, I need you for this. Join me.'

Sunday August 26, 1923

It was Mary's thirty-fourth birthday. How long would they be together? John was fifty-four – when would she tire of the age gap? Would he always be able to keep her satisfied in the ways he could now? Had the deprivations of his childhood left him with a mortal weakness that could strike at any time? The question repeated itself over and over as the trembling excitement built to a crescendo like a great piece of symphony music reverberating through the core of him.

He watched Mary step down from the train with Ronny in her arms. The boy had a pair of reins over his collared woollen sweater and, when she let him down on the floor, he turned towards the engine with his hands over his ears trying to squirm away. Mary, in her trademark black straw bonnet, was stooped and broken as she looked around. John hurried up to them with Danny hop-skipping in tow.

'Have you left your things on the train?' John said.

She looked up. Evidently a night of crying had scrubbed her face raw. She shook her head. 'We couldn't bring anything other than what we are wearing. I didn't want a scene with...' She couldn't continue for crying.

'Mary, my poor wee thing,' John said, as he took her in his arms. He could hardly bear to imagine it. Mary stealing the boy away early in the morning, leaving behind three bewildered children who would only now be realising that they were abandoned.

She shrugged him off and nodded pointedly at Ronny. John turned to him. 'Hello, young man,' he said with forced brightness. 'Was it your first ride on a big train?'

The boy pulled in behind his mother's skirts.

'Say, good morning to your Uncle John, Ronny.'

There was a squeak from behind the skirt.

'And you know your Uncle Danny.'

This time the boy leaned out and allowed Danny to ruffle his hair.

John took Mary by the arm. 'Come now, Mary. The boy has another adventure. We're going to take the underground electric railway to the new house.'

John gave Ronny a running commentary on their descent by lift to the underground platform but all conversation ceased when the train thundered in to the crowded station.

When they emerged blinking into the daylight and relative peace of the Clapham Road, John said, 'What do you say to that adventure, Ronny? What do you think of a train that spends all of its time in tunnels?'

'We both thought it was awfy noisy,' Mary said. 'I don't think you will put me in one of those again soon.' She touched a hand to her breast. 'We were so crammed in those lifts! I have never been so close to total strangers.'

'I believe the underground railway is a truly socialist method of transport. Did you see how all manner of people were in the same carriage? It's transport for the proletariat.' He pointed north. 'We're going this way. The house is in a new scheme called Atherfold Road. But before we head off that way I want you to know that the open space of Clapham Common – as big as Glasgow Green – is less than half a mile in that direction. To reach it you pass along the High Street which has all the shops you could ever want.'

'Is that where the River Thames is? Down by the common?'

He laughed. 'No! London is a very big place, Mary. There is space enough to have parks all over the city, not only around the river.'

She looked about her. 'Well this is very nice, with the trees lining the road.' She took a deep breath. 'It's more like Bishop Loch than a city, the air is that fresh.'

'There are parts of London especially to the north and east by the docks that stink every bit as badly as East Glasgow. They have industry there and the people packed into wee houses like sardines in a tin, but here it's civilised enough. Come on, we're holding people up.'

The four of them walked less than a hundred yards before turning into Atherfold Road, an avenue of new terraced, double-fronted houses. It was still unpaved. They stopped outside number 45. 'Here we are.' He handed Mary a set of keys. 'These are yours, Mary. It's your house. My solicitors have acted for you in the purchase.'

She looked at him shaking her head. 'Are you mad, man? This must cost a fortune. I can't take it.'

'You already have. You have to sign some papers with the solicitors to make it legal and so on, but you are the owner. It's all yours. And let us not hear any more about it.' He pulled her arm close to his side and patted the back of her hand. 'Call it a birthday present.' He waved her to go ahead. 'Now, go along and open the door so we can all have a cup of tea.'

Mary led the way up the tiled pathway tugging Ronny by the reins. She opened the door onto a hallway already equipped with a dresser.

'I took the liberty of buying the furniture in a job lot, I hope you don't mind,' John said.

Mary merely shook her head leaning forward from the welcome mat to peer up the stairs. She ran a gloved finger over the surface of the hallstand table and inspected her finger. 'This is far too much room for us, John,' she said. 'We could have managed in something less than half this size.'

'Think of it as an investment, Mary. A new house in a good area. It will do well for you.'

'I don't know what to say.'

John laughed. 'How about, "I'll put the kettle on and make us some tea".'

'I will have to fire up the range first.'

'Oh no you won't. This house is fully equipped, look.' He flicked a switch. 'Electric lights!'

She flicked the switch with her tiny gloved fingers and held the other hand to her mouth, 'Oh my! Just like at work.'

'And the kitchen has a gas range. Instant!'

Mary was shaking her head again.

'The solicitor told the agent you are a war widow and your dead husband's family have paid for the house.'

'But what about the boy? He is too young for the story to make sense.'

'Many a soldier died from his wounds after managing to father a child – just another tragic war story.'

She bent down to unbuckle Ronny. 'You go and explore the house.' He clung to her skirt. She pulled herself upright. 'You seem to have thought of everything, John.'

'So are you happy?'

She turned and looked at Danny as if seeking his approval. He bent forward and picked up the boy who, to John's surprise, made no protest. 'Come on, Ronny. Let's you and me see where you're going to sleep in this grand house.'

Immediately their voices were lost at the back of the house Mary's features crumpled. Her voice cracked. 'I have left my children. How can I ever be happy? I telt them as I put them to bed last night. Can you imagine the pain of it? Tom is seven years old. I told Ella to look after them as I would be going away for a while. She's only ten and I asked that from her.' She sobbed openly. 'Goodness knows how they will grow up with a drunkard for a father and Lou the only woman to care for them. What have I done?'

John's heart ached at the sight of it. He pulled her to him, brushing his hand over her hair, making shushing noises. His responsibility for her pain speared through his chest. The weight of her body surrendered to him. Without his arms around her she would have slumped to the floor. He sought something to comfort her with. 'You can make a home for Ronny here. Perhaps one day, when they are older...' As his voice trailed off he sensed her body straightening as if somehow he had imbued her with a new resolve.

'Aye, it's my only hope. One day they will understand.' She snuffled the handkerchief against her nose and pulled away from his embrace. 'But for now, John, you are going to stay here as you promised – as the lodger?'

'If you will have me.'

'And the other Glasgow members will come here for meetings?'

'The important ones – Maxton, Kirkwood, some others.'

'And you want me to be there when you talk – to contribute – to be part of it?'

'If they'll have you. I will have to persuade them.'

'You *must* do it, John. This is my only consolation – the work for the party, for the women back in East Glasgow. I will never forget the tenements as long as my three children ...' She stepped forward and pushed herself into his arms. 'I can deal with the pain as long as I have you and the work for the party.'

She looked up at him and he wondered again at all that had brought them here.

'We must get started,' she said, kissing his cheek and then pulling away. 'Show me to the kitchen and I will make that cup of tea.'

John led the way and watched as she investigated the cupboards to find what was needed to make the tea. All the while, she commented under her breath about his poor choice of this piece of furniture or how it would have to be moved as she started to make a list of the provisions they needed.

As he watched her bustle around to take over her house, John concluded that, despite the pain that was ravaging both their insides, in all his fifty-four years, he had never seen a more heart-warming sight.

Three

John stood at the window of the parlour looking out on Atherfold
Road. He knew the others would arrive by taxi and wanted to
be at the front door before they knocked. He was worried they
would see Mary before he had time to explain. His waistcoat
felt tight about his middle. He had put on weight in the weeks
since he had come to live with her in the house.

As far as Catherine was concerned he had come down to
London before the end of the recess because he needed to
organise new living arrangements. Staying in hotels was clearly
unsatisfactory and he had secured lodgings in a Clapham
house run by a war widow. He and Danny were the only guests.
He had not given her the telephone number on the basis that,
if she did not know it, she would be unable to share it with
others in Shettleston. As far as he was concerned, constituency
business was never so urgent that it could not be dealt with by
mail or, in an emergency, telegram. The same went for family
and business concerns.

The civil servants at the House of Commons had a different
story. As far as they were concerned, he was still resident at
the Cosmo Hotel in Marylebone. It suited him for them to think
this and it gave him an excuse to keep Danny there, away from
Atherfold Road. All correspondence and telephone calls to
John at the hotel would be directed to Danny. With a telephone
installed in Mary's house (which is how he saw it), it was very
easy for Danny to say that John was away temporarily and
would return the call.

Now though, he would have to tell the core of the Clydesiders

168

about his true arrangements (up to a point) so they could allow Mary to play a role in their meetings. He would have to trust them not to disclose his living arrangements to anyone outside their group. Could he keep all these plates spinning? He sighed and pulled at the points of his waistcoat. Only time would tell.

A black cab turned into Atherfold Road and puttered sedately along. He imagined his comrades counting the numbers. As it pulled up outside, John hurried into the hallway. 'They're here!' he shouted towards the back of the house where Mary was in the kitchen. The smell told him there were scones in the oven.

He opened the door. It always warmed his heart to see his colleagues and he spread his arms as they came up the path. The tall, stooping Maxton shook hands and stepped inside, removing his trilby. 'My, oh my, something smells good, John. I didn't know Danny was an accomplished baker. Very nice house, by th'way. How many properties is this, now?'

'Just the two,' John said. 'Ach, it makes sense for me to have a permanent base here.'

Geordie Buchanan was next, his boyish grin matching the sparkle in his eyes. 'Your house here is bigger than the place where we have our rooms.' He laughed as he shook hands. 'You could fit all the Glasgow members in this one, John. How about it?'

John knew better than to react to their joshing and turned to Campbell Stephen whose chin jutted even further than normal, which John took as disapproval for living in such opulence. He began to think that it was going to be an even more difficult morning than he had imagined. Davey Kirkwood brought up the rear. His expression was difficult to read. His lips were drawn back in a grim smile beneath his heavy moustache, but his nose was wrinkled as if he had discovered something disgusting on his shoe.

John shut the door and turned back to the congested hallway. He signalled to the coat stand that partly obstructed their progress into the house. 'Coats on there, boys.' He stooped as if he would have to shoulder them aside to make a passage to the rest of the house. 'Let me through and I'll lead the way into the parlour.'

'Parlour!' It was Kirkwood who imitated him, his moustache trembling as he snorted in derision.

Maxton spun to face him and, with a furrowed brow, gave a single shake of his head. A clump of dank hair fell forward over his brow and he swept it back.

John went to the window and turned back to them, directing them to sit round a low table set with a patterned damask cloth on which stood a tray of tea things in matching china. Maxton led the others in and took one of the dining chairs. Stephen and Buchanan sat on the sofa. Kirkwood shook his head to decline a second dining chair and perched on the arm of the sofa. When they were all settled, John took his seat in the single high-backed easy chair. He had made sure earlier that this did not put him at a height disadvantage.

'Before we bring the meeting to order I want to deal with one or two off-the-agenda items,' John said. 'First, of course, I want to welcome you to my new London base. I have felt for some time that we need a place apart from Westminster where we can meet comfortably to discuss the future direction of our informal group of Glasgow city members as we seek to influence the direction not only of the other Clydesiders but the Independent Labour Party and the Labour movement in opposition.' The group members nodded their agreement.

John drew a deep breath, his mouth had suddenly dried and he was aware of a bead of sweat which had released itself from his armpit and was trickling down under his shirt towards the restriction of his waistcoat. 'The other item is a favour I wish to ask of you, comrades.' He had their full attention. He took another deep breath. 'You need to know that I have been joined here in London by Mary Ireland, who has had to leave Glasgow because of difficult circumstances in her married life. She and her young son live here under my protection.' This evoked puzzled looks. 'Some of you will remember that comrade Mrs Ireland played a key role in the 1915 rent strike, mobilising the women of Parkhead and supporting the action in Tollcross and Shettleston.'

He watched as his colleagues flashed glances in each other's direction. Kirkwood shifted his bottom on the sofa arm as if he wished he had chosen a more comfortable chair. Campbell Stephen reached for his pipe and started fussing with a pouch of tobacco.

John's face was burning. He forced his voice to stay even. 'She was one of the small band of women in George Square on Bloody Friday and is a hero of that infamous day.' He looked at each of them in turn. 'I would like you all to welcome her into our meetings.'

There was a full minute's silence during which Buchanan's boyish features stayed suspended in a state of surprise, his eyebrows arched and his cheeks reddening. Kirkwood stroked the ends of his moustache. Stephen lit his pipe and drew noisily on the stem held between gritted teeth. One by one they turned to Maxton. He passed his hand down the bottom half of his face as if straightening a beard that wasn't there. He coughed. All the while his eyes were fixed on the two empty dining chairs drawn up the table.

John had put one out for Kirkwood, who had chosen not to use it, and the spare was for Mary. He cursed his presumption.

Maxton cleared his throat. 'John, we have always thought of this as a natural group of the representatives of the five most deprived divisions in Glasgow. It's a parliamentary group. As such, we had never envisaged inviting people who are not in parliament.' The others had solemn faces as they nodded in agreement.

John fought to keep his voice even. 'Come on, Jimmy. You know we are nothing grander than a talking shop. Yes, we work out strategies on how we shall act together in parliament – those knaves and fools on the government benches won't forget the 27th of June in a hurry.' He hoped his mention of the infamous day would bring them to his side again.

Kirkwood, who was always touchy on this subject spoke up. 'I called them murderers too, John. The Speaker must be deaf in his left ear if he says he never heard me.'

John smiled broadly. Kirkwood had unintentionally lightened the mood. 'We know you shouted as well, Davey. We all heard it. Trouble is, your accent is the most difficult for the Sassenachs to make sense of. The poor Speaker probably didn't understand you.' He waited for the chuckling and the elbowing and pushing between Kirkwood and Buchanan to die down. He stood up. 'But back to the business in hand, Mary Ireland would bring a fresh perspective to the table without opening our little group wider within the established party. Surely, it can only be a good thing.'

Campbell Stephen put down his pipe in a manner that suggested he had considered the matter and was now ready to speak. 'This is a delicate matter for us, John. There were rumours...' He looked round for support and when none came coughed and started again. 'If anybody outside this circle knew...'

Again there was silence. Buchanan spoke up. 'Aye. What damage would it do to us, to our cause?'

John frowned to show he was considering their concerns. 'As far as the people here in Clapham are concerned, Mrs Ireland is a war widow and this is her house. I'm her lodger. All is above board.'

'And at Westminster?' Buchanan asked.

'For them, I'm still at the Cosmo with McAleer.'

Maxton looked down at the tablecloth and his tone was questioning. 'It's a complicated web, John. But if it's *so* important to you, John, I say let her in. If it blows up in our faces we'll have to deny all knowledge. You understand, don't you?'

John nodded. 'It's a matter of my making. I take responsibility.'

Maxton looked round the table. 'What say the rest of you, then?'

There was a muted but positive response. John rubbed his palms together. 'Thank you, Jimmy.' He bowed his head. 'Thanks to all of you. I'm sure you won't regret it.' He paced to the door and, holding the doorknob, turned back to the room. 'I shall ask Mary to bring in some tea and she will stay and take it with us while we decide how we are going to approach the next session.'

The Clydesiders inner circle thus became six with Mary Ireland joining Wheatley, Maxton, Kirkwood, Buchanan and Stephen.

Of course, Mary's role on the first day was to serve the tea to the men and, once they had settled in, Stephen with his pipe and the others with cigarettes lit, persuade them to take slices of Victoria sponge or scones with cream, which they had no intention of declining. Once she had sat down and pulled her skirt around her legs, she was merely an observer.

The group agreed that the thrust of their attacks should continue to be housing, health, education and unemployment, all areas in which provision in Scotland in general, and Glasgow in particular, fell woefully short of the national average. Millions north of the border had no prospect of improvement and the flimsiest of social support.

The group had allocated roles to each other as if they were a shadow of the opposition front bench and their energies were not merely to decry the government's lack of action but also to keep relentless pressure on Ramsay MacDonald and the other prominent Labour members to fight for the cause. This made them unpopular in the House, although Maxton and Wheatley in particular were admired for the passion of their oratory and the logic of their argument.

Wednesday October 17, 1923
John, having persuaded the others to accept Mary, became concerned that, by the end of the second weekly meeting she attended, neither they nor she were benefitting from her presence. The next morning after breakfast, before he left for the House, while Ronny pushed his wooden cars around the back parlour rug, John broached the subject. 'How long have you been down here now, Mary?'

She clenched her hands together, each palm rubbing furiously on the knuckles of the other. John noticed how the skin was no longer cracked and raw as it had been in the early days.

'Seven weeks and two days.'

He put his hand across the table and placed it over hers. The movement under his palm was like the trembling of an injured bird. His chest seemed to empty of the life force that kept him moving forward.

Her eyes appeared to focus on his wedding band. 'It's fine. I like it well here. What is there I could not like? I have a fine house. The boy has forgotten what it's like to sleep in a drawer. He is safe.'

'And you have the meetings.'

'Aye, the meetings. It's good to hear what you boys are plotting.' She smiled. 'Who would have thought it? Here we are in London keeping a fire burning under Ramsay MacDonald so he can never sit down.'

'It's the only way to push our cause. We can't let them forget us.'

She cackled and it reminded him of the tenements. 'There's no way any of them will forget the plight of the people of East Glasgow while you and Jimmy Maxton have a say in things, John.'

'What about you, Mary? Are you happy you came?'

She pulled her back up straight. 'I am a soldier for the cause. I came where I thought best for many reasons – not only for the boy. But every weekend, when you go back to Braehead House and this place rattles with me and Ronny, it's very lonely.'

'What about the neighbours?'

'They're not from my class, John. They know well enough there's something fishy going on here. If you are the centre of gossip, it's no' easy to make friends.'

John's eyes misted over. 'I didn't know.'

Her voice was flat. 'How are you meant to know? You leave us on Thursday morning and I don't see you again until Monday night. Most days you are out of here before lunchtime and God knows what time you get in. When do we have time to talk?'

He stooped his head to make eye contact. He waited until her dark eyes were staring back at him. 'You don't know what it means to me to have you waiting for me when I get home. To snuggle up and –'

She looked away. 'That's well enough and I'm not saying...' She pulled out a handkerchief and wiped her eyes. But they filled and brimmed over straight away. 'When I take Ronny to the park I see other mothers with their children. Older girls like Ella and Millie, boys like Tommy. It makes me so desperately sad.' She sighed. 'I'll get over it. I'm here because I had to come; for Ronny, for you and for the party.'

'And for you, Mary – and for you.'

'Aye,' she said smiling like the child at a Christmas party who sees the presents run out before her turn. 'Aye, I have my selfish reasons. But add all of them together and they're not enough for three children to see their mother walk oot the door and never go back. That's what I have to live with here in my fancy house in London.'

He remembered why he had started the conversation. 'About the meetings, Mary. The six of us at the core of the Clydeside fight. Do you still want to be part of it?'

She looked at him as if he was the one deserving of pity. 'You don't understand, John, do you? I'm here because I'm a comrade to all those women I've left behind in the tenements. As much as you men won't let MacDonald forget East Glasgow, I am not going to let you forget the tenement women.'

'But you haven't said anything about them.'

'Not yet, John. I'm still new to it. But when my time comes, you and the others will know, all right. Don't be feert, I'll not stay quiet when it's my time to speak.'

Four

Tuesday October 23, 1923

John was dressing for the third meeting of the parlour cabinet when the telephone rang in the hallway. He heard Mary's voice, the Glasgow clipped out of her language to answer. 'Yes, Danny. Yes I'll tell him this very moment. Yes. As soon as you put the telephone down.' His hands were still stationary, each holding an end of his tie as she entered their bedroom.

'That was Danny,' she said.

'Yes?' His heart fluttered. 'What is it?'

'Ramsay MacDonald's office telephoned to the hotel for you. They want to have all the members in early.'

'What is it?'

'Danny asked but they wouldn't tell him. They said it was very urgent, though.'

The telephone rang again. Mary looked at him, her eyebrows raised and he shrugged nodding to the tie ends in his hands. She turned and left. Again she used her strange telephone voice unnaturally loud and cod-English. She called out. 'It's Jimmy Maxton. They caught up with him before they left his digs. The boys are going straight to the House.'

John gave up on his tie and negotiated the landing and stairs carefully. When he reached the bottom, Mary gave him the receiver.

'What is it, Jimmy?'

'The rumour from MacDonald's office is that Baldwin is going to call an election.'

'It's suicide!'

'It's the honourable thing,' Maxton said. 'If he brings in

trade protection, it's in direct contravention of Bonar Law's manifesto. He has no alternative.'

'But he can't win.'

'He must think he can. Anyway, MacDonald wants us all in now. We're going straight there.'

'I shall send for Danny in the motor and join you as soon as I can.'

'Are you too grand for the underground train, John?'

'Don't be silly. There's work on our line. It will be another year before Clapham is open.' He returned the earpiece to its cradle and placed the telephone back on the hall table.

Mary's eyes were wide, her eyebrows raised. 'What is it, John? Who can't win?'

'Baldwin is going to make an announcement in the House. They think he's going to call an election.' He took the stairs two at a time doing his best to knot his tie as he ran. He called over his shoulder. 'Telephone Danny. Tell him to contact MacDonald's people and tell them I'm on my way. As soon as he is done he is to motor over here as fast as he can. I shall be ready by the time he gets here.'

His heart was racing as he turned at the top of the stairs and watched Mary pick up the phone and ask the operator for a connection to the Cosmo Hotel.

Later that day John relaxed into his seat in the back of the London car, as Danny grandly called it, and looked out at the crisp October evening. He shivered. Parliament had had another momentous day.

The light was still on in the hallway when John stepped down from the Morris. It was not as well appointed as the Wolseley, but it was more in keeping with his status as a Labour MP. He leant in to the open front window. 'We're finished for the night, Danny. Go back to the Cosmo. Be here at the usual time tomorrow.'

Danny put a finger to his cap. 'Right-ho, boss.' He crunched the gears before juddering the motor away from the kerb.

John shook his head. Danny was developing some strange London expressions from the chauffeurs he communed with in

St Stephen's yard. With his abject driving ability and tenement ways, Danny was rougher than the drivers he shared time with. John wondered about letting him go. Perhaps if there was change of government…

He opened the front door and shuffled round it trying to minimise the noise. Mary emerged from the back parlour wiping her hands on her pinafore. 'Well?' she said.

He held out his arms and drew her to him. She lifted her face and they touched lips momentarily. He pulled his head back. 'You shouldn't have stayed up.'

'I had to know. The BBC announced it – Baldwin called the election.'

He spun her round and patted her bottom to urge her towards the back of the house. 'Let's have some drinking chocolate while we talk.'

He listened to her busying herself in the kitchen while he sat at the back parlour table. He rubbed his hands together and looked at the empty grate. 'Did you fall asleep?' he said, raising his voice over the roar of the gas ring.

'Yes. Sorry, I let the fire die out. The milk will be ready soon.'

John heard the dry grind of the wooden spoon in the saucepan and the smell of hot chocolate wafted into the room. He licked his lips and praised God for his life. He admitted its unorthodoxy not only in his living arrangements but also in the business that had financed everything. He was certain, though, that as long as he felt the Christian compulsion to share his sins with a priest in the privacy of the confessional booth he would be redeemed. His past had brought him to this point and the means of arriving here counted for nothing as long as he had God's favour and Mary's love.

He rehearsed the day's discussions again. Surely, Baldwin had made a huge tactical error. With the Liberals split and the country in favour of free trade, how could he expect to win the country round on a protectionist platform? This was the breakthrough moment. Everything pointed to a reduction in the Conservative vote. Even if there was another anti-Labour coalition, there would be sufficient support for social reform in the Liberal ranks for the Labour Party to push forward improvements in the lot of working people throughout the country, especially in East Glasgow. He was on the doorstep of destiny.

Mary carried in the tray set with a jug and two cups with saucers. 'I have made it with the sugar as you like it so there is no need to add more,' she said as she poured. 'So tell me what happened.'

John took a sip and winced as the thick liquid scalded the tip of his tongue.

'Careful. It's hot,' she said.

He smiled as he replaced the cup. 'It could be sweeter.'

'You're sweet enough!' she said.

'If you say so, woman.' He leant across and put his hand on her arm and patted it. 'If you say so.' He straightened up. 'To business. It was an anticlimax after Ramsay had us prepared. The House was bursting. Members sat on the stairways, stood at the bar, behind the Speaker, anywhere there was a space there was a man. Baldwin stood up and moved forward to the Dispatch Box and the House went quiet. He explained that the government wished to introduce a tariff reform bill but that this was in direct contravention to promises made to the electorate by his predecessor, Bonar Law –'

'The Right Honourable Member for Glasgow Central –'

'Aye, Mary, exactly as you say it. The poor man is on his death bed, I understand.'

Mary reached for her cup and took a sip. She pulled back her head sharply and made a show of pouring a mouthful into the saucer, blowing on it and sipping it from the edge.

John nodded towards her. 'You will no' receive invitations to polite society with your tenement manners, Mary Ireland, by th'way,' he said.

She looked back at him as if to stare him down. 'So you're thinking of having me invited alongside you, is it?'

He wiped a palm across his forehead as if to wipe away sweat. 'I was telling you about Baldwin. What the Conservatives now want to do goes directly against their election promises so he is seeking a new mandate. You can imagine the response.

Huge cheers from us and the Liberals and cries of "shame" from his own side. When it quietened down, Baldwin explained that he had been in correspondence with the King and His Majesty had agreed this was the correct constitutional approach. Therefore he was going to leave the House forthwith and see the King to seek dissolution with a view to an election on the 6th of December.'

'So soon?'

'Our problem is we spent all our election funds only a year ago. He must think we won't put up a fight.'

Mary straightened her back and he recognised the woman whom he had seen giving the ruffians what for outside his house over ten years before. 'Well he has another think coming, has he not?' she said.

Thursday October 25, 1923

John hurried across Parliament Square to the flower stall outside Westminster Abbey and bought a dozen red roses. He stood by the kerb and signalled to Danny to pull across the traffic and pick him up. When the Morris was alongside, he opened the rear door, placed the flowers on the back seat and climbed in himself. 'Clapham,' he said and waited for Danny to incline his head to show he was listening. 'I shall want you to wait two minutes for me outside the house and then we go on to Euston.'

Danny reacted with the slightest shake of the head.

John felt the irritation of Danny's sullen insubordination twist his insides. 'I know it's not the straightest route but with the railway out this is best for me. I have to see Mary first.'

At the end of the journey to the southern suburbs John walked up the path carrying the roses in front of his stomach like a pregnant bride. Mary opened the door the moment his key touched the lock.

He closed the door before proffering the blooms. 'For you, Mary. I'm so sorry I shall be away and you will miss the cut-and-thrust of the election. Of course you could always join the local party here in Clapham – help the local effort.'

She took the flowers, smiled and held them low. He offered

his cheek and she touched it with her lips.

He leaned down to Ronald who, as always, was entangled in his mother's skirt. 'Uncle John has to go away, Ronny,' he said. 'You be good for your mother.'

The boy smiled and put his head out to one side as if John was about to join in a game of peek-a-boo. His blue eyes clouded when there was no response.

John took Mary by the elbow and ushered her into the back parlour where it was warm. 'I have to go back to Shettleston today, Mary. There's no time to lose.'

Mary wiped her hands on her pinafore. 'Of course.'

'I would love to have you with me, you know that.'

She came up close and straightened his tie. 'John. These past few months have meant everything to me. I didn't think I could ever be happy again after leaving my bairns in Glasgow but you, the party, the MPs meetings here, it has all meant so much. What if you lose?'

John laughed and hugged her. 'Sweet, sweet Mary. I'm not going to lose. You should be thinking, what if Labour wins?' He pulled her to him. 'Now, Danny has the motor outside. I have a train to catch. Look after yourself.'

She stood on tiptoes to peck him on the lips. 'You too, John. Come home safe to me.'

'One last hug now and I must away.' He pulled her close. 'Look after the boy.' He drew back. 'I really have to go. I will call you when I get the chance.' He hurried back along the passage to the front door and turned. 'Next time we meet, Labour will have won the day.'

He hustled himself into the Morris. 'Euston, then.' He looked through the rear window. The tiny figure of Mary stood beside the gate with Ronny tugging at her skirt.

He closed his eyes and recalled the meeting that had started it over again – January 1919. It was the first time they had made love for three years or more. She had been so passionate, so giving.

He had been shocked when she slid down in the bed and started kissing him down there. She had taken him to the point and beyond and he had experienced such elation and despair.

She had tempted him so thoroughly; here was so much sin. They had made a travesty of God's gift. As he rocked on the edge of sleep in the back of the car, he remembered Bloody Friday as the day he lost his soul.

Five

Thursday December 6, 1923
John spent all of November in his constituency following his well-established pattern for electioneering. The days would be spent touring the factories, addressing groups of men called from work by their union leaders or standing at the stump as they came off shift. He sensed the separation from them that his position as the incumbent member created and he always reminded them of his working-class roots. The language he used on those streets would have been unrecognisable to his Clapham neighbours.

He felt this estrangement from his roots even more keenly when he attended the funeral of John Maclean who died at the end of the month. Much of the rhetoric there denounced the 'so-called socialists' who had pandered to the 'English' parliament. These parliamentarians had betrayed the revolution with their talk on Bloody Friday when, had Maclean been there, Glasgow's revolution would have sparked an independent socialist state of Scotland. John kept his head down hoping to stay inconspicuous among the thousands who were there to pay their respects.

After constituency strategy meetings or gatherings of the party faithful he would meet with Catherine and the children before spending time in his office to discuss the two sides of his business interests with Paddy and Patrick. Then he would retire to his bedroom and, at last, have time to think of Mary who waited for him in London.

As the day of the election approached, he prayed for the brighter weather, cold but dry, to continue so that his working men would not be deterred from making their way to the polling stations.

The day came and stayed clement. He attended the count with Catherine and made a gracious acceptance speech congratulating his opponent on the conduct of the campaign. Catherine kissed his cheek as they left the stage. Danny drove them both back to Braehead House.

Later, alone in his office, John telephoned the house in Clapham. He kept his voice low. 'I won, Mary. The majority was over four thousand. It looks good for the other Clydesiders. We're all coming back, I think.'

'And the party?' She sounded wide awake despite the late hour.

'Are you still up, Mary?'

'I couldn't sleep until I heard from you. I've been listening to the wireless.'

'What have you heard?'

'I knew you were in. And Jimmy. Davey, Geordie, Campbell. You are all re-elected. It's a good night for Labour – the Liberals will be in third place. They are saying no party is going to have an outright majority. The Conservatives will probably have the largest number of seats. We'll know by midday tomorrow.'

'Let's all have some rest then, Mary.'

'Aye, and you must come down and see us both soon.'

'I will, Mary. As soon as everything is clear. Good night, now.' He kissed the empty air in front of the mouthpiece.

Her voice sounded tender all those miles away. 'Good night, John.' There was a crackle and a click and she was gone.

Sunday January 6, 1924

It was the day after the twelfth night and a gusting fire in the grate was warming the front parlour. The group sat around the dining table: Davey Kirkwood, Geordie Buchanan, Campbell Stephen and Jimmy Maxton, John leaned back expansively in one of the carver chairs. Mary had placed the tray of tea things in the centre of the table and joined them.

John took the letter from its envelope. The chatter died. All eyes were on the cream paper with its green House of Commons crest.

'Ramsay is asking if I would be prepared to serve were we to form a government.'

Jimmy Maxton leaned forward and like a conjurer produced an identical envelope. 'I received the same note.'

John looked round the room, squinting through his lenses. 'Any others?'

Kirkwood, Buchanan and Stephen looked blank.

'Have we heard from any of the other Scots – Shinwell?'

They shook their heads.

Mary nudged John with her elbow. 'Tell them when you received the letter, John.'

He looked at the date, even though he knew the letter by heart. 'It's dated 17th December. It was delivered here the next day. Yours, Jimmy?'

Jimmy flipped his fringe back from his eyes. 'I was still in Glasgow. It reached me there a few days before Christmas.'

'So Ramsay was thinking about a minority government since very nearly straight after the election,' Geordie Buchanan said. If anything the rigours of a successful election campaign appeared to have stretched his smooth skin even tighter across his boyish cheeks.

'I hope you said you would serve, Jimmy, as John did,' Mary said.

'Of course,' Jimmy said. 'Do we think two of us is sufficient representation for the Clydesiders?'

Campbell Stephen took his pipe out of his mouth and tapped its side against the ashtray. 'We have to be realistic. Ramsay will be aware that the English will count the Scots in his Cabinet. We're not going to get more. You two have the City Council experience.'

'We must hold out for at least one Cabinet post,' Mary said. 'We'll not be fobbed off with a couple of junior positions because MacDonald is feart of annoying the English.'

John patted her hand. 'Quite so, Mary. Jimmy or I, or both, will serve in the Cabinet should he decide to go for government.'

'We have to shift Baldwin out first. There's no way he can last with only two hundred and fifty seats,' Jimmy said.

'Nearly seventy more than us.' Campbell had a match to the bowl of his pipe and blew out a cloud of fragrant, blue smoke with his words.

'Aye, but he has no appetite for a coalition with the Liberals,' John said. 'As soon as he tries anything, we and the Liberals will bring him down. It's only a matter of time.'

Tuesday January 22, 1924

Two weeks later, John was woken by the sensation of lips brushing his cheek. He opened his eyes and saw the blurry outline of Mary's face. He reached for his glasses with his left hand while the right reached behind her head and they kissed. He remembered how he had come in from the House the night before and Mary, responding to his elation, had made love to him. He revelled in the mystery of her attraction to him.

His wife had always regarded the physical aspect of their marriage as a duty yet here was a woman, twenty years younger, taking the initiative and using his body for her gratification, taking and giving pleasure in equal quantities. He imagined the spring he was going to have in his step when he took the detour to Westminster Cathedral to confess the sins of last night. She kissed him back, pushing the tip of her tongue against his closed lips. His body reacted in anticipation of more sinning. He pulled her close.

She mumbled something against his neck.

He pulled back. 'Say again?'

'Government. When do you think you'll hear from MacDonald?'

He laid back on the pillow and chuckled. 'I thought it was me you wanted but it's the idea of sleeping with a Minister of His Majesty's Government.'

'And what if it is? Here you are, a miner from a one-roomed cottage in Baillieston and me from a Parkhead tenement and you are soon to kiss the hand of the King. Oh, John, I bless the day I stood up for you in Anstruther Street.'

'No more than I do, Mary.'

'So!' She leaned in and punched the pillow into shape beneath his head. 'When do you hear?'

'It could be any time this morning. I should stay by the telephone.'

She flung back the covers. 'What are we waiting for then? Up we get! I'll wake Ronny and make us some breakfast. You prepare what you are going to say.'

The telephone did not ring that morning. John had been out to buy a copy of *The Times* and was trying to read its coverage of the previous day's events, which culminated in Ramsay MacDonald's trip to Buckingham Palace and a request to form a minority administration – the first 'Labour Government'. Merely reading the words created a wellspring of excitement in his gut that spread upwards constricting his chest and the muscles of his neck. He wondered whether he would ever relax enough to make a speech from the front bench.

He had watched Mary dust the hallstand twice and, on the pretext of untwisting the chord to the telephone's ear piece, check that they were connected to the operator. He counted back the twenty years from his own age. She was only thirty-four! Despite having four children, her waist was still slim. She had put a layer of padding on her hips since the Glasgow days but, if anything, it added to her allure. They swayed enticingly as she ran the polishing cloth along the dado rail.

Shortly after midday the door-knocker sounded. He followed Mary as she rushed to open it. Over her shoulder he saw the stooped figure of Jimmy Maxton. His head was low, his face dark beneath his trilby. Raindrops fell from its brim onto the tiled step.

'Has he heard anything?' Jimmy said to Mary.

'Nothing. You?'

He shook his head. 'I've told our landlady to give Downing Street this number if they call.'

He shook off his raincoat and stepped inside, wiping his feet on the mat. 'Ah! You're there, John. I was saying to Mary, it's not good if we don't hear something soon. The major posts are allocated first.'

John folded the paper. 'We have to stick by what we agreed. The Clydesiders have to have a full cabinet seat. Perhaps Manny Shinwell has something and we have been left out.'

'We would have heard –'

The telephone rang. John nodded to Mary. She shucked off her pinafore and straightened her back before lifting the apparatus. 'Danny. Yes, he's here.'

She passed the telephone across and John put the earpiece to his ear. 'Danny?'

'There been a mix-up here at the hotel, JW. The Downing Street switchboard still has this as the contact number.'

'So?'

'They first called over an hour ago. It's been regular since then. The reception manager here has been doing what we said. They've been holding any messages until they saw me. I have only moments ago come in. I stayed with a friend after dropping you off last night.'

'The hotel people didn't tell them I was no longer staying there I hope.'

'No, they followed the instructions – hold your messages for me. I'm sorry, JW. I didnae realise today would be important.'

'It's not your fault, Danny. I should have told you to make sure you were by the telephone. I will call them from here.' He slammed the earpiece down on the cradle. 'Damn!' he lifted it again and asked for 10 Downing Street.

'Prime Minister's Office.' The man's voice was clipped and militaristic.

'I believe the Prime Minister is trying to contact me... John Wheatley.'

'Yes, Mr Wheatley, I *have* been trying to find you. The Cosmo Hotel has been most uncooperative. They have merely said they would hold messages for you. I don't think it's very satisfactory. I'll put you through, but first you must give me the telephone number you will be at for the rest of the day.'

There were clicks on the line as the connection was made. John recognised Ramsay MacDonald's voice. 'John? Are you there?'

'I'm here, Prime Minister.' John realised he was standing to attention. His heart was fluttering. Mary came alongside him and hugged his arm to her bosom.

'We're not putting up a very good show, I'm afraid. The civil

188

servants who run this office expect all my candidates to be sitting by their telephones. It's not a good start.'

'I'm sorry, Prime Minister.'

And drop the Prime Minister, will you?'

Of course, Ramsay.'

'Now I have you pencilled in for the Health Ministry. Under-Secretary with Trevelyan as Minister. What do you think?'

Jimmy stood eyebrows raised, hopping from foot to foot. 'What is it?' he mouthed.

'Have you anything in mind for any of the others from Glasgow, Ramsay?

'I'm not really able to share anything until it's all decided but, if you accept, you won't be the only Under-Secretary from Glasgow.'

'So nothing at full cabinet level for Glasgow?'

Jimmy shook his head. Mary looked up at him her eyes wide and fearful.

'Not in the current plan.'

'Then, I'm afraid I have to decline your offer, Prime Minister. I like Health, of course I do. I could do so much about housing from there. But not as an Under-Secretary.'

'Then I'm sorry, John. There doesn't seem much else to say. I shall see what I can do but...'

'I understand. Thank you anyway. And good luck with the rest of your plans.' He returned the earphone to its cradle. 'Let us go into the parlour. Mary, I think we need a cup of tea.'

They sat round the table in the back parlour, each with a cup of tea in front of them. Jimmy was still shaking his head, eyes blank. 'So it's nothing for Glasgow, then?' It was the third time he had said it. Each time he sounded more incredulous.

Mary patted the back of John's hand. 'You were absolutely right to turn it down. Let's hope the other Glasgow man is as principled.'

If it's Geordie or Davey, boys who don't have any expectations, they'll be delighted with an Under-Secretaryship. They won't be asking questions,' John said.

'Manny or Campbell, they would smell a rat, though, wouldn't they?' Mary said.

'Campbell would. Manny has never been close with us. He might take it.' Jimmy said.

'We've been let down.' John spoke sharply. 'We should get the six of us together tonight. We need to discuss how we are going to react. We must not take this lying down. Glasgow has to have a seat at the table.'

'You're right, John,' Jimmy said. 'A meeting here?'

'Of course here,' Mary said.

In the silence that followed, the telephone rang. Mary raised herself deliberately from her chair and walked out of the room with an even pace. John could hear her voice in the hallway but could not make out the words.

She scuttled back. Her voice was strained and tremulous. 'It's the Prime Minister's Office again, John!'

John swept out followed by the other two.

'Hello?' he said into the mouthpiece.

It was the military man. 'Mr Wheatley? I have the Prime Minister for you.'

'Thank you.'

'John?'

'Ramsay.'

'I have spoken to Trevelyan again. He has been very accommodating.'

'Yes?'

'It means I can offer you the Cabinet post of Minister of Health. Would you like to think about it?'

'No, Ramsay.' Mary and Jimmy slumped in reaction. 'I am delighted to accept the post of Minister of Health and look forward to serving in your government.' The two figures in front of him jumped into the air and Mary clapped her hands together silently.

'That's settled, then.' There was a pause and rustle of papers. 'Now, I understand Maxton is there with you.'

That is correct, Ramsay.'

'Then please pass him the telephone.'

John watched the expression on his friend's face as he spoke. 'Prime Minister, very well, Ramsay.' There was a long pause during which Jimmy's heavy eyebrows lowered. 'I am sorry but no... I appreciate it would be in John's Ministry but no' even then. I am obliged to decline.' He shook his head. There were tears in his eyes. 'I was hoping for a cabinet appointment... next time, perhaps... thank you, Ramsay.' He put the earphone back on its cradle and his shoulders slumped.

Six

Tuesday June 3, 1924

John paused at the white line marking the bar of the house. The sight of the green benches always made his blood quicken and he ran a finger round his stiff collar. It felt tight. Despite the rule against it, he could not resist a glance up towards the Ladies Gallery. He had a clear view of Mary in the third row. She put a finger to her brow as if to straighten an unruly hair and the movement turned into a suppressed wave. Had she been afforded the recognition he craved for her, she would have had a better seat, but he was glad to see that she would have a clear view of proceedings.

He shuffled purposefully to his seat on the front bench. Ministers usually entered from behind the Speaker's Chair in order to avoid the possibility of tripping over colleagues' feet. Now, as he passed between the table and first row of seats, his colleagues patted him on the back and there were murmurs of 'hear, hear'. Oswald Mosley, never one to concern himself with the rules, brazenly stood to make room for him, drawing a murmur of dissent from those around him. 'Knock 'em dead, John,' he said.

This was the first test since his appointment. It had not always been plain sailing and he had not always received the unequivocal support of the Prime Minister, but the scorn from the benches opposite always strengthened his resolve.

No, this was the auspicious day. He had prepared his ground totally. He had the full support of his colleagues on the Front Bench and more importantly, from his point of view, the contributions from his parlour cabinet of Mary and the key

Clydeside MPs. Today, he would lay before the House for the first time the fruit of their labour, the terms of his Housing Bill. Procedurally, he was doing this in response to a motion regarding the finance for the existing 1923 Act, but it was no less momentous for that.

His hand shook as his name was called. He stood to a clamour of 'hear, hear' from his own side, but could only see the cold eyes of the members opposite.

If he succeeded in gaining Parliament's support for his measures the result would be the construction of 190,000 low-rent council houses in 1925, with the figure growing over the next ten years to half-a-million new homes annually. John's name would go down in history as the man who cleared the slums.

He placed his notes on the dispatch box and glared through his glasses, pursing his lips. His start was faltering, commenting on the disruptive tactics used by the opposition. His voice gained strength when he moved to the concrete proposals of his new bill. 'The House will expect me to present, as far as one can in general terms, the Government proposals on housing and the reasons which led to their adoption by the Government. Perhaps the first point to which I ought to address myself is whether the Act of 1923, as it now stands, is not sufficient for the solution of the housing problem. I take it that Members in all parts of the House will agree that it is not. I count, at any rate, on the acquiescence of the party opposite to that statement.' He smiled grimly when this was greeted with hostile shouts of dissent from those in front of him. He jerked back his head in mock surprise. Now he would make them sit up.

John and Mary sat in a corner table at the ABC tearooms in Victoria Street. Mary had taken off her gloves and was pouring tea. 'I had to stop myself from applauding when you told that Tory that if he lived in a slum for a week the problems would all be solved.'

'That was Ormsby-Gore, next in line to a Baronetcy, I believe. But trust me, Mary, he's not the worst of them.'

'And I heard Davey Kirkwood butt in with his 'hear, hears,'

but I couldn't hear what you said before. It's awfy difficult to keep up in those seats.'

'I said I wouldn't give them sob stories about the poor again, as I didn't want to repeat the offence of assuming Conservatives have souls as well as pockets.'

Mary laughed and patted a hand down on the table. 'Och! That's a good one right enough, John. You seemed so comfortable giving them whit for.'

He patted her hand. 'My parlour cabinet prepared me well.'

'You have come such a long way, John. Look at you, Minister of the Crown.'

'Aye and you, Mary Ireland, with your little finger out as you sip your tea from a fine china cup and not the saucer.'

'If we are talking about getting above our station, John Wheatley, I will remind you it was you who kissed the King's hand.'

John shook his head. 'I still blush with the shame of it. Give me my due, though, I refused to wear the frock coat.'

She pushed a finger into his side. 'Would they be able to find one big enough for you?'

John glanced around the crowded restaurant. Nobody seemed to be taking a special interest in them.

Mary hung her head. 'Sorry, John. It's so difficult not to show affection when we're out. And with Ronny not with us for a change.'

'Let's hope he's enjoying his day out in the car with Uncle Danny. ' He patted her hand again, longing to take her in his arms. 'If only we could be more open, Mary. I would have liked nothing better to have you as my escort on these occasions. You mean so much to me. You are so much more than a wife could ever be.'

'I'm sad because it feels so much less.'

The silence hung between them as he watched her eyes fill with tears and the pain in his chest boiled up.

She smoothed down the skirt of her dress and lifted her chin. 'I thought you were very strong at the end of the speech, "taking the population out of the shadow of the slum". Is that what you said? Do you really believe the Wheatley Bill will have that effect?'

'If it becomes law, Mary, my Housing Act will transform the lives of the working classes but we have to stay in power and for that we are relying on Ramsay MacDonald.'

Seven

Tuesday October 7, 1924

'So this Countess of Caernavon or wherever sent Catherine a letter.' John took a sip of his tea. 'I had met her at some ministerial function or another.' He broke off to make sure he had the attention of the four men around the table. He raised his nose and put on a strangled toff's voice. '*I was very disappointed not being able to meet you, Mrs Wheatley, when I met your husband at the Palace last week. I would like you to know I will be at home in London on the afternoon of Tuesday the ninth.*' He resumed his normal voice. 'Which is posh code for inviting her round for tea.'

A rippling sound started in his throat which threatened to burst through his lips, which were making a sissing noise as he struggled to contain a full-blooded laugh. Again he checked his audience to ensure they were primed for the climax. 'So what did Catherine do? She sent back a letter saying she would also be at home that afternoon – at the family house in Shettleston!'

John led them as they threw their heads back and roared.

'That showed her well enough!' Davey Kirkwood, his moustache hanging over his open mouth, slapped his palm down on the tabletop and the teacups rattled.

Jimmy Maxton shook his head, sending a lank of hair from side to side across his brow. He wiped a tear from the ledge under his eye as it threatened to dislodge and fall across his hollowed-out cheek. 'Yon Catherine can still wield a good put-down.'

The faces round the table fell into silence. John wiped his hand across his mouth as if to wipe away the last trace of a smile.

The door opened and all five heads swivelled to the figure entering the room. 'What were you all laughing about?' Mary carried a tray with a fresh pot of tea.

'I was telling them about how I made Joynson-Hicks look a fool in the committee stage of the Housing Bill.'

She switched the teapots and placed the tray on the sideboard. 'Aye, well when somebody is born as stupid as that body it isnae difficult for you now, John, is it?'

John noticed the men around the table give each other sharp glances. They had never accepted Mary as an equal as he had and, even though they fully understood his domestic situation, he felt their disapproval lurking below the surface.

'Let's start the business of the day. Since we came back from the recess, all the talk in the House has been of the Prime Minister's dispute with the Attorney General.'

'Not Ramsay's best performance.' Campbell Stephen puffed out a cloud of sweet-smelling pipe smoke that hung heavy over the table.

Maxton leaned forward, his face sharply shadowed in the electric light. 'Is this the time to strike? You have distanced yourself from him since he failed to support you over the Poplar Board of Governors so why not make him pay now for his indecisiveness?'

'Would a fight for the leadership no' force an election?' Geordie Buchanan's shoulders were hunched over at the prospect, his boyish features troubled.

Mary shook her head. 'There's no guarantee that if Labour had another leader, the King would accept another minority government. He could refuse to appoint a successor as Prime Minister and force an election, couldn't he?'

Kirkwood leaned in. 'Rumour has it you are a favourite of the King's, John. If he was to accept anybody in the party as Prime Minister, it would be you. He would have you rather than that Welsh windbag Thomas.'

John shook his head. 'I'm not so sure. But I can't, by my principles, stay in Cabinet if MacDonald throws the Attorney General to the wolves to save his own skin.'

Jimmy patted him on the arm. 'Nor should you, John. We would all support you if you felt you had to resign.'

'We'll see what he has to say when he makes his statement tomorrow.'

'Has he given any indication of what he's going to do?' Mary asked.

Kirkwood snorted. 'He has to own up to misleading the House.'

'We don't know the detail of it, but yes –' John nodded towards Kirkwood '– he is going to say he inadvertently misled us.'

'Inadvertently!' Campbell Stephenson coughed smoke around the table.

'And will the Attorney General support him?' Mary seemed keener than the others to know the exact position.

'We can't tell for sure. I am not even sure that Ramsay's position is supportable,' John said.

'So the leadership is in question?'

'Aye, Mary, the leadership could be there for the taking but who would like to be seen to be sticking a knife in the back of a wounded animal?' John said.

'For the good of the party, comrade –'

'Even for the good of the party.'

Maxton sat straighter in his chair and topped up his teacup. 'Mary's right, John. With a leader who has the approval of the King we could still stay in power.'

'You are the man-in-waiting, John.' Buchanan's eyes shone. 'Beatrice Webb, whose opinions count for something, by th'way, called you the new star of the Commons and a rival for the leadership if MacDonald breaks down –'

Maxton sucked noisily at the teacup. 'There is no question – MacDonald is breaking down.'

'What was it Charles Masterman said in *Nation*?' Kirkwood pulled out a cutting. 'I have it here. I will ignore the part where he describes you as a "benign Pickwick", John' – he paused to allow the chuckles to die down – 'here it is: "he possesses a perfect Parliamentary manner... da da da... confident without arrogance... da da da... a capacity for convincing statements".

Masterman may be no fan of Labour but he is a fan of you, John.'

'You are the only one in the Cabinet who is leadership material, John,' Jimmy said.

John pushed back his chair and stood up. There was silence while he poured his fresh tea and added milk. 'What about Mosley?' he said.

The men shook their heads. 'It's too early for him,' Maxton said.

'He's on the wrong side of the class war for my taste,' Kirkwood said.

'And for me,' Buchanan chipped in.

'As it happens I agree with Jimmy on Mosley,' John said. 'I think one day he will make a fine leader of a socialist Labour Party – even a government, but he doesn't have enough allies yet. I also happen to think it's too early for me. If MacDonald resigns tomorrow we must be ready to act straight away. We would have to stage what amounts to a coup in the party to have a leadership election and have a man in place in time to put a case to the King for a continued Labour government. Frankly, I'm not sure it can be done. But I am willing for you boys to make the soundings. If you scramble all over the House tomorrow, perhaps we shall have a good idea of where we stand.'

'It will get back to the Whips and then to Ramsay,' Jimmy said.

'We must take our chance.' Mary said it with a firm nod of the head and the men stayed silent.

Friday October 10, 1924

'Careful, Ronny!' John ran forward to catch the boy as he teetered on the edge of the Long Pond at Clapham Common. 'Mary, he could have fallen in.'

'Och, and he would have a cold walk home in wet shoes. See how shallow it is.'

'Let me go, Uncle John. I want to feed the ducks.' Ronny had no trace of his mother's accent.

John patted his head, pulled his scarf tighter and tucked the loose ends into the belt of his herringbone wool coat. 'You're right, I was panicking.' John returned to the bench. 'You know we should get the boy one of those wee model yachts. The ones with the wooden hull and the real cloth sails. We could come down with it in the spring.'

'Ach,' Mary said shaking her head. 'It's too late for his birthday so perhaps you could look for one for Christmas. Though I will be the one down here sailing it with him on a freezing cold Boxing Day morning. You'll be tucked up in Braehead House.'

'Not now there is going to be an election, Mary. In government or out, I shall be dealing with the aftermath through to the New Year.'

'Did we ever stand a chance?'

'Of taking over from Ramsay, do you mean?'

She nodded before sinking her neck low into her coat's fur collar.

'No. The boys found no appetite for a challenge. Mosley is the only enthusiast in the Cabinet. He's stifled by Ramsay's slow progress too. But with a minority Government...' He clapped his gloved hands together.

'So it's an election in a little over two weeks?'

'Yes, which is why I have to be away to Glasgow later today. Catherine will already be asking why I didn't leave first thing.'

Mary's eyes appeared to be focused on a point far away over the head of her son who was rationing the crumbs amongst the small huddle of ducks at the water's edge. 'And will you get in?'

'I should be safe. Although Fred Cooke has already sent a telegram to say that the Conservative candidate is determined to play dirty.'

'What do you mean?'

'Questions about how I made my money.'

'Can you see him off?'

'I'm sure of it, Mary. Don't you mind it.'

'But what happens if you lose?'

'I have my business interests; you have the house.'

'But you won't have a reason to come to London.'

'I shall come down to check on the business – Edgar's.'

'But not for the week, not like now.'

He sighed. 'Let us cross that bridge –'

'No, I have to know. What about me?'

'I can't...' He looked at his feet as he scraped the pebbles underneath the bench.

'You won't ever leave Catherine though, will you?'

'I can't –'

'You won't –'

'I can't.'

'Your church...'

'Yes.'

'You're a hypocrite, John Wheatley.' She said it angrily and almost at once put her gloved hand to her mouth. More softly she said, 'It's a puzzle to me why I love you.'

John was stung by her comment. He knew the truth of it. If his love for her was a raft in choppy waters, his inability to be fair to her was a fatal flaw that threatened to sink them both. He could not own up to it. 'I love you too, Mary. We shall find a way to be together. Even if I am not re-elected to Parliament, we will still find a way.'

'I hope so, John. I dearly hope so. I'm putting all my trust in you.'

John looked around to make sure they weren't being watched and put his arm around her back. He pulled her to him and kissed her on the lips. The boy was still engrossed with the ducks. 'I'm going to have to go now.' He signalled to the north side of the pond where Danny stood waiting. He folded Mary inside his arms for a last hug. Tears fell down both her cheeks.

He touched a gloved finger to the end of her nose. 'Don't forget to vote, Mary.'

'As if I would. Who wid have thought, me a householder with a vote? But I won't be satisfied until women have the same voting rights as men.'

'Quite right too. Neither of us is the type to pull the ladder up behind us. It's why we work so well together.' He looked across at Danny who had his pocket watch out. 'Now I must go.'

As he hurried away without looking back, he felt a tightening in his chest and this time knew it was more than an emotional response. It felt as if a vice was squeezing his lungs and heart together into something the size of a cricket ball.

'Goodbye, Uncle John. See you soon.'

He wanted to turn back to wave to Ronny but the pain in his chest was so bad it took all his will to force himself to walk in a straight line to Danny and the waiting Morris. He resolved to see a doctor when he was safely back in Glasgow.

Eight

Tuesday October 28, 1924

John drew the heavy curtains across the wide window and turned back to face into the room. 'Give that fire a poke, Danny.' He rubbed his hands. 'Let's see if we can get some heat into this room.'

'Shall I put on some more coal, JW?'

'We should turn in early, but why not? After today I think we deserve a wee nightcap.' He took a decanter from the sideboard and removed the stopper. He held the bottle so it was between him and the rekindling fire. The spirit within glowed as the flames scattered in the cut glass. The colour drained as the dark figure of Danny stepped in front of the fire and there was the sound of coal chuting into the grate.

The smell of coal dust filled the room and transported Wheatley back forty years to the time he was a pit boy. He shook his head to escape the reverie and poured two glasses. He placed Danny's on the far side of the desk and took his seat in the high-backed seat in front of the curtained backdrop. 'You can stop your fussing over there now, Danny. Come and sit down.'

Danny did as he was told and lifted his glass. 'Slanje!'

John raised his glass in response without leaning forward. He took a sip.

'Will you do it, JW – tomorrow?'

'It's a tight one, Danny.' He sipped at the whisky again, allowing it to stay on his tongue so he could feel its heat before letting it slide to the back of this throat. 'What with my church attacking me from the one side and that Orange bastard, sorry my "honourable opponent", from the other I feel like a punching bag for all of them.'

'You must be doing something right if you have them both at your throat.'

'Sometimes I wish I was still a simple man with none of this,' Wheatley spread his arms wide. 'Campbell Stephen doesn't have his church telling him he is too radical to be a good Christian. Jimmy Maxton's Tory opponent isn't defaming *him* like Reid Miller is me.'

'You wouldnae swap places with Jimmy, boss. Look at the sadness he has had to endure.'

John sighed. 'You're right, Danny. He was a broken man when his wife died, but I've made sacrifices as well, for the church, the party and for my wife.' He stopped abruptly. He had allowed the whisky and the comforting warmth of the room to loosen his tongue.

Danny looked up sharply.

Wheatley held up his hand. 'Best to ignore that last remark, Danny. But you know well enough I would have liked to have had comrade Mary Ireland at my side as we fought this campaign. She would have connected me to the tenements. They can see I've lost touch with my roots. A better Tory candidate than Reid Miller would have made more of it. He doesn't need to try to blacken my name. All he has to do is paint a picture of the man in the manse who plays at being a socialist.'

'Nobody doubts your sincerity. Look at your record – the Housing Act.'

'You know it, I know it and perhaps even Reid Miller knows it, which is why he thought my business record was a softer target.'

'He disnae understand the folk in East Glasgow.'

'Thank God!'

'So you think you're safe?'

'Safer than many Labour candidates. The working men of this city are dyed-in-the-wool Labour voters. The traditional liberals are outnumbered. But in constituencies where Liberal voters switched to Labour in 1922, the Zinoviev nonsense will have scared them back to Asquith. I'll win but I'm not sure

Ramsay MacDonald will be Prime Minister by the end of the week.'

'You said the Zinoviev letter was a forgery.'

'Look, Danny, even the Russians are not stupid enough to write to the Labour movement in Britain urging us to acts of sedition and revolution four days before an election and allow the letter to fall into the hands of the British secret service, are they? It will prove to be a forgery, I am sure. But with all the attention it has had in the *Daily Mail* and *The Times* it's going to split the Labour vote and let Baldwin and the conservatives back in.' He slugged back the remainder of his whisky. 'It's time you went to bed. You have a lot of driving tomorrow and it'll be long day. We have to make sure Labour voters do their duty even if you have to chauffeur every last man of them to the polling station.''What about the fire?'

'Leave it. I have a few things to do here before I go up.'

Danny clipped the joint on his brace and heaved himself up. 'If you don't need anything else, boss?'

'No, on you go.' He waited until Danny closed the door behind him and picked up the telephone mouthpiece and tapped the rest impatiently. When he heard the operator's voice he gave her the number for the house in Clapham. He heard the connection being made to the London exchange and then the sound of the telephone ringing in Mary's house. It seemed to last an age before there was a click on the line and the operator said, 'I'm sorry, caller, but there is no answer.'

Wheatley jammed his elbow onto the desktop and ran his free palm across his eyebrows. 'Please try it for longer,' he said.

This time he realised that the clicks meant he was put through. He heard the confirmation from the distant operator, 'You are connected Glasgow caller.'

'Thank you,' he said. 'Mary?' He waited for the clicks that told him both operators were no longer listening in.

'John?' She sounded as if he had woken her.

'It's good to hear your voice, Mary.'

'And you. How has the campaign been?'

'I was saying to Danny, it could have been worse. It'll be

tight.'

'You'll come through. You have the working men behind you.'

'Not the church, though. And Reid Miller has been digging the dirt.'

'The working men care less for the church and the dirt than you think, John. They know you're the right man for the job.'

'I wish you had been here, Mary.'

There was a silence and she said, 'I know that, John.'

He cast around for something to change the subject. 'And you? Have you been working for the local man?'

'We don't stand a chance against the Tory. But my work with the League of Youth is bearing fruit. We have thirty members already.'

'I needed your energy here, Mary.' There was silence. 'Mary?'

'You only have to ask, John.'

He sighed and felt the familiar ache in his chest. 'I know that, Mary. I love you so.'

'That's as maybe. You need your rest now. It will be a long day, tomorrow. Please call me as soon as you know. I don't think I could bear it if you didn't win. Would I ever see you again?'

He didn't know what to say. 'Mary...'

'Goodnight, my love.'

He heard the clicking sounds as each connection closed down in turn.

What had she said? *I don't think I could bear it if you don't win*? It was equally true for him. He had cut his connection with the loan and betting networks in East Glasgow run by Paddy Meechan. John's old share now went directly to Catherine.

John's brother, Patrick, had sole charge of Hoxton & Walsh. The dividend from his shares, together with income from his investments and a salary from Westminster – should he be re-elected – were, in total, more than sufficient for John to transfer to London and make a life there with Mary. It was not as if he and Catherine were living as man and wife. Why could he not make the break?

He poured himself another whisky and placed it in the

centre of the blotter on his desk. He placed an elbow either side of the glass and held his head in his hands, his fingertips smoothing his eyebrows in a steadily repetitive motion. If only he could stop believing. If only he could convince himself that the happiness in this life would not result in certain damnation in the life hereafter.

His relationship with Mary put his mortal soul in danger, but he believed God recognised his human weakness and took him to be a good man at heart; certainly a better man than the factory and mine owners who lived off the blood of working men and their families. But he was certain he would fall from the delicate state of grace he had achieved if he sought a divorce and took Mary as his wife. God had put Mary as a temptation in his way and, while he could rationalise the relationship they had, he could not bear the thought of the excommunication that would follow a divorce.

Mary wanted more. It was something he knew but couldn't trust as much as he could his faith. As he approached his sixties surely she would recognise the twenty-year age gap more and more and he would lose what attraction he still held for her. In winning her in the short term, he would lose everything and not only in this life. No, he had to win the election; it would allow him to defer a decision once again.

Monday November 3, 1924
The train slowed alongside the platform and John, leaning out of the window, saw Mary standing by the barrier at the far end, hand in hand with Ronny. John was reminded of the first time he had seen them in Euston when they arrived a year or so before with nothing but the clothes they were wearing. He stood back to allow the guard to let the window down to its lowest level and fuss with the outside door handle. John stepped down as soon as the train stopped and walked briskly towards her. It had been over two months since they had parted on Clapham Common. They embraced and he kissed her cheek.

'Uncle John!' Ronny held his arms out demanding a hug.

John stooped and put his arm around his shoulder. 'Look at you, young soldier. You have sprung up since I was gone. You mother and I had better talk about your schooling when we get home.' He glanced up at Mary. She was looking at him with a quizzical set to her eyes.

He swept them both through the ticket barrier. 'Come! We must have tea. I could eat a horse sandwiched between two omnibuses. Have you eaten yet?'

Ronny's bare legs worked fast to keep up. 'No. Can we go to a Lyon's Corner House? Can we?'

'If your mother says we can, then of course we can, my boy.'

He realised what he had said and wondered why he had allowed the euphoria of the moment to loosen his tongue.

Mary merely gave him a conspiratorial smile that made him puff out his chest like a peacock. 'If Uncle John wants to take us for a special tea who am I to stop it?' she said. At that moment she saw a family of ragamuffins standing lost on the platform. There was a mother and three girls, ages ranging from around twelve years down to about six. The woman looked harassed as if she had been abandoned there. The girls huddled around her like ducklings with only their wide eyes establishing a link to the world outside. Mary's small feet stilled their clicking step and she stood transfixed. Her eyes filled with tears and she wiped them with a gloved hand. John pulled a handkerchief from his pocket. 'Here, Mary dear, take this.'

'What have I done, John?' she said.

'What you had to, what was best for everybody.' Was it true? Had he been selfish, dangling the possibility of political influence in front of her, knowing it would break up her family? No, when he considered what would have happened to Ronny and how she would have been tortured by her youngest child's misery, how could it have been selfish? Hadn't she ended up a woman with a property? Where was the selfishness in that?

'It may have been the right thing for Ronny, John. It may even have been the right thing for Ella, Millie and Tom. But it wasn't the right thing for me.' She leant her forehead against the lapel of his topcoat. 'Not for me.'

John put a hand to each of her trembling shoulders. He spoke softly. 'Come now, Mary. Chin up – for Ronny's sake.'

She shook her head. Wiped her eyes and blew her nose on John's handkerchief. She offered it back with a brave smile but he waved it away. She nodded her head and her feet resumed their brisk short paces across the concourse. 'Come along, both of you, a grand tea awaits.'

Nine

Tuesday March 10, 1925

The four other MPs in John's parlour cabinet: Jimmy Maxton, Davey Kirkwood, Geordie Buchanan and Campbell Stephen, were all returned but with Baldwin's Conservatives boosted by over a hundred and fifty seats and Labour down by forty, there was no hope of Ramsay MacDonald forming another minority government. Asquith's Liberals lost over a hundred seats so it was Labour that formed His Majesty's opposition.

The six figures sat around the table in the front parlour in Atherfold Road bent over, reading intently. Maxton, who had drafted the paper, sat back in his chair. 'I had a secretarial agency make these copies. You are the first to see it. I'm not sure whether I should call it *"Twenty Points for Socialism"* or *"Socialism in our Time"*. What do you think?'

John held up a hand. 'Patience, Jimmy. Let us read it first.'

One by one the members sat back in their chairs. Mary was the last to finish. John noted how the others now treated her as an equal. Campbell Stephen lit his pipe, shrouding them in fragrant smoke.

'Well, what do you think?'

Geordie Buchanan bowed in Mary's direction, his youthful eyes bright. 'Ladies first.'

John sensed her reticence and nodded encouragingly.

She cleared her throat nervously. 'It's a fine socialist document, Jimmy. You will have no problems seeing it through the *Independent* Labour Party meeting next month but it's too strong for MacDonald. The parliamentary party will not adopt it while he is leader.'

The others nodded.

Kirkwood put his hands flat on the table. 'This is exactly the lead the ILP should be taking in the party. We have to shake up these pragmatic labour men.'

Campbell Stephen chapped his pipe against the ashtray. 'This comes from the heart, Jimmy. We can all see it but is the party ready?'

John stood and shuffled to the window. He looked through the lace curtains to the road where children were kicking a ball. Ronny was in the front garden playing alone with a toy tipper-truck, running it up a mound of soil he had constructed. John imagined the brmm-brmm noise accompanying the lorry's progress. The room was silent behind him, expectant.

He turned round to face the seated figures. 'Mary's right. The ILP will take to this as a duck takes to water. It will scare MacDonald and his cronies on the right. But we are now in a different position. We are in opposition. We can return to a fighting policy such as this –' he pointed to the document on the table '– *Socialism in Our Time*". With the loss of government goes the responsibility to be statesman-like. We are playing to different rules. What say you to that?'

Mary stood up and clapped her hands together. 'Yes, John! It's time to fight for what we believe in.'

John's heart surged. With Mary at his side he felt capable of anything.

'Are you no' forgetting something?' Maxton's deep tones interrupted the euphoria. 'What about MacDonald?'

Kirkwood hadn't spoken since deferring to Mary. Now he leaned forward and scratched the industrial rash that had never left his dry hands. His accent was no less edgy than it was the first day he arrived in London. 'Ramsay MacDonald has never been comfortable leading this party of working men –'

'And women –' Mary said.

He smiled. 'I stand corrected – and working women. I wid rather see a toff like Mosley, who has belief and vigour, as the man. MacDonald was soft and outsmarted on the Zinoviev letter and it cost Labour seats in the English constituencies. We need new leadership.'

Campbell Stephen's cracked voice came in. 'Davey, you do know that the toff you're so fond of lost his seat to Chamberlain?'

'Don't take me for a fool, Campbell. The Zinoviev forgery did for Mosley as it did for many a good socialist. I ken that without a seat he can't lead the party, of course I do. I used Mosley to make the point about MacDonald.'

'It was a good point, Davey,' John said. 'Mosley's Birmingham declaration has much to commend it. A Labour Government must operate a planned economy with central direction of credit and output. He doesn't mention wealth redistribution and we should take him to task on this but much of his thinking is sound.'

John sat down. Who would say it first? The last time they discussed the possibility of replacing MacDonald they all assumed him as the heir apparent. Did he detect a new reticence? Had he lost them? Maxton had put forward the policy. He was the only one among them who had prepared for opposition. He had consulted John about the general direction and some of the points of detail but it was Maxton's work. Was it *his* bid for leadership? Had Maxton outflanked him?

'Surely the next leader of the party is sitting in this room?' It was Mary, dear Mary. 'From the day you boys left St Enoch's station in November 1922 one among you has made his mark in London consistently. Even that business when you were suspended –'

'Not all of us,' Stephen interrupted, puffing his pipe smoke into Kirkwood's rosy face.

'Aye, not all of you, but of those that were suspended, only one enhanced his reputation as a parliamentarian. One of you has made his mark and been commented on in the newspapers as a possible leader. One of you has been a Minister of the Crown and steered through the only truly socialist measure of the last parliament against the wishes of a hostile majority opposition. When we discussed this last year only one name was on our lips. It's as clear to me as the sun shining through those curtains and showing how much dust there is on my window ledge.'

The shouts from the boys playing outside suddenly became

the only sound in the room. John could hear the scrape of their boots as they ran and then heard the noise of the motor car that had evidently interrupted their game, puttering as it passed the window. How would they react to Mary leading the way? If they had decided on Maxton already would she have said enough? He sensed his hopes were teetering on a cliff-edge.

Buchanan blushed as he turned to examine the window ledge. Kirkwood shuffled his papers and ran a forefinger along the trimmed edge of his moustache. Cambell Stephen put down his pipe.

Maxton's spindly body lifted from his chair as if he was a puppet manipulated by someone in the room above. He leaned forward and flicked back the lank of hair that had fallen forward over his forehead. The other hand was placed thumb forward above his hip as if he was testing a pain in his kidney. John felt as powerless as a cork tossed on the ocean. Maxton had the power to sink him or raise him to new heights. he was the god of the moment.

Maxton spoke. 'Mary is right. It has never been in doubt as far as I'm concerned. If the parliamentary party is to be an effective party in opposition, John Wheatley should be the man to lead it. I would be content, have always been content, to stand for leadership of the ILP. As for this paper,' he flicked at it with the back of his hand, 'it was always a work of collaboration between myself and John. He has been and always will be my mentor, my leader. What say you, John?'

The three other men and Mary greeted Maxton's words with a round of applause. Kirkwood clapped him on the back. Maxton sat down.

John rose. He felt the colour drain from his face as he understood the enormity of their decision. 'Of course it would be an honour to serve you and the party as leader. But the party already has a leader and the future is not decided in this room but in the wider party where MacDonald has many allies and where we have made some enemies. This is not a short game like football. This is a long game like the Englishman's cricket. We have to establish our position as leaders of thought. We take their minds first and when MacDonald shows a fatal weakness we strike. What say you?'

The men round the table stood and cheered and Mary came to him and kissed him on the cheek. She nodded towards the window. Ronny was there. Intrigued by the noise, he was squinting in through a gap between the ledge and the lace. Mary gave a wave but he did not respond.

Ten

Tuesday April 20, 1926

John stood in the members' lobby of the House flipping the back of his left hand with the envelope in his right. The Serjeant at Arms had handed it to him as he passed through St Stephen's Hall. It must be important for them to be lying in wait for him. He read his name on the front – it was handwritten and he recognised the Leader of the Opposition's pen.

He moved out of the traffic of the lobby and stood in the corner by the Government Whip's office. The high marble walls echoed to the sounds of the members' shoes as they click-clacked to their offices. A mumble of conversation sounded as two Tories in full court dress made their way to the Central Hall.

John slit the envelope with his thumb and unfolded the paper. The letter was no more than a terse request for a private meeting the following day. John hurried to the staircase so he could signify his agreement to MacDonald's private secretary.

It had been over a year since John's parlour cabinet of Clydesiders had agreed to promote him as the party's next leader-in-waiting. In that time Jimmy Maxton had been elected leader of the Independent Labour Party and his document *Socialism in our Time*, amended in collaboration with the other members of the parlour cabinet, had been adopted as the credo of the left wing of the parliamentary party that sat in an uneasy partnership with the majority on the right.

Slowly, like a seashore building an accretion of flotsam at every high tide, the radicals gathered more and more MPs around them every time MacDonald displayed another bout of indecision. At first, it was the Scots from the outlying constituencies who joined, then the Welsh and the northern English put their weight behind the Clydeside militants.

MacDonald's lukewarm response to the proposed General Strike astonished those members of the party who had their roots in the working classes and John and the Clydesiders became more and more critical of his stance

By that April, a significant section of the party, led by John, was snapping like a sheepdog at MacDonald's heels, trying to herd him into the corral with the mining, engineering and transport unions planning to call a General Strike in May.

Wednesday April 21, 1926
In the small hours of the day of the meeting, after the House had completed its business, the principals of the parlour cabinet, Maxton, Mary and John, met in Anstruther Street

'What does he want?' Maxton asked, the low light from the shaded lamp making his hollow cheeks and pale skin even more ghost-like than normal. He sipped tea from a bone-china teacup.

'There's no hint in his note.'

'Could he be preparing the ground for resignation – establishing whether he should anoint you his successor?'

John snorted. 'Mary, you always try to see the positive side to everything. If he were standing down I would be last to know. It's Snowden he sees as his natural successor. He would talk to him first.'

'You have been critical of his response to the strike.'

'Aye. Maybe he's had enough and wants to pull me back into line.'

'Perhaps the time is now.' Maxton positioned the teacup on its saucer as if he was placing the final piece in a jigsaw.

'What do you mean?' Mary said.

Maxton inclined his head towards John. 'If he wants to pull you back into line, perhaps it's time to break out. Tell him, unless he's prepared to put the party wholly behind the miners and other striking unions, you'll come out into the open as an alternative leader and challenge him at the party conference in October.'

John put his forefinger to his lips and sucked in air around it. 'Do we have enough support?'

'I would say we do.' Maxton started jotting some numbers down on the back of a receipt he found in his jacket pocket. 'The ILP is strongly behind you and gives us a sound platform. Thanks to your alliance with Mosley you will carry those who would have supported him and many of them are from the English constituencies. Would Mosley openly support your candidature?'

'He's in print as saying that John is the only member of the party who can get things done. He called John a master of facts and figures.' Mary's voice cracked with pride.

'We're both on the platform together at Manchester Free Trade Hall next week. I can ask him then.'

Maxton wrote with a flourish a final figure in his calculations. 'I estimate you'll have a majority of at least twenty members if it comes to a leadership contest.'

John was still unsure. His brain seemed crowded with possibilities. 'What if MacDonald stood down and left the field clear for Snowden?'

Maxton's voice rose. 'You would do even better.'

'What about –?'

'There's no alternative candidate but you,' Maxton said. 'We have to thank our stars Mosley is out of the race. We have to act before he gets a by-election. If he had a seat –'

Mary interrupted, clenching her fists and John was reminded of the first time he had seen her, when she was ready to take on Bobby Craig '– Mosley might take back a few of the English but the Celts would still be firmly with us. John would still take it.'

Maxton shook his head. 'I'm not so sure. We shouldn't take the chance. It may be now or never, John. What say you?'

John stood up and took a pace to stand directly in front of the fire. He turned his back on it and clasped his hands behind him, sweeping back the wings of his black jacket. They both looked up at him, waiting.

He already knew his answer but allowed the tension to build. Finally he spoke. 'If MacDonald asks me to come back into line I shall tell him his views on the strike are not representative of the party at large and ask him to step down so we can have a leadership election in the Autumn. If he declines, I shall tell him that I will set in motion an official challenge to his position with a view to replacing him at conference.'

His closest comrades rose from their chairs and came over to hug him, the tall spare figure on one side and the small woman on the other. John felt the warmth of their love for him and was ready to take on the world.

Later John and Mary lay in bed alongside each other. Neither was able to relax enough for sleep to engulf them. He took her hand, rubbing his thumb across the ring he had given her to support the pretence she was a war widow. 'I was reminded today of the first time ever I saw you, Mary. Do you remember that day?'

'When I nearly provoked Bobby Craig into burning down your house?' She chuckled and moved in closer.

'You were a brave wee soul that day, Mary, and you have been my saviour enough times since then to make me forget what could have happened that day.'

'Danny was a Godsend John.'

'Aye, I owe him my loyalty. You don't think I keep him on for his driving skills, do you?'

'We've been like the Three Musketeers. All three of us from the tenements.'

'Strictly speaking, that's not true. I was born in a miner's hovel. Far lower down the pecking order than the worst tenement.'

She dug him in the ribs. 'We should not compete on levels of poverty, John. My parents' cottage in Dundee was probably no better than your miner's cottage.'

'But you didn't have to share with seven brothers and sisters –'

'Yes, yes.' There was an impatient edge to her voice. 'But look where we are. Danny spends most of his days driving your motor around London and his nights in a swish hotel. I am a woman of property. You are on the brink of leading this great party of ours. You could be Prime Minister inside five years.

Danny and I have a lot to be grateful to you for. We have come this far attached to your coat tails. I fear you must leave me behind.'

John pulled her close and kissed her forehead. 'I would not do it to you. Are you not one of my closest advisers? Why should that change? I promise you this Mary; if ever I have the keys to 10 Downing Street you shall be my confidante. Lloyd George had his Miss Stevenson, I shall have my Mrs Ireland.'

'But what of Ronny?'

'The boy will be ready for boarding school by then.'

She pulled back. 'I couldn't... not again...'

'Hush, dear one. We have so much more to worry about first. Remember only this. You are my chosen companion for whatever life holds for us. You know I can't change the realities but it's what is in my heart that counts.' He felt the tension leak out of her little body and in a few moments there was the merest hint of a noise as she drew breath regularly through her open mouth.

Eleven

Wednesday April 21, 1926

A few minutes before midday, John strode along St Stephen's Lobby and turned up the stairs to the floor above the chamber. He knocked on the door to the Leader of the Opposition's office as Big Ben struck noon, a sound that made the fabric of the building tremble.

'Come in!'

MacDonald was behind his desk while the Chief Whip, Arthur Henderson, a neat man with the appearance of a bank clerk, sat in the visitor's chair. The mullioned window revealed only blue sky. John tried to imagine which aspect this room gave on to. Did it have a view of the river? How pleasant it would be to be able to ponder a party leader's decision while watching the gay river traffic pass by beneath the window.

MacDonald waved a hand in the direction of Henderson. 'Be so kind as to leave us, Arthur. John and I have private business to attend to.'

The two visitors nodded to each other as they passed; John held the door and closed it carefully after the smaller man had passed through. He took a deep breath and then turned to face his adversary with what he hoped was a disarming smile. 'How are you, comrade?' he asked.

Well, John, very well. And my old friends in the ILP, what of them?

'As you would expect, Ramsay, we miss your counsel.'

MacDonald waved a dismissive hand. 'I think not, John. Now you are joshing me.'

John let it go. Why should he pretend? 'You asked to see me,

Ramsay.'

'Quite right, John, ever the man of action.'

Again John chose not to respond.

'Indeed, indeed.' MacDonald looked around him as if for inspiration. 'Would you like a cup of tea? I could ask someone to fetch one for you.'

'No, thank you.'

'Something stronger?' He took the fob watch out of his pocket. It glinted in the light through the window.

John allowed an edge of impatience to grate in his voice. 'You know I took the pledge, Ramsay. Many years ago.'

'Indeed. And you are a man who sticks to his principles.' MacDonald ran his thumb and forefinger across the grey moustache that almost covered his mouth.

For the first time John had the unpleasant sensation of being on the back foot. What was MacDonald hinting at?

MacDonald cleared his throat. 'This is going to be an unpleasant interview for both of us, John. But I hope you understand I have to protect my position.' He paused as if waiting for an answer.

John's brain was tumbling with possibilities. What was this all about? He sensed a tightening in his chest. What did he mean by 'unpleasant'? If MacDonald was launching into something that would 'protect his position', would it in some way impair his own ability to manoeuvre for leadership? John decided to go onto the attack. 'I know you're an honourable man, Ramsay. Perhaps you may regret it if you take this interview further. Would it be best if I leave this office now and nothing more be said?'

MacDonald stood and was silhouetted in the window. 'No, John. I'm determined in this course. I will come to the point.'

The sense of dread grew in John's brain and manifested itself in an ache behind his eyes. He removed his glasses and rubbed his eyelids. It succeeded in removing the immediate pain.

MacDonald turned so he was half looking out onto the scene below. 'It's not common knowledge and it's not likely to be something you'll experience, but, on the day he is asked to form a government by the King, the new Prime Minister receives a visit from the head of the nation's Intelligence Service. The Prime Minister is made aware of the matters of immediate concern – Ireland for instance.'

The mention of Mary's surname sent a jolt of fear through John's body that dissipated immediately he realised his mistake.

'In addition, the Prime Minister receives relevant intelligence regarding possible traitors to the country. The irony in my case is that the files I received included those on all the leading members of the Independent Labour Party. I had the dubious pleasure of reading my own file.'

John hardly heard the final sentence. What would the Wheatley file have revealed?

'Most of the files contained nothing more than tittle-tattle that you and I would regard as legitimate political activity. There was some particular concern about some of our Glasgow colleagues' activities during the war and around Bloody Friday but, frankly, I regard those activities, including yours, as honourable and appropriate.

John's breathing was shallow. How he wished the old windbag would get to the point.

'Yours was the thickest file by far, John.'

John nodded. It was no more than he expected, nevertheless the floor seemed to be slipping away beneath his feet.

'You were first put under surveillance when you became a councillor in 1910. It was soon apparent that your business activities were questionable, to say the least.' He turned back to the desk and consulted a piece of paper. 'Of course, as Leader of the Opposition, I no longer have access to the file but I have kept a record. Let me see... ah, yes, it talks of your illegal race-betting business and of running a loan book charging excessive rates of interest. There was a publishing business underpinned by a subscription-funded newsletter where maintenance of subscriptions was enforced by low-level thuggery and violence. Your man –' he consulted the paper running a nicotine-stained finger down the page '– Daniel McAleer, was your first street enforcer but his role was largely taken over in 1912 by one

222

Robert Craig. Does all this ring a bell?'

John shrugged his shoulders, his head was spinning. 'What can I say? I pulled myself up by my bootstraps. I reached a position where I could help the poor. Any misdemeanours are well in the past.'

'It's true that they are now at arm's length, John. But now you operate through your brother-in-law Paddy Meechan and your wife, Catherine. When we lost office last year you were still benefitting from questionable activities which prey on the poor of East Glasgow.'

John leaned forward. 'I deny all of this, of course.'

MacDonald nodded. 'I expected no less. Let us move on.'

'Please do.'

MacDonald stared at Wheatley. 'I am enjoying this no more than you are,' he said.

'Then, pray, let us get it over quickly. What do you want?'

'Unfortunately, what you have heard so far is only the half of it.' He pulled back his chair and sat down. 'Do you remember the charade we went through when I appointed you to my Cabinet? How I called you at the Cosmo Hotel?'

John nodded with a growing sense of dread.

'I had already received the intelligence that you were in fact living in your...love nest in Atherfold Road, Clapham with your mistress and your illegitimate child. We called the Cosmo merely to keep up appearances.'

When John heard the words 'love nest' his stomach surged and a wave of nausea rose in his chest. He was light-headed. He took out a handkerchief to wipe cold sweat from his brow. He felt like Alice in Wonderland, the room was growing larger or he was reducing in size. MacDonald and the desk seemed to tower over him.

'It's common knowledge that *my* mother was never married. I am illegitimate and I own that I have been scarred by the fact. You cannot expect me to think lightly of a man who puts a woman, whatever her status, in the position my mother was in. How much worse it is for you who calls himself a man of faith.'

John needed to make him stop but he had no idea how to answer. Perhaps, if he interrupted, something would come to him. 'Ramsay –'

'Let me finish! You have, at least, provided for the woman and her son but in doing so you have deprived three other children of a mother, not to mention your own fractured marriage and how all this has affected your poor wife. I don't have to tell you, you have behaved despicably. You have had your days in the sun under my patronage and protection, but your actions over the past few months betray you as clearly positioning yourself to challenge me for the leadership.'

'Ramsay, I –'

'There is no point in denying it, man. You are not fit to be the leader of the Labour Party and I will see it does not happen.'

John rested his hands on his knees to try to arrest the trembling that affected his lower limbs. 'What will you do?'

'Before I tell you that, there is one more thing. How is your health?'

John's brow creased with confusion. 'Why do you ask?'

'I was still Prime Minister when you went back to Shettleston to fight the last election. I still received intelligence reports. There's no need to dissemble, John. I know that your doctor is concerned about the state of your heart. I assume you haven't told your colleagues in what you laughingly call your parlour cabinet.'

'How do you –?'

'It's not important. As a gambling man would say, your cards are on the table and I see you have no more than a busted flash –'

'Flush –'

'No matter, you have nothing to take a stand on.'

'What will you do?'

'Nothing.'

John mopped his brow again. 'Then why tell me all this?'

'Because it allows me to dictate the terms of what *you* will do.'

'Which is?'

'Firstly, I have already prepared a letter you will send from the Cosmo hotel telling me about your ill-health and your intention to retire from politics at the next election.'

'But I have no such intention –'

MacDonald held up a hand to silence him. 'That is of no concern to me. You could decide, after all, to stand whenever it may be. The letter will be sufficient to remove any ambitions you may have for leadership. Nobody will support a candidate who is on the verge of retirement because his health is suspect.'

'And that is it?'

'Oh, no! I have to be sure, John. I am a man who has always believed in the benefits of a belt *and* braces. So secondly, you will charge Mr Reid Miller, your opponent in the last election, with slander.'

'Why in heaven would I do that?'

'Is it not true that Reid Miller has made remarks alluding to your dubious business activities, your connections with tenement loan books and illegal off-course betting?'

John shook his head. 'Nothing damaging, he's no more than a bag of wind. If I took him to court it would have the opposite effect to what I intended. It would propagate the rumours he is spreading and bring them to national attention –'

'Exactly the effect I want.'

'You dog!'

'Careful, John. I am the leader of your party and I intend to remain so. I may be, as you say, a dog, but the walls around us have seen far darker deeds done in the name of democracy.' He held out two sheaves of foolscap paper with handwritten notes. 'Here are your instructions: the wording for your letter and the line for you to take with your solicitors in pursuit of Reid Miller. I suggest you follow them to the letter or...'

'Or what?' John was seized with a moment of elation. He saw the flaw in MacDonald's plan. 'If I do this, you have played your cards. If, as you say, I somehow engineer to regain my health and decide to return to the main fight; if the action against Reid Miller succeeds, you shall have nothing left.'

'It's a lot of *ifs*, John. Look here, the gambling analogy is becoming tiresome. But let us prolong the agony one last time. You are forgetting my ace in the hole, your mistress and the boy. Any leadership bid would not survive the scandal of their existence, of your sham marriage. If they are made public, if

Mrs Ireland's conduct in leaving her children is attributed to you, you'll be finished. Even if your political career does survive the buffeting you are going to inflict on it over the next twelve months, you may still have a slim chance of enhancing your position but only if you give up Mrs Ireland and the boy. Are you prepared to do it?'

John stood and snatched the papers. 'I will find a way.' He turned towards the door.

MacDonald's voice trailed after him. 'Not much of a parting shot, John. Farewell.'

Danny was lounging in the back of the Morris reading a newspaper. He jumped as the door opened. 'You're early, boss.'

'I'm going to take a short walk. I shall be back here in ten minutes. Be ready to go to Clapham.

John strode off in the direction of Westminster Bridge. His mind was tripping over itself trying to think of a way out. He was only dimly aware of the bright sun shimmering on the river. He looked back over the bridge parapet. Could he work out which of the hundreds of windows had looked down on him dispassionately while he was being dissected by MacDonald's scalpel? Was the leader watching him now as he scurried like a doomed beetle into a corner? John reached the public telephone kiosk that had recently been installed at the end of the bridge and pulled open the door.

He waited until the clicks had finished and he was confident the connection was closed. Even then he was circumspect. 'Mary, I am afraid I have bad news from the meeting today. The great ditherer has acted. He's taking me out of contention.'

'What? How can he?' Her voice sounded high-pitched and strained at the other end of the line.

'He's using my past against me.'

'Is he threatening you? Is he going to the press?'

'No. It's worse than that. I'm coming home.'

'Take care, John. I love you.'

He replaced the instrument to its cradle, left the kiosk and hurried back over the bridge to St Stephen's yard. He stood at the gate and watched Danny manoeuvre the car towards him.

'Get going Danny,' he instructed miserably. He sat back in the seat and went over the meeting in his mind. Even before they had passed over the bridge he had decided to give Mary a partial version of events. But what to leave out? He had never asked how much Mary knew about his business activities in the early days. She was from Parkhead so she must have been aware of rumours. There would be no point in withholding anything about them from her. She would work out for herself that any action against Reid Miller would be a sham designed only to bring those rumours out into the open. There was no point in being anything other than honest about this element of MacDonald's terms.

John's thoughts were interrupted by a movement in front of him as Danny shifted in his seat and removed his cap. They were eye to eye through the medium of the rear-view mirror. 'Something wrong, boss?' Danny said.

John shook his head. Why should he share his troubles with the driver? 'The meeting with Ramsay MacDonald did not go well.'

Does it mean trouble for you?'

John wondered why Danny was being so solicitous. 'It's all and nothing. I'll come through. You know me.' He smiled at the eyes that flashed between the mirror and the road in front.

'Is it all over for us down here?'

Wheatley was puzzled as to why Danny was inferring so much. Had his movements since emerging from the House been so unusual? 'Why would it be?'

The big man drew a deep breath. 'None of us is getting any younger, JW. You didnae look well when you came out to the car. I've seen you taking the pills you carry with you. I worry for you and I'm sure Mary does as well. I wouldnae mind if you took us back home – tae Glasgow.'

'If you think I'm going to give all this up when Labour can form the next government, you have another think coming, my lad.' He straightened up. 'No, I'd gladly die in the service of this party, in the service of the working class in Scotland. And you'd do best to remember your place. I'll hear no more talk of going home, do you ken? '

The eyes nodded. 'I mind what you're saying, JW. I mind it well.' He straightened up and his eyes returned to the road.

The Morris passed The Oval cricket ground. They would soon be in Clapham High Road. John pondered what Danny had said about his health. Did Mary worry about it? She had never given him reason to think she did. Using one's health was a useful formula when composing a resignation letter. He could simply tell her it was not true. He could keep the visit to the doctor in Shettleston from her, at least.

Then the final question, MacDonald's 'ace in the hole', was Mary and Ronny's existence in London. Would he tell her MacDonald knew? He only needed to worry about this if, somehow, he survived the Reid Miller action and could re-establish himself as a contender to succeed MacDonald.

Danny manhandled the Morris with a gear-crunching fanfare into Atherfold Road. John had made his decision. He would protect Mary as much as he could.

She stood at the door her brow creased, drying her hands on the hem of her pinafore. He dismissed Danny for the day and ushered her inside. With the front door closed behind them, they embraced.

John placed his bowler hat on the stand by the telephone.

'Was it awful? Come into the back parlour. There's a pot of tea.' She placed the flat of her hand on his back and steered him down the hallway towards the back of the house.

She poured the tea as John warmed his hands by the fire. He felt the flush swell in his cheeks as the heat took the tension out of his neck.

'Tell me what happened, John. What was it all about?'

John let go a weary sigh and slumped into the easy chair. Mary placed the cup alongside him and sat on a kitchen chair by the table. She smoothed the patterned, cotton tablecloth with the flat of her hand and tugged at the corners.

'Stop your fussing, woman, and I'll tell you.'

She looked up with hurt in her eyes.

John removed his spectacles and rubbed his eyes. 'I'm sorry, Mary. That was uncalled for.'

Mary held her silence.

John sipped his tea as he told Mary of the meeting, how MacDonald had insisted John should use his health as the reason for his pending retirement from politics emphasising there were no grounds for him to do so. He recounted MacDonald's insistence that he sue Reid Miller and how it would probably backfire on him. 'And there you have it,' he concluded, 'MacDonald takes me out of contention for the leadership without lifting a finger. His hands are clean.'

Mary stood up and came alongside John's chair. She put one arm around his shoulder and ran a finger across the short hairs above his collar, a touch he always took comfort in. He pushed his head back like a cat.

'What did he say about us, John?'

John stiffened. 'Nothing.' He kept his voice steady.

She bent down so her face was directly in front of his. With his spectacles removed he could see the powder in the pores on her cheeks, the tracery of veins reddening her nose. 'If you have been under surveillance, he must know about us. What about the times we met in your apartment in Ingram Street? If they've been watching you since 1910, it will all be on record. He must know you live here.'

'He didn't say anything about us, Mary. He didn't need to. I will be destroyed by my own hand without you and Ronny being brought into it.'

Mary returned to her chair. 'Hmm. His own illegitimacy may mean he is sensitive to Ronny's position.'

John reached for his spectacles. 'And his mother. He must have sympathy for you.'

She looked at him sharply. 'So you say he's not using us against you?'

'No. There's enough in my past to do the job without you being involved.'

'You're telling me everything, John, aren't you? You haven't been asked to give me up. I couldn't stand it if you had to give me up.'

John moved across to her chair and his knees snapped as knelt alongside her taking her hands in his. 'I could not give you up, Mary. If they offered to make me King of Scotland, I would turn it down if it meant losing you. We can't guess what MacDonald knows but he may think so little of me, he believes you and Ronny are expendable to me, that I would gladly give you up to further my position in politics. If so, he misjudges his adversary. No, the truth is that MacDonald does not need to test my resolve as far as you are concerned. He has enough.'

He felt her grip on his hands tighten. 'Then there is a flaw in his plan. If you refuse to write the letter about your health, if you refuse to sue Reid Miller, what can he do? Don't you see, John? You don't have to do anything he says.'

John imbued his voice with all the calm and sincerity he could muster. This was his one chance to convince Mary that her part in his life was immaterial to MacDonald's plan. 'One way or another, Mary, my business past will be made public. MacDonald is offering me the honourable way out. I retire because of my supposed ill-health and I appear to be acting rationally to stop the slurs to my reputation by suing Reid Miller. Both effectively remove me from any hope of the leadership without any mess that could blow back on him and the party. What appears to be the flaw in his plan is actually its strength.'

Mary shook her head. 'You seem to take it so lightly, John. You're so close. You could be the Prime Minister of the next Labour government.'

John shook his head. Tears brimmed out of his eyes and tracked their way down his cheeks. 'It was a dream, Mary. Given my past, it was always a dream.'

Twelve

Tuesday April 28, 1926

'It's political suicide, John.' Maxton's hair was swept back to reveal the furrows of puzzlement on his brow. The lines either side of his mouth were scored deep in his sallow skin.

'It's something I've been thinking about for months. Remember how I tried to flush out Reid Miller and his people last autumn?'

Maxton tutted. 'I was against that tomfool scheme then and I'm against this now.'

Mary came into the room bearing a tray with tea things for the three of them. 'What were you against, Jimmy?'

'Your man here telling Reid Miller and his people to put up or shut up.'

'I thought a thousand pounds would force them into the open; I would test the weight of their evidence.'

'And what did it do in practice?' Maxton stood, took the tray from Mary and placed it in the centre of the table. 'It reminded the ordinary people – your voters and supporters – about your less than snow-white past. Have you thought that without you going public, inviting people to put up or shut up may have provided MacDonald with ammunition to use against you?'

The irony of this was not lost on John and he caught Mary's eye and winked. 'Well it hasn't come to that, Jimmy. No, I am tired of all this. I am feared for my health. I shall write to Ramsay as leader of the party and tell him of my intention to stand down. Then I shall go back to Glasgow one last time to clear my name and send Reid Miller and his Orange blackguards on their way.'

Maxton was in the act of sitting but jerked upright. 'What do you mean, "one last time"?'

John leant across the table and put his hand on Mary's. 'This is for your ears only, Jimmy. When this is all over. When I have stood down. I will stay with Mary, down here in London. I'm an ex-minister of the Crown – Ramsay will have to make me a peer. I shall spend my years tottering from here to the House of Lords.' He felt Mary's grip tighten in response.

'Then our work together is finished, John.' Maxton said. 'You have always been the link between the radical left and the parliamentary party. You were the right man to be our next leader. What alternatives do we have without you? Better the pragmatist Ramsay MacDonald with what is left of his Scottish left-wing instinct than an Englishman. You're putting us back to square one. Will you no' reconsider?'

'It's the way out for me and it gives me a way to stay with Mary. I shall relinquish all my connections in Glasgow. I shall bring Danny in from his exile at the Cosmo Hotel and set him up here as well. I shall see out my days here.'

'Good God! You are talking as if you have lived your three score and ten. You are not yet sixty, man.'

John chuckled. 'No, I have a few years yet until that milestone but it's time for me to take it slower.'

Maxton stood. 'Then there is no more to be said.'

Mary waved a hand across the table. 'Jimmy, you haven't had any tea. Sit down and take a cup. There's Dundee cake.'

He smiled at her brushing the hair back from his face. 'I seem to have lost my appetite, Mary. But, thank you. Will you try to make him see sense – understand what he is throwing away?'

John stood and moved across to stand behind Mary, placing his hands on the chair back. 'Given everything, I can only see what I am going to gain.'

Maxton shrugged into his raincoat and twisted his trilby hat into position capturing the lank of hair inside the brim. 'I will see myself out.' He was already through the parlour door and called back. 'Leave it to me to tell the others. We shall see you in the House.' The door slammed behind him.

232

Wednesday September 14, 1927
Life in the Atherfold Road house was returning to normality after nearly eighteen months of disruption. Firstly, the Clydeside parlour cabinet had disbanded. With the left wing of the party leaderless, MacDonald did not press John to act immediately but merely reminded him of his commitments.

Towards Christmas in 1926, Oswald Mosley had won the Smethwick by-election and, after the recess, MacDonald, seeing a new danger to his authority, decided to ensure John's elimination. So it was in March 1927 that John wrote his letter relinquishing his seat at the next General Election because of ill health.

He had expected MacDonald to make it public but he received a hand-written note explaining that there was no hurry to announce anything as the election could be up to two years away. For the moment he was grateful for John letting him know his intentions. He thanked him for his years of service and wished him well for the court case against Reid Miller. He signed off with a hint that, upon his retirement from active politics, John could count on the offer of a peerage.

With the need for the pretence that John still lived in the Cosmo Hotel long gone, Danny McAleer moved into a bedsit room in the attic of Atherfold Street in time to spend Christmas with Mary. John returned to Shettleston for the holiday and spent the time preparing for the court case, which was due to start early in the New Year.

The case was adjourned and when it resumed in July, as MacDonald had expected, the airing of John's dirty washing was sufficient to discredit him. There were no direct accusations in court concerning John's early business affairs but stories about the loan and betting books that made him rich before the outbreak of the war ran through East Glasgow like a wind-fanned fire.

When John returned to London at the end of that summer, with his political career ended, he decided he would wait until the next election and then cut all his links with Shettleston and settle down with Mary at last.

He immersed himself in his dual life as before but without

the hurly-burly of office and the machinations of the parlour cabinet he was able to spend much more time with Mary. Ronny, now seven years old, attended a local primary school and it was 'Uncle John' who escorted him there some weekday mornings. On this day, John had just returned from the school when the telephone rang.

He recognised the clipped patrician voice of Oswald Mosley. 'John, old man. You seem to have dropped out of the game just as it's gettin' excitin'. We ought to meet. But not at the House. Where do you know that's safe?'

Tuesday September 20, 1927

Nearly a week later, John opened the glass-panelled front door to reveal the suave, moustachioed figure of Sir Oswald Mosley who smiled broadly. 'So this is where you've been hidin' yourself.'

John led the way to the front parlour. Mary served an afternoon tea tray in silence and withdrew. John fussed with the teapot and strainer while Mosley helped himself to a slice of cake and chomped into it messily. When he smiled he revealed a wedge of fruit stuck in the large gap between his front teeth. John decided not to remark upon it.

'Frankly, John, I had expected you to be leadin' this great party of ours by the time I got back into the House. I often described you as the only man of Lenin quality in the party. The closest thing we have to a practical revolutionary. A man of vision, with an executive streak. Surely, last year around the General Strike, while I was out in the wilderness, that was the time to make your play. Why did you not see it through, John? Why step back when it was within your grasp?'

John took a deep breath. How much could he tell him? Mosley was no friend to MacDonald but he was also a notorious gossip. Could he trust him? 'It's good that the people of Smethwick had the sense to vote you in, Oswald. How long ago was it now?'

Mosley's smile looked more like a sneer. 'You know very well when it was, John. Nine months ago. Let's call it a gestation period.' He sniggered.

John refused to react. 'And it has taken all this time to seek me out?'

'You had your court case, John. You have to admit you have been lyin' low.'

'And now, here I am, back in London and what you might call a busted flush – certainly as far as any hopes of the leadership are concerned.'

'Hmm. Look here. Do you mind if I smoke?' Without waiting for an answer, he extracted an exotically-coloured cigarette from a silver case, tapped the end twice and inserted it into a monogrammed holder. John declined the one Mosley proffered towards him but took an ashtray from the window ledge and passed it across. Moseley lit his cigarette and puffed away releasing clouds of smoke charged with a strange perfume that John had not encountered before. Mosley waved the cigarette idly. 'Yes, you did rather shoot yourself in the foot with that court case. Whatever possessed you?'

'I felt I had to clear my name.'

'Hmm. And you told MacDonald to drop you from the Shadow Cabinet while you fought the case. I'd say you lost out pretty much all ways round.'

'Is this what you came to tell me, Oswald? You think I hadn't worked it out for myself?'

Mosley stubbed out the cigarette even though he had smoked no more than a third of it. 'Let's start again John. I'm not here to make judgements but as an admirer of yours who's disappointed that you appear to have lost your way.'

'I'm sorry, Oswald. I am defensive when it comes to my own failings. May I pour you more tea?' Mosley pushed his cup and saucer forward. 'I appreciate what I have done has effectively ended any hopes I had for leadership, but I felt my honour was at stake.'

Mosley affected a serious demeanour. 'Quite so, John. Honour, quite so. And is your honour intact do you think?'

'I leave it for others to judge.'

'Hmm.' He took another bite at the cake and sipped some tea.

John had become tired of the slow progress of their conversation, he put down his cup smartly enough to make the china rattle in protest. 'I would be grateful if you would get to the point, Oswald. Why are you here?'

'You're right. We have danced around each other enough. I will get to the point. It will not surprise you to know that I see myself as a future Prime Minister of Great Britain.'

John smiled. 'You have never hidden your ambition.'

'Quite so. Frankly, as my record shows, I have no great concern about which party I lead when that ambition is realised, although I am a socialist at heart.'

'Now it may be your turn to be surprised – I believe you.'

'Yes, thank you for that.' He bowed his head. 'I believe the Liberals are finished. Future elections will be between a polarised reactionary party – the Conservatives, and a socialist progressive party – Labour. Labour will win the next election, even if it's held before 1929, and I intend to be its leader by then.'

John shrugged. 'This is no great revelation. You have always been open about your ambitions.'

'I'm going to be frank with you, John. Perhaps more frank than I have been with anybody because I believe we are peas from the same pod.' He took a second cigarette from its case and went through his routine of tapping it twice before placing it between his lips for lighting. 'Of course, we come from very different backgrounds but we share a number of experiences. For instance, back in '18, I defended myself, like you, against slander from a pigmy of an opponent whom I had seen off in the polls.' He sparked a match, held it to the tip of the cigarette and drew heavily.

John nodded. He remembered it was the first time Mosley came to public attention. He smiled. 'You were a Tory in those days, if I remember.'

Mosley grinned. 'Couldn't resist it could you? Actually I was part of Lloyd George's Coalition. But let us not split hairs. We both supported an Irish Free State and deplored the activities of the British Army in Ireland.'

'Which led to you crossing the floor.'

'Indeed. You may not know that, again like you, I have dipped my toes into the publishing business. My interests were not as extensive as yours in Glasgow and London. But I owned the *Harrow Gazette* briefly in '21.'

'You're right, Oswald. I didn't know.'

'There you are! I'm surprisin' you with how very alike we are.' He leaned an elbow on the table and leaned forward. 'Most importantly we see eye to eye politically. We detest the living conditions endured by the working classes. We both believe in a state-controlled economy with planned incomes and government control of finance and the means of production. We both understand the simple but effective palliative of artificially creatin' full employment thereby stimulatin' manufacturing to meet the needs of a country in work. It's the socialist virtuous circle that puts the needs of our country first.'

'I couldn't put it better myself.' John drained his cup. 'But where is all this going?'

Mosley looked out of the window and across the small patch of garden to the street. 'This is the part I have shared only with Cimmie, my wife. I have an alternative plan. Should the Labour Party not have the vision to adopt me as its leader before the next election I have the financial backing to form a breakaway party – a new socialist party.'

John frowned in consternation. 'Should you be telling me this?'

'Very much so. I am takin' you into my confidence because I want you to share the socialist future Cimmie and I are mappin' out for this great nation of ours. You should be my right-hand man.'

John's first thought was that Mosley had lost his mind. Was he serious? Had he come to his house to make fun of him? Was he hammering nails into the coffin fashioned by MacDonald? He put his hands up. 'Slow down, Oswald. You're going to have to give this old man time to catch up. What exactly are you trying to say?'

Mosley nodded. 'You're right, John. I get overexcited when I talk about my vision of the future.' He took a theatrically deep breath and placed both hands flat on the table. 'What you have just done, the way you reined me in, illustrates exactly my argument. You are a thinker of quality. You are the perfect foil for my... let's call it impetuosity. If I am Prime Minister you will be my Chancellor of the Exchequer. If I am forced to create a new party you will be the unshiftin' rock on which it's founded. You are the sound man I must have at my side, John. What d'you say?'

John realised his mouth was gaping and he broke off a piece of Mary's Dundee cake as if it had always been his intention to take a bite. 'You honour me, Oswald. I don't know what to say. I was not prepared for this.'

'This is all in confidence, of course. I have support from within the party – my dear Cimmie of course, John Strachey who will bring in more once he declares and we already have young Robert Forgan from your neck of the woods. I'm pretty confident your Kirkwood is one of us too. Of course, it would strengthen our position if you were to declare for me at some time in the future. It would bring in the other Clydesiders – except for Maxton perhaps. Poor Jimmy has too many principles to be a truly successful politician – not like you and me, what?' He chuckled, blowing more of the sweet-smelling smoke up into the electric light fitting.

'I have told MacDonald that I am considering not standing at the next election.'

Mosley spluttered the cigarette smoke and picked a speck of tobacco from his tongue. 'But you must stand! Why would you not?'

'It's a complicated situation.'

Mosley's eyes brightened and he shuffled his chair forward. 'Let me guess. Is it something to do with the little woman here in Clapham?'

John's head snapped back. 'What do you mean?'

'John, John. You don't understand the rarefied circles to which I have access. The intelligence file on you is no secret. Do you think I would come here laying my confidential plan before you without the knowledge of how far you have been compromised? It's of no concern to me how you live your life. I want you with me because we share the same ideals – a socialism based on full employment at home, restrictions on imports, more spending power for the working man and full production – socialism that benefits this nation.' He slammed his hand down on the tabletop. 'Let the politicians in Europe look after theirs, we fight for the workin' man of Britain.' His chin jutted forward as he finished.

John sighed. 'Spare me your tub-thumping, Oswald. It's true I've come round to the need for a national solution first and that internationalism can follow in good time. You and I see eye to eye, on this and many other things – including impatience with MacDonald's appetite for change. But we come back to the fact that I am a millstone liable to drag down any cause. I'm not the man I was.'

'You do yourself an injustice, John. You are still the man you ever were. It's MacDonald who has changed. He has cut you adrift. It was his patronage that made you immune and he chose to withdraw it when you became a threat.'

John wondered how Mosley could know this.

'Consider how many on the government benches have made their fortunes out of far worse crimes than the peccadilloes that paved the path to your fortune. As your leader, I will smooth the way for you – and for Mrs Ireland.' He waved his hand flashing the rings on his fingers. 'We'd find something for her – an official advisory role, a safe seat, even the upper house for God's sake. There'll be no need for you to live a lie, John. Join me, both of you, and help me build a new socialist Britain!'

John closed the door. His heart was fluttering. He leaned his forehead against the cool frosted glass. Oswald Mosley was an unscrupulous cad, he had no doubt of it. But the man's knowledge of MacDonald's actions demonstrated how he was connected to the top tables. Did he have enough support to be realistic about a challenge for the leadership? The list of supporters he had reeled off, headed by Cimmie and John Strachey, was lightweight but they were the next generation, eager and ambitious.

It was logical for Mosley to look for a statesman with gravitas to be, as he himself put it, the 'unshifting rock' on which he could build his bid for power. Mosley was right about the alignment of their political beliefs. He was also correct to think that, if John moved in with Mosley, much of the Celtic ILP would follow.

John steepled his fingers against his chin. Could it be true? Would Mosley's hunger for power give him and Mary a renewed political career? Had God worked mysteriously to detach him from the fading lights of MacDonald and his dear friend, Maxton, and attach him to this rising star of the political firmament? In a moment of prayer-generated enlightenment his doubts about Mosley's character were obliterated by his belief that God had dealt him a new hand. He punched the air with both fists. Yes!

'Mary, Mary! Where are you?'

'Up the stair, John.'

'Stay there. I'm coming up.'

He climbed the carpeted stairway and turned into the front bedroom. The sun shone through the lace curtains. Mary was on the other side of the bed fussing with the counterpane.

'What did Mosley want?'

He walked across to the window bay and turned the chair in front of the dressing table so that it faced into the room. 'Sit down.'

John sat on the bed and saw in Mary's look an admonishment for disturbing the cover. He ran his hand over the pattern feeling the contours of the needlework. 'Mosley is a man destined for leadership. We have all known it. You remember our parlour cabinet acknowledging as much when we talked of me taking over from MacDonald.'

Mary straightened her back. Although she had her back to the window her eyes shone at him. John marvelled at her capacity to be as excited as him about his calling.

'He is going to make a play for the leadership when the time comes. It may be before the 1929 election or it may be some time after. If Labour wins he shall be Prime Minister.'

'A socialist party led by a toff!'

'Come, Mary. He may have been born with a silver spoon in his mouth but he is a good socialist.'

'So, Oswald Mosley could be the next Prime Minister. Why are you so excited?'

'Because he wants me at his side. He says I have "Lenin

quality" – a socialist vision but an executive efficiency. He thinks I can bring him the Clydesiders. He mentioned Chancellor of the Exchequer.'

'Is he serious?'

'Deadly serious, he's already gathering support. He said Davey Kirkwood is with him – John Strachey – others.'

'But what about MacDonald; he will ruin you as soon as he hears you're part of an opposition to him.'

'We have taken it into account in Mosley's plan. I'm to lie low until he takes over. Until then I will be surreptitiously persuading others to the cause. I'm confident I shall be able to deliver all the Scottish Labour men and a good proportion of the Welsh as well. He will reveal me as his man only when he has the leadership. Anything MacDonald can do after would harm the party. He would have to act merely out of spite. He would not do it.'

Mary turned to look out the window. John followed her gaze. The late summer sun was low, peeking from behind clouds edged salmon-pink. Where the sky was clear it shone a bright aquamarine. It had the makings of a red sunset. 'Let's suppose the plan works and MacDonald is sidelined and doesn't detect your hand in the plot. Can you trust Mosley? He's betrayed colleagues in the past.'

John shifted across and dropped to one knee in front of her. He took her hands in his own, forcing her to look down at him. 'Mary, I truly believe this is our chance. Mosley knows about you.'

'You told him?'

'No, he already knew. People like him have spies everywhere. But that's not the point. He wants you to play as active a role as his Cimmie does. They, the Mosleys, will come here to make plans for the new socialism. It will be like the old days with the parlour cabinet, Mary. You and me, together.'

'But Mosley can't erase your history, can he? You have a wife. I will have to stay hidden in the shadows.'

'Mosley says he will find a proper position for you. There are paid advisers to the Cabinet. He's talking about a seat – either in the Commons or even the Lords. You'll be recognised for what you have been to me. You will take on our work after I am gone.'

Her eyes were shining with tears. 'How can it happen, John? Given your past – and mine.'

'The war has brought so many changes. The old values don't count as much as they once did. Mosley is not troubled by these things. Our new brand of socialism recognises the frailties of past conventions. Mark my words the next decade will see this progress taken even further. Your past and mine – they'll be irrelevant in the new order of Mosley's vision.'

'And us, John?'

He took her hands, 'I shall stand again at the next election. There will be no more pretence. I shall move out of Braehead House. I will take an apartment in Shettleston for when I need to be in the constituency. Paddy Meechan can take the East Glasgow business and good riddance. For the rest of the time we shall live here openly as man and wife with Ronny acknowledged as my son.'

Her voice was flat. 'But you will not get a divorce.'

'I'm sorry. It's a step too far.'

She had agreed. John closed the bureau front and scraped back his chair. In his mind, he went over the wording of their joint letter to Mosley. It outlined the terms of their agreement paying particular emphasis to Mary's role as an equal partner as the four of them draw up the manifesto and implementation plan for a new vision for Labour, in opposition or in government, after the next election. It specified that she should have a role independent of John in any administration they formed.

Wheatley had not told Mary about the plan should Mosley not have sufficient votes in the parliamentary party to defeat MacDonald. There was no need to scare her with the possibility of breaking away from Labour and forming a new party. He could see how difficult it would be to convince her that it was the right thing to do. His own mind was made up. If the Labour Party was stupid enough to vote for the dithering MacDonald again, instead of the vigorous Mosley, it deserved to be broken up and a new nation-first socialist party take its place, especially if John and Mary had leading roles.

He heard the front door close and went across to the window. He shifted the curtain. Mary was dressed in her black coat with a close-fitting black straw bonnet. She held the letter in her gloved hand and turned right out of the garden gate towards the post office. John would far rather Danny had been sent but Mary insisted that, with her brisk step, she would have no problem catching the last collection.

He watched her retreating figure and recalled the last words of their discussion. They had stood up and embraced. 'Trust me, Mary,' he had said, 'the future of the Labour Party is in our hands.'

She had pulled him to her and they had kissed full on the lips, lingering. She had backed away and fixed her dark eyes on his. 'It's hard to believe. Am I truly to be part of it at last?'

He had hugged her so tight, 'God willing,' he had said. 'God willing.'

Ronny

One

Wednesday May 14, 1930

Ronny had never crossed London in a taxi before. It was difficult to keep up with the sights passing the window. He skittered from side to side in the back of the cab, pointing to each famous building and asking his mother to confirm its identity. But the adventure, the knowledge that they were to travel the length of Britain in a train, only became certain when the taxi drove through the arch at the entrance to Euston station. He had only ever seen structures like it in books about Rome. Here in London, the arch's columns, which rose high above the side of the taxi, were black with soot.

The driver stopped the motor and, without leaving his seat, unhitched the leather strap that secured their bags in the open platform alongside him. 'Here you take your case, Ronny', Mary said.

She led him across the hall to the Scotland platform. His heart thumped in his chest as he hurried along. Perhaps *The Royal Scot* itself would be pulling the train. He couldn't wait to find out. As soon as they were through the barrier, he ran ahead, ignoring the alarmed calls of his mother.

Now Ronny's mind could only cope with the enormity of the prospect of standing alongside the steam engine. He dismissed the niggles at the periphery of his consciousness telling him his mother would be angry. At ten years old, surely you should be allowed to wonder at the power of the locomotive before getting on the train? His head slumped at the thought of sitting in a compartment with his mother for a whole day. Even more hours than he spent at school. She had been so low since Uncle John died. He tried to shake the doubts away, nothing should dampen the thrill of *The Royal Scot*, there at the end of the platform.

It was too late. The mood was lost. Ronny could only think of the dark happenings that had brought his mother down. It had started when Mr Maxton had called to tell her about Uncle John. He had said John had been taken ill with a minor stroke – something to do with bleeding in his brain. He had been fit enough to make the journey back to Glasgow but, after a second stroke, he had died in his house in Scotland.

The news made Ronny sad. As his mother's lodger, Uncle John had been a constant presence in the house. They had, all three, sat together at breakfast on weekday mornings and Uncle John had often taken him to school. He didn't stay in London at the weekends though and his duties as a Member of Parliament meant they seldom met after Ronny returned from school.

Uncle John had been good to him. He always brought him Edinburgh Rock when he came home from his weekends away and last Christmas he gave Ronny the biggest Meccano set you could buy. He was sad that Uncle John had died but it was only when he saw his mother's grief that his eyes filled with tears and a new experience of desolation wrapped around him like a cold, damp sheet.

He was now near enough to hear the hissing and see the clouds of steam as if a great beast with a huge snout was breathing fire. His heart lifted and there was nothing he would rather do than examine the monster that was going to pull them all the way to Glasgow. He could see now that it was not in the distinctive red livery of *6100 The Royal Scot* itself but one of the original 4-6-0 series, *6115 Scots Guardsman*.

He hoisted up the skirt of his macintosh and felt in the back pocket of his shorts for the notebook. There were other boys around him gawping at the huge locomotive and he had to jostle them to make room so he could write down the name and number in his book. Around him, faces turned at the sound of a woman yelling his name. His face reddening, he turned away reluctantly and dawdled back to Mary who was waiting by an open door.

'Come along. There are seats here in a non-smoking compartment.' She pushed him in the back as he heaved himself into the train.

He sat alongside her facing the engine. A hooter shrieked and he felt the first stirring of movement beneath his feet and the seat back seemed to press forward. He looked out of the window. The newspaper kiosk on the platform moved backwards imperceptibly at first, then inch by inch, then foot by foot. In no time it was behind them and the carriage moved into a cloud of steam and smoke where the *Scots Guardsman* had stood. They were on their way. He turned to Mary. 'Is it on time?' he asked.

A man opposite had drawn his watch from his pocket at the first sound of the engine's whistle and he looked across and smiled. 'Right on time, young man,' he said. '*The Royal Scot* at ten – never lets you down.'

Ronny was soon engrossed in the comics Mary had bought at the station kiosk. He liked the adventure stories in *The Champion* but the Greyfriars School in *The Popular* was his favourite. He wondered whether he would have liked to go to a boarding school like Bunter's and decided he had to put up with enough ribbing at day school. They made fun of him for not having a dad, even though many of them were in the same boat. He had made up a story that his father had died heroically in the war but they seemed to sense it wasn't true.

For as long as he could remember, Ronny had known that he had a father in Scotland but never understood why he didn't live in Clapham with them. Ronny knew better than to ask. Something told him, if he did, it would only annoy his mother and he would be in trouble. After John died, Mary had told Ronny they were going to the funeral and would visit his father. He was going to see a brother and sister he never knew. It was the first time she had mentioned them. It was very strange.

The journey took all of the day. Mary had made them sandwiches for lunch and he managed to have a sleep afterwards but the chuff-chuffing of the engine and the percussion of the wheels on the tracks seemed to go on and on until it echoed inside his head. He read every single word in his comics over and over, even the advertisements for the jokes and tricks like sooty soap and x-ray glasses.

Finally they arrived at St Enoch's station and he was able to unfold his stiff limbs and climb down onto the platform of a station in Scotland. The first thing he noticed was the smell. It was horse dung mixed with rotten eggs and it made him wrinkle his nose. When that didn't help, he pinched his nostrils together. The stink was so oppressive that Happy Harry, one of the characters in his *Crackers* comic would have put a clothes peg over his nose.

Mary jiggled his hand. 'You think the smell of Glasgow is bad, Ronny? I tell you it seems fresh as the seaside compared to the way I remember it. Come on, we must catch a tram.'

They stepped over a drift of horse droppings and Ronny noticed how many more horse-pulled carts there were than in London. There it was only the rag-and-bone, milk and coal tradesmen who could not afford motor-vans. He would see the occasional cart piled high with furniture when a family was flitting from one house to another, but most of the traffic was motor-driven. Here in Glasgow, which he had already labelled the smelliest city in the world, there were as many horse carts as there were motors.

They turned a corner and waited at a tram stop. The people were talking a language he hardly recognised as his own tongue. It was as if they had stopped up their noses and were singing from the backs of their throats and the words they were using were totally different to the English that Ronny knew.

Mary pulled him aboard the tram and bought tickets from the conductor. He noticed how her voice, too, had changed. It was higher, more singsong. But at least he could tell what she was saying. The others in the tram gabbled so furiously it made him certain: he *was* in a foreign country.

They left the tram at Parkhead Cross and Ronny felt cold despite his tightly buttoned and belted school macintosh. The sky was darker here. It was as if a black cloud hung over the place and the smell like in his school chemistry laboratory was so strong it made him cough. 'Where are we going, Mum?' he asked as they crossed the road behind the tram. The air was stinging his eyes.

'We have a room booked.'

'In a hotel?'

'A guest house.'

He went quiet.

They crossed the road to a tall redstone building with streaks of black down the front. Mary made him wait in the hallway while she went with the landlady to check the room.

When they returned, Mary gave the lady some money. The woman said they should be back down at six-thirty for tea. Mary led the way up the stairs. It was a simple room with two single beds. The walls were thick with scarlet and pink roses twining up to the picture rail.

'We are only here for one night, Ronny, so don't you bother unpacking your things into the drawers. The bathroom is down the hallway. We're sharing it with other people so mind you leave it clean. Your towel is here. Don't forget to take it with you. And bring it back again – don't leave it there.'

The tea was boiled ham, which Ronny thought was over-salted, with potatoes and cabbage. They had some bread and jam for pudding and it took the taste of the ham away. Mary said that the bread was from the Co-op down the street and you couldn't beat it. The butter was more yellow and saltier than he was used to.

After tea, Mary told him they should wait in the lounge, for they were going to have a visitor. They had only been in there for a few minutes, with Mary sitting straight-backed in a soft chair while Ronny looked in the sideboards for something to read, when the door opened and Danny McAleer clumped in.

'Uncle Danny!' Ronny jumped up and threw himself at the broad-chested figure who filled the doorway. Danny held on to him and spun him round. Ronny felt the spin going out of control. Danny staggered backwards.

'Mind the furniture!' Mary shouted.

'You're getting too big for this,' Danny said and let him down. He led Ronny to a chair and sat in the seat opposite Mary, fiddling with his calliper and bending his leg. 'Are you all set, Mary? Is this place all right?'

'It's fine, Danny. Everything is spotless, as you said it would be.'

'Aye, I ken Mrs McNair would meet your exacting standards. Well, it's good. Now tomorrow, I will be with the procession from the house. You be at the cemetery in good time. There are going to be thousands of mourners. Working men from all over East Glasgow will leave their toil to be there.'

'And afterwards?'

Danny shifted his backside on the seat and twisted his cap in his hand. 'Aye, afterwards. You must walk back up the London Road to the house in Duke Street. I have told the man to mind he is sober for your visit. The children will be there. His sister across the landing will look after Ronny if you don't want him to go in with you.'

'Why wouldn't I, Mum? Why wouldn't I go in with you?'

She sighed. Her eyelids seemed to have become heavier since John died. She sounded tired all the time. It seemed to be an effort for her to answer him. 'It's your father's house, Ronny. You won't remember him and you won't remember the house. Maybe it's best you don't go in.'

'Does that mean I won't see the brother and sister you told me about?'

'I don't know. It may be best if you played in the close.' She looked at Danny. 'What do you think?'

He shook his head. 'Glasgow's a lot different from London,

hen. Those weans have a lot not to like about having Ronny in the house. Perhaps best if he stays with you – or the sister.'

She stood up and Danny followed suit, stooping to fix the joint in his leg brace. 'It's decided then,' she said. 'He'll stay with me.'

She put a hand out and rested it on Danny's arm. 'I'll try to fit in a visit to the Necropolis beforehand – to see Ella. It's two years now and I haven't been yet.' Her face crumpled.

Danny looked awkward. He stooped and held out both arms as if he was ready to catch her if she fell. 'I'm so sorry, Mary. It was as I said, by the time Bobby Craig told me she was already buried.'

'I know, Danny. I don't blame you. ' She took a handkerchief from her cuff and dabbed at her eyes before straightening her back and lifting her head. 'Afterwards, Ronny and I will visit the house together. We'll have a fish supper in town and meet you at the station. Are you still going back on the night train?'

'I'll be there looking after you, Mary. You can depend on me.' Something in the way he said it made Ronny look at his mother and he could see she noticed it as well.

Thursday May 15, 1930
The next morning, Mary checked that Ronny had put on a clean shirt and she brushed down his school blazer.

'Should I have a black tie for the funeral?' he asked.

'We are not in the official party, son,' she said, straightening the knot on his school tie. 'This will do fine.'

They left their bags behind the desk in the hallway and went out into the drizzle. Mary put up an umbrella and they waited at the tram stop.

The tram came to a clanging halt and they bustled their way inside. It was crowded with men all wearing dark suits with black ties. There were women too in dark coats and black cloche hats like Mary's. They were packed as tightly as a cattle truck heading for the abattoir. 'As crowded as when the Celts are playing at home,' one man said. But the others met his remark with a frosty silence.

The man next to Ronny smelled like the men who delivered

coal down the chute into the cellar in Atherfold Road. The coal dust shone in the fibres of his jacket. Ronny began to make out more smells: hot metal like in the metalwork room at school; the fried-onion smell of sweat; and the tang of sulphur mixed with the nasty one of rotting eggs.

He knew better than to make a fuss. Since he came to Glasgow he had realised that the people in this city were less lucky than they were in London. There didn't seem to be any way of getting out from underneath the bad air, to get away from the smell of men who worked in factories or in mines. In London, there were as many men with sharp suits and cardboard collars travelling on trams and the underground trains as there were the down-at-heel workers or layabouts.

'Cemetery gates!'

People all around him turned to the exits and then stepped down. The passengers surged around the tram and crossed the road in front of it and behind. Ronny was surprised to see the men at the front of the crowd step into the road with their arms up and stop the traffic so the rest of them could cross. He had never seen that before – they stepped out like policemen and the motors had to stop.

Once they were through the gates, Mary halted to survey the lay of the land. Ronny looked to the right and saw the open grave straight away. It was the first in from the cemetery wall but down a slope from the main path. It looked like there was a stream the other side of the grave. Ronny wasn't sure it was a good thing to be buried so close to water. It would be awfully damp.

The higher ground to the left was like the terracing at a football match and it was already covered with people. The men were bare-headed in the light rain. A row of policemen kept the crowd off the pathway. Ronny saw how the procession would come in the main entrance behind them, go a hundred or so yards towards the building at the far end and turn right and right again so as to double-back along the lower path to the grave. He took his mother's hand. 'Let's stand here behind the gate Mum. We won't be able to see them come in but we'll have a good view when they come back along.' He tugged at her sleeve and they pressed against the wall.

A man with the same idea as Ronny turned and nodded as they squeezed in alongside. He had thin gingery hair and twirled his flat cap in his hand. He touched a finger to his forehead. 'Mrs Ireland, Mary,' he said. Ronny stared wide-eyed at him. A strange man so far from London who knew his mother!

Mary looked up at the ginger-haired man and her brow creased.

The man turned down the sides of his mouth, made a sniffing noise, and shook his head. 'Aye, you won't remember me, Mary. I've kept ma head doon most times we've been near.'

Ronny could hardly make out the language. He leaned towards the man to hear him better.

'I was scouting you for Danny McAleer years back. Ah wis his ear on the ground in Parkhead, so I was. Don't you mind me?'

Mary's puzzled look disappeared. 'Why if it's not Bobby Craig. Danny told me he kept in touch with you. When was it we last met?'

'Ah ken that day well for the sherricking you gave me, ye mad harridan,' he said, smiling.

Mary smiled too. For a moment her old worry-free complexion shone out. It was the first time Ronny had seen her smile in days. 'Nothing more than you deserved, if I remember. But we did bump into each other after that, I'm sure.'

He looked sheepish. 'Aye, mebbe. Once or twice by your close.' He nodded towards the hole in the ground. 'They had your man wrong that day in Shettleston. Ah'm glad we didnae put him oot his hoose.' He put his hand on Ronny's head. 'This is the boy, then.'

She put one hand on Ronny's shoulder and took off his school cap with the other. 'Aye, this is Ronny.'

While they were talking, the beat of a bass drum had grown in volume and now a hush descended on the crowd. A man tried to shuffle across in front of them and Bobby Craig stepped forward to push him back. 'You stay there and make sure nobody crosses in front of you. This woman here and the boy need to see this.' The man shrank back and then stood to block any more entering the corner area which now belonged to Bobby Craig, Mary and Ronny.

The slow shuffle of hundreds of footsteps sounded behind them on the other side of the wall. A motor-hearse appeared through the gates and started down the main path. Heads bowed on all sides. The drum stopped and there was total silence except for the scuffling and scraping of slow-marching boots. Mary reached for a handkerchief and put it to her face. The men around Ronny, their faces stubbled and thin, were letting tears fall down their hollowed-out cheeks.

As Ronny had predicted, the procession went away from them and they had to wait for it to double-back before they could see what was happening. Ronny didn't recognise the widow, following behind the hearse. He only saw that she was an older lady supported by a woman a few years younger than his mother. Then there were more of the family. They were led by a young man, who could have been the younger woman's brother, followed by a group of others from the older generation.

These all passed before Ronny saw people he recognised. The Prime Minister, Mr MacDonald, led the non-family mourners. Ronny had seen his picture in the newspapers. Next to him was Mr Buchanan and then Mr Maxton. Both of them had been to the house. Mr Kirkwood and Mr Stephen, all of Uncle John's political friends had come up from London. There was Mr Mosley and not far behind him Uncle Danny, his bad leg straight out. All of them were bareheaded in the drizzle.

Seeing Oswald Mosley reminded Ronny of the number of times the famous man and his pretty wife, who had insisted Ronny called her Cimmie, had come to their house in Clapham. The adults would all go into the front parlour and sit round the table making plans. Ronny had to stay in his room when they were there.

One day, after one of their visits, his mother told him he must not tell anyone about them. She said it was a secret but she could tell him that they were very important people and one day Mr Mosley would become Prime Minister. When it happened his Uncle John would be Chancellor of the Exchequer, she had said, and there would even be a place for her on either the red or the green benches in Westminster. Ronny wondered now why the colour of the seats was important and why she thought it was good to have one reserved for her.

As if she could tell what he was thinking, Mary bent towards him and whispered, 'You remember Mr Mosley, Ronny? Uncle John and I had hoped he would be Prime Minister instead of Mr MacDonald. He's missed his chance now Uncle John has died. There's talk he's going to leave Labour and start a new political party. See here. The people who make British history are burying your Uncle. Your mother has been part of it.' She had her eyes fixed on the coffin and it sounded as if she was talking from far away. 'We're finished now, Mr Mosley and me – both of us left high and dry.' She stood up straight again and Ronny watched her tears tumbling down behind her veil.

The crowd closed across the path behind the tail of the procession. The coffin was on the shoulders of six men. From his position above the path, Ronny could see everyone clearly. The six men manoeuvred the coffin into place and lowered it on top of the open grave where it was supported by two planks. They all stood while the priest said some prayers. Ronny felt an ache rising in his chest and soon his tears brimmed over as well.

The coffin was lowered in and the priest said a final prayer. The widow stepped forward and took some dust from a box offered to her and threw it on top of the coffin. She glanced away and her eyes seemed to snag on the group by the gate. It looked like her features were carved in white marble. She did not continue her sweep of the scene, she still looked their way.

Ronny realised she was looking directly at him. Why was she staring? He hadn't done anything wrong. He decided to do what he would have done in the playground. He stared straight back at her, daring her to blink first.

Two

Bobby Craig drove them to the guest house in his Austin Seven to pick up their bags and then to the Necropolis.

'You stay in the car, Ronny. I'll only be a few minutes.'

Ronny watched her buy a bunch of flowers from a stall and go through the gates and up towards a low building.

'Where's my mum going, Mr Craig,' he asked.

'It's the plot where your sister is buried,' the man said in a way that persuaded Ronny not to ask anything else. He realised that this must be the Ella that his mum had talked about with Danny. He was still trying to work out his feelings when Mary emerged from the building and walked purposely away along the main path. She turned to the right and disappeared behind the high grave markers.

She returned to the car without the flowers and with her eyes rimmed with red. 'Okay, Bobby. Thanks. Let's go to Duke Street.'

He stopped at the corner. 'I won't come in. The Spaniard and I are not exactly on speaking terms.'

'Who's the Spaniard?' Ronny said.

Mary straightened his coat. 'Thanks for the ride, Bobby. You've come up in the world.'

'Thanks to your man Wheatley. Meechan's been in charge of business in East Glasgow since Wheatley went legal, but it was Wheatley and McAleer gave me my break.' He held up his right arm and gave a bitter smile. Ronny saw for the first time that it was bent strangely at the elbow and he realised that he hadn't gripped the steering wheel properly with his right hand when he drove the motor.

'So the business, as you call it, goes on?'

Bobby Craig got out of the car and looked up and down the road. He took Mary by the arm and steered her close to the wall. Ronny shuffled along behind near enough to hear even though Mr Craig was talking directly into her ear. 'You still have to be careful what you say and how you say it, Mary. Life up here hasnae changed for the working man as you'll find oot when you see your husband.' He made a show of spitting on the ground and Ronny stepped back making a face. 'The Wheatley family still runs money-lending, betting and many a bar in this part of the city and has done for as long as I can remember.'

Ronny could see Mary trying to pull away but Craig had gripped her arm hard.

'It's the simple pleasures of the Glasgow working man have kept him – and, I dare say, you – high on the hog down there in London. They all respect the man for what he made of himself and it seems he never forgot where he started out, but that fancy house in Sandyhills needs to have fancy gates and it's not to keep the Wheatleys and the Meechans inside.'

Mary pulled her elbow away, 'You've had your say, Bobby. The boy and I will be out of here tonight and, trust me, I won't be back again except to put that man up the stairs in his grave.'

'If they'll let yer!' He spat again, turned to the car, eased himself in and drove away.

Ronny took Mary's arm. 'Are you all right?' he said.

She leaned down, straightened his tie and smoothed down the front of his macintosh. Her hands shook and there was a waver in her voice. 'You mind your Ps and Qs when we get upstairs. Remember, whatever state the man is in, he's your father. We're not going to get a welcome here because I took you down to London when I did. These here think I did a wrong thing, so it's not going to be easy. But I need to see the children – your brother and sister. Come on. Let's get this over with.'

It was a dark man with dark eyes and black stubble thick on his chin who opened the door. He could have passed for a pirate. 'Mary,' he said gruffly and stepped back into the room.

The first thing that struck Ronny was the heat and the smell.

It was the hottest place he had ever been in and he had been in the hot plant room in Kew Gardens. The smell was of cooked cabbage and it seemed to be seeping from the walls.

'Your coat?' the man said.

Mary looked round and after a pause unbuttoned her coat and pulled it off. She signalled to Ronny he could do the same.

'Where are the children?' she said.

'Children?' He scratched his cheek and the rasping noise filled the room. 'Millie's a young woman of fifteen and Tom's only a year younger.'

She nodded and her shoulders, which she normally held so rigid, slumped. 'You don't have to remind me, William. I have thought about them every day.'

He snorted. 'Aye, so you say.'

She sighed. 'I don't want an argument. I just came to see how all of you are keeping.'

'I am no' bad for a man who has raised three bairns on his own.'

There was a long silence. Mary's shoulders shook like she was sobbing. Ronny tried to hold her hand but she pushed him away. 'About Ella,' she said.

The man felt behind him to check the chair was in place and sat down. 'There was no time,' he said.

Mary made a wailing noise. Her nose was running and she wiped it with her glove. Ronny realised then how bad she must have felt; she would never have let him get away with that. 'You should have let me be there. It was cruel of you not to tell me until it was over and she was in the ground.'

'We thought she would get better. We couldn't afford to call a doctor out – by the time we did it was too late. It happened too quickly.'

'I should have known.'

'You chose your path and it didn't include the bairns. I did what I could for them. I was on my own.'

'You had your sister.'

'Her name's Lou.'

'I ken well enough her name.'

'Ah'm just saying it's no thanks to you. You left us in the

258

lurch from the start – the bairns had to make do with Lou for a mother because of yer politics years before that fat bastard took you away.'

She straightened up, pulled out a handkerchief and wiped her face. She sighed again, more wearily this time. 'You're right, William. Please let it be so as we're not shouting at each other when they come in. Can we try to be civilised?'

'You had to mention the girl.' He nodded and looked at him. 'This is the boy, ken? Still has the blue eyes. Glasses an' aw. My eyesight has never troubled me, by th'way. You did the right thing taking him to London. The little runt wouldn't have lasted five minutes up here.'

She reached for her coat. 'William!'

He put his hands up. 'Okay! I wis just saying. I'll call in the others. They're hiding over the landing.'

Mary held up her hand. 'Before you do, I want to know something.'

He turned away and stirred the fire with a poker. 'Here we go,' he said.

'I only want to be able to say, now they're older, that they'll be able to visit me in London, if they want to. Will you let them?'

'Ah'm no' gonna stop them, am I?' He left the room

Mary pulled a hard chair away from the table. She ran a finger across the seat, inspected it for dust and sat down. She waved Ronny in alongside her and he stood behind the chair.

When the door opened, two young people, as dark as the man, stumbled in. Tom came first. He was wearing a suit and tie and his hair was slicked back with grease. He swaggered up to the chair. Ronny straightened and realised he was nearly as tall but the other boy already sported a man's five o'clock shadow. He stopped a foot or so in front of Mary's chair and tucked his thumbs behind the lapels of his jacket. 'All right, Ma?' he said.

Millie wore a brown dress with a clean white apron over the skirt. Her black hair was cut short and hung loose over her ears. She hung back behind her brother but she was a clear head taller. Her face was the colour of strong tea and her eyes, as with her brother's, were so dark that the outside was the same colour as the middle part.

'Millie, Tom, it's good to see you.' There were tears in Mary's eyes.

The girl was brimming tears as well. 'You too, Ma,' she said.

Ronny watched as his mother took the two strangers in her arms and held them close. The boy and the girl stood rigid, arms stiff by their sides. Ronny waited while they spoke together, struggling to make sense of the rolling burr of their language, giving up in the end, focusing instead on the glowing embers in the grate of the range and thinking how very strange the visit to Scotland had been.

Mary was sobbing as they went down the stairs and Ronny realised that nothing he could say or do would make her feel better that day.

They spent an hour or so dawdling about the shops in Sauchiehall Street. Mary showed Ronny the department store where she had worked and took him to a big square. She stood him on a plinth there, next to the entrance to the City Chambers, and told him about the riot that had happened. She tried to make it exciting by describing the blood on the men and their injuries after the police had finished with them but Ronny's tummy was rumbling and his mind was on the fish supper she had promised.

He was disappointed when they took a table at the Lyons Corner House. He would have much preferred to eat his fish and chips out of newspaper as they walked to the station.

Afterwards, Danny was waiting for them at the barrier for the night-train. 'Do you have everything, Mary?'

She answered wearily. 'Aye, let's get out of this place, Danny.'

Ronny followed them, still savouring the taste of the fish and chip fat coating his mouth. Danny held the door open and he followed Mary into the compartment. Ronny sat next to the window, but it was already dark and he could only see his reflection. His glasses glinted back and he swept back the curls of mousey hair that tumbled over his forehead. He had seen posters for something you could use to flatten your hair called Brylcreem and wondered whether it was what Tom used. He thought about the one-room that those three people lived in.

He turned back into the compartment. 'Where were the beds, Mum?'

'What do you mean, where were the beds?'

'The beds in the room. Where do they sleep?'

'Who?'

'You know, where we went this afternoon?'

Danny leaned forward to look past Mary. 'They live in what they call a single-end, son. Did you see the doors of a big cupboard flat against the wall?'

'Yes.'

'That was a bed behind there. I think probably Millie would have that one. I bet they had two big chairs by the range with flat cushions.'

'Yes, they did. How did you know?'

'Most single-ends have them. They fold out into beds for the men.'

'Why don't they live in a big house, like us? I have a bedroom of my own.'

'You've been very lucky, Ronny. There are many families much bigger than the Spaniard's who live in single-ends. It's all they can afford. But it's a lot better now than it used be. They have social housing now in Glasgow and all over the country thanks to...' he looked at Mary.

She fussed with her gloves. 'Thanks to your Uncle John, Ronny.'

Danny nodded his head slowly. 'Aye, thanks to your Uncle John.'

He opened his mouth to ask why Danny called his father the Spaniard when his mother held up a hand. 'That's enough questions now, Ronny. It's way past your bedtime.'

He snuggled his head into the corner and closed his eyes. Despite all the strange things that had happened and the whirling thoughts that spun around him, he couldn't keep his eyes open and he was already half-asleep and only dimly aware of the noise and movement when the train pulled away.

Ronny woke up to the low murmur of voices. Something made him keep his head still and his eyes closed. The carriage rocked from side-to-side as it negotiated some points. The familiar rhythm of the clattering wheels resumed.

'He's out for the count.' Danny said.

Mary sounded testy. 'I still don't want to talk about it.'

'But you have no reason to stay in London now and neither do I. There's nothing for us in Glasgow either. D'you think I want to work for the Meechans?'

'Because I *can* move out, it doesn't mean I have to. What about Ronny?'

'It's Ronny I'm thinking about as much as you... and me.' he said.

'I could put Glasgow behind me once and for all. I could do it without blinking. I have seen today there's no way I can make it up to the bairns. Maybe one day, when they are grown up, they'll forgive me.'

'They will, Mary. When they're adults, they'll understand.'

Mary started sobbing softly so Ronny could barely make out what she was saying. 'Not Ella, though. She'll never grow up to forgive me. How could William and Lou not tell me she was ill?'

Danny's voice was soft. 'Mary, hen, she had the pneumonia one week and was gone the next.'

She blew her nose. 'I thought my heart would never mend from losing her and now I've lost John as well. What will I do, Danny?'

Danny's voice was a low rumble. 'I made an offer once before. D'you ken? It was after the election in '22. I said then I had put money by and we could have a life together. I have never changed the way I feel about you.'

'I know Danny, but –'

'Let me finish. You don't need the big house in London. You could sell it. With your money and mine we could buy a lovely house by the sea. We could run it as a guest house, if you like. We could pay for Ronny to have the education we never had. Like his father –'

Mary's voice cut in with the hard edge Ronny recognised

from when she was going to smack his leg. 'Don't you ever mention that, Danny. It's why it would never work. You know everything about me – all the things I've done wrong. Do you think you could hold back from using them against me? You know what I've done, what I've been, yet you still want to be with me. Why?'

Danny's voice was flat and quiet. 'I do, Mary. That's all I know.'

'Well, I'm sorry for you. You're the kindest man I have ever known. But I'm sorry, Danny...' She continued to sob. 'I don't love you.'

For what could have been minutes Ronny heard only the sounds of the train rattling along. Then there was a scratching noise and Ronny realised it was Danny rasping his hand across his cheek. 'You once told me I was too kind,' he said. 'That there was no bad side to me. But you were wrong.' He was whispering gruffly. He sounded as if he was having trouble breathing. 'When I told you before I had money saved up, enough to buy a place in Ayr, where did you think it came from? I've enough money now to buy a guest house down south. How is it, d'you think?'

Mary didn't answer.

Danny's voice caught in his throat. 'Oh, Mary! You've no idea. I'm not the man you thought I was. I never have been. I lied to you, to JW, to everybody.'

'Hush, Danny. You'll wake the boy. What d'you mean?'

Danny sniffed and Ronny imagined the familiar hard face with the mouth turned down. 'Ach, Mary. Almost from the day JW first took me on, when he first started in the politics, they came to me and offered me money–'

'Slow down, Danny. You're not making sense.'

There was the sound of Danny taking a deep breath. 'I have been in the pay of the intelligence service, Mary. It was me. I was the one who reported back every move JW made. I told them about you. The report Ramsay MacDonald had was all from me. JW was ruined because of it. And, do you know, after you started up with him, I was glad to do it, Mary. I was glad to tell them, knowing it was bad for him. It was because of you. There, so now you know.'

Ronny strained to hear the response but there was only the repetitive snare-drum beat of the wheels on the track.

The rasping noise came again and Danny's voice sounded normal. 'So there you have it, Mary. Danny McAleer is not so perfect after all. Does it make me bad enough for you to care about? Does it make you want me as I have wanted you for nigh on twenty years?'

Mary's voice was low and she hissed words as if each one carried a poisonous dart. 'So it was *you*, Danny. You were the one stopped my man reaching his destiny. You did for me too, Danny. Don't you see? John was taking me with him – not Catherine. *I* was his right hand – his confidante. Your spying brought him down – and it broke my heart to see him lose out. He was never the same after MacDonald told him what he knew. You might as well have stuck a dagger in his back.'

In his half-awake state Ronny could only half-understand what he was hearing.

'Aye, and how many nights have I lain awake knowing it, Mary? But no more than I've hoped one day what I did would bring us together.'

'You idiot! How could that ever be? I'm sorry, sorry for you and your guilt. Sorry for your dashed hopes. God knows, John's past was his own making. He chose his route to the top of the heap. You had nothing to do with that. If you hadn't spied on him, there would have been hundreds in East Glasgow queuing up to take your place.'

'Do you forgive me then, Mary?'

'No. What's the point? If I could push you out of this carriage so you die under the wheels I would, but what purpose would it serve?' She was crying and Ronny's heart ached with the sound of it. He wanted to sit up and tell her he would look after her but he could see he would be in trouble for eavesdropping. He kept his breathing regular and his eyes tight shut.

Mary rummaged in her handbag and Ronny heard the sharp click of her compact being opened. He imagined her pursing her lips as she looked at her reflection. She snapped the compact closed. 'You'd better get used to this, Danny. I don't love you and that's the end of it. My mind was made up even before I left

London yesterday. I'll stay in Clapham, take a job, perhaps, or move to a smaller house – one where I could take in a proper lodger. I'm well set up, thanks to John. Ronny will finish school and have an apprenticeship. Tom and Millie, maybe one day they will come to London for jobs – they'll be much better off down there. You never had any part in my plans.'

Danny's words strained as if he was being strangled. 'But we've been close for nearly twenty years, Mary. That has to count for something.'

She gave a very deep sigh. 'You had your hopes, Danny. I was foolish enough to have mine. It was Glasgow – we all had to look out for ourselves. It was Glasgow and it's all in the past.'

'Will you still see Mosley and his wife?'

She snorted. 'You think they will want me to be part of their circle now? You saw how I was treated at the funeral. There's nothing for me in the party. No, what I do with my life from now on is up to me and me alone.'

'The intelligence people – they want me to work for Mosley. To spy on him. You're sure you'll have nothing to do with him?'

'Not now he's leaving the party. Go on. Do for Mosley what you did to John and good riddance.'

'You'll be on your own, Mary. Who will look after you?'

'You don't understand, Danny. I didn't go with John because I needed looking after. I didn't desert my bairns only because I loved him. The work was part of why we had that love. We thought we could change things. One of the reasons I loved him so much was because, from the very first day outside his villa in Shettleston, he was the one man who treated me as an equal – both as a person and in the politics. It was the politics. We thought we could make a difference. I thought *I* could make a difference.'

'Is it over, then?'

Mary's voice was hard and strong. 'Aye, I'm finished with it. I don't need it with John gone.' Ronny imagined how his mother's back would be stiff and her chin would be jutting out. 'I was nothing more than the Spaniard's wife in Glasgow. In London and around the Labour Party I was John's bit of skirt – aye, I had a brain too, but as far as the Clydesiders and Mosley were concerned it made me more of a circus trick than if I was there just to keep John warm in his bed. John was the only one who understood my real worth.' She clicked shut her handbag. 'From now on I will be my own person. I shall make a life for me and my son. There's no place in it for you, Danny, or for any man.'

The words spun round in Ronny's head. He didn't understand half of what his mother and Danny had said but the last words were easy enough. He would stay in London with his mother.

He smiled and slipped into his sleep, lulled by the lurching train and the rhythmic clacking of its wheels.

-- The End --

Books about the time, people and politics that influenced the author's approach to writing *No Mean Affair*

Jim Allen: *Days of Hope* (Futura Publications 1975)

Arnold Bennett: *Riceyman Steps* (Cassell & Co Ltd. 1923)

Gordon Brown: *Maxton* (Mainstream Publishing 2002)

Maggie Craig: *When the Clyde Ran Red* (Mainstream Publishing 2011)

Jean Faley: *Up Oor Close* (White Cockade 1990)

David Howell: *MacDonald's Party: Labour Identities and Crisis 1922-1931* (Oxford University Press 2002)

Thomas Kenneally: *The People's Train* (Sceptre 2009)

David Marquand: *Ramsay Macdonald: A Biography* (Jonathan Cape Ltd 1977)

A McArthur and H Kingsley Long: *No Mean City* (Corgi 1957)

Iain McLean: *The Legend of Red Clydeside* (John Donald Publishers 1983)

Robert Keith Middlemass: *The Clyde-siders* (Hutchinson 1965)

Robert Skidelsky: *Oswald Mosley* (Macmillan London Ltd 1975)

Rhona Wilson: *Old Shettleston and Tollcross* (Stenlake Publishing Ltd 1998)

Barry Winter: *The ILP Past & Present* (Independent Labour Publications 1996)

Ian Wood: *John Wheatley* (Manchester University Press 1990)

Acknowledgements

I would not have been able to develop the story of Mary Ireland's life without my mum's ability to remember conversations she had with Dad's relatives over sixty years ago. Mum is 90 yet combines the intellect of an Oxbridge don with the wit of a snippy teenager.

This book was my final project for my National Academy of Writing diploma course at Birmingham City University and I am grateful for the support from the faculty there, especially Nicola Monaghan and Jackie Gay who gave me the confidence to call myself a writer. Fellow students: Edmund Bealby-Wright, Bobbie Darbyshire, Ryan Davis, Kathleen Donnelly, Tina Freeth, Federay Holmes, Geoff Mills, Nick Le Mesurier, Tamsin Walker, Sophie Ward and Emma Whittle all offered support and guidance. Special thanks to Bruce Johns who gave freely of his time, initially as a fellow student and later as a good friend. Ben Evans of Addison & Cole advised me on how to shape the story.

Staff in the British Library and the Mitchell Library in Glasgow were unstinting when I needed help with my research into John Wheatley. The Transport Museum's Michael Kitchen made special efforts to keep me on track regarding the London Underground. Ian Arnott, a native of Glasgow, read the manuscript and advised me regarding locations and vernacular.

I owe a huge debt of gratitude to Foxwell Press, the first publisher to show faith in my work. Foxwell's Founding Manager, Fiona Joseph, is an entrepreneurial and uniquely gifted writing colleague. Thanks to Clare Christian, Stuart Bache and Adam Davis for, respectively: editing, cover design and book design. The professionalism of their collective work is in your hands.

How do I adequately thank my family for fathomless support and love? Val, David, Ruth, Charlotte – here it is; we did it.

Lightning Source UK Ltd.
Milton Keynes UK
UKOW02f0808280415

250479UK00003B/107/P